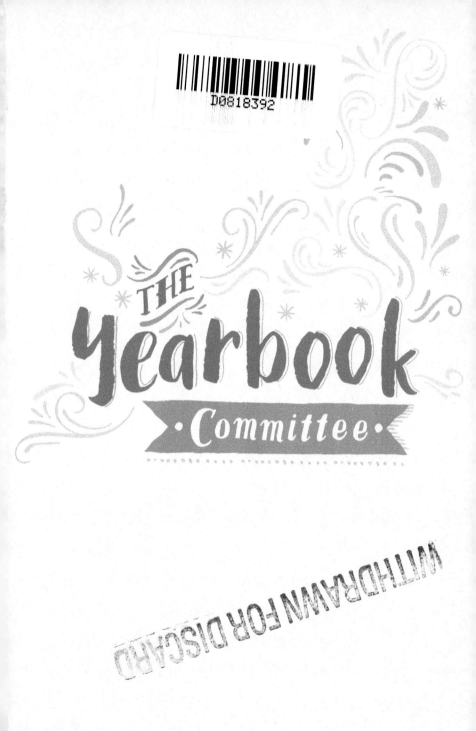

THE Yearbook · Committee ·

Books by Sarah Ayoub

Hate Is Such a Strong Word
The Yearbook Committee

THE
Yearbook
·Committee·

written by
Sarah
Ayoub

HarperCollins*Publishers*

HarperCollins_Publishers_

First published in Australia in 2016
by HarperCollinsPublishers Australia Pty Limited
ABN 36 009 913 517
harpercollins.com.au

HarperCollins_Publishers_
Level 13, 201 Elizabeth Street, Sydney, NSW 2000, Australia
Unit D1, 63 Apollo Drive, Rosedale, Auckland 0632, New Zealand
A 53, Sector 57, Noida, UP, India
1 London Bridge Street, London SE1 9GF, United Kingdom
2 Bloor Street East, 20th floor, Toronto, Ontario M4W 1A8, Canada
195 Broadway, New York, NY 10007, USA

National Library of Australia Cataloguing-in-Publication data:

Ayoub, Sarah, author.
   The yearbook committee / Sarah Ayoub.
   978 0 7322 9685 8 (paperback)
   978 1 7430 9917 9 (ebook)
   For young adults.
   Interpersonal relations in adolescence.
A823.4

Cover and internal design by Stephanie Spartels, Studio Spartels
Cover image by BONNINSTUDIO/stocksy.com/428487
Author photo by Simona Janek, GM Photographics
Printed and bound in Australia by McPherson's Printing Group
The papers used by HarperCollins in the manufacture of this book are a natural,
recyclable product made from wood grown in sustainable plantation forests. The fibre
source and manufacturing processes meet recognised international environmental
standards, and carry certification.

For Danielle-Nova Najem, Tammi Ireland and Viola Bechara —
the friends I found in unlikely circumstances.

And for my siblings, Milad, Marie-Claire and Josie —
the friends I was lucky enough to be born with.

You are the best team-mates a girl could ask for.
I hope you are all in the yearbooks of the rest of my life.

Prologue: November

I stayed with David after everyone had disappeared. It didn't seem right to call them friends now — sitting in the living room and looking around the empty house that was littered with bottles and plastic cups and vomit, it was obvious that they were just revellers who were only there to celebrate when it was all fun and easy. I wanted to say 'I told you so' to David, tell him yet again that you had to be careful, but even after the events of that night I was still wary of David's criticism. Fun police, he'd called me earlier. And maybe I was.

Until, of course, the real police had shown up.

I sighed and reached out to rub David's back. I wondered if I should stop — it seemed like a really girly gesture — but David didn't say anything. He just sat there, shoulders hunched, unusually silent.

'Maybe you should go call your parents,' I said.

David looked up and nodded. 'Do you think it will make the news?' he asked.

I shrugged. 'I don't ... don't know.'

'I'll call them just in case,' he said, rising.

He returned a few minutes later, a look of shame on his face.

'They're on their way,' he said, tossing his phone down onto the couch.

'Are they mad?' I asked, regretting the words as soon as they came out.

'What do you think?' he growled, his eyes flicking up at me. 'Come on, let's sit outside. I need some air.'

'I'll be right out,' I told him, as I looked around the room. 'Let me tidy up a little more.'

I threw some more things in the garbage bin against the outside back wall, then followed David back up to the front entrance of the house, where I joined him on the cane chairs and waited. Waited for news from the hospital; for trouble to come knocking; for his parents, who would probably say that this was the last straw in his long line of bad behaviour.

David's voice cut through the silence.

'You should say it,' he said. 'Tell me I was wrong to invite everyone on my Facebook list.'

I scoffed, but said nothing. That wasn't the only issue, I wanted to say. There was no security, no order, no one keeping watch. Just a bunch of dumb, hammered teenagers who thought they were so much older than their actual age. But there didn't seem to be much point in saying any of that now.

Still, not everything that had happened had been David's fault. Nothing about this party seemed different to any of the other parties we'd been to as seniors at Holy Family High School. Sure, there were a few extra people in the mix, but the basic ingredients were the same: smuggled booze and clueless kids high on hormones, their parents' cash and the quest for high-school popularity.

Prologue

But something must have been different this time; none of the other parties had ended this way before. Maybe it was the excessively hot November weather; maybe we should have paid more attention in that first-aid lesson; maybe it was that end-of-year fever that had everyone thinking a little more recklessly.

It was hard to think through the sirens still echoing in my ears, even though the ambulance had long gone. Moments later, David drifted off, and eventually so did the moon, a large beam of light shrinking into the bay before me as the hours passed. But my eyes wouldn't close.

I was glad of that — if they did close, I'd see it all again. The police notebooks being flipped open, my classmates' faces contorted with shock, the limp body strapped to the stretcher. Still, zombie-like, almost shrunken. Even with the minor signs of life that flickered on the monitor as the paramedics shut the ambulance doors, I knew there was no guarantee.

Everything seemed uncertain, different, damaged. Just like the promise of our youth, now irreversibly changed due to a night whose sinister warning had been brewing steadily beneath the surface of our teenage dreams.

Charlie

Nine months earlier

Charlie Scanlon Three. Terms. Left.

Pete Brady likes this.

The car that's been tailing me for the last hundred metres slows down further, and I go from mild concern to panic. As a petite seventeen-year-old on a deserted suburban road at 6.30 a.m., I am the perfect candidate for a sexual predator. Great. I'm going to disappear and there will be no clues or witnesses. I'll become another unsolved mystery.

I curse myself for starting the day so early. Then again, I didn't have many options. Mornings at home were super awkward now that my mum and my stepfather, Stan, were trying for a baby. The kinds of noises that came from their room … Let's just say I'd rather listen to static.

I sneak a very subtle look through the camera in my phone and freak out when I can't see through the tinted windows. There's probably more than one of them; my chances of escape are reducing by the second. I take a deep breath and quicken my pace, imagining the headlines: 'High-schooler found strangled in bushland', 'Student raped on walk to school', 'Parents shoulder blame for move that cost daughter's life'. Well, maybe not that last one, but if I do die today, at least Mum and Stan will live out their days in sorrow, knowing it was their selfishness that brought death closer to my door.

Then the door opens, and I stop, steadying myself for a fight. I'm like an atheist Joan of Arc going into battle — except I'm too afraid to turn around. A hand reaches over my face, and I react, elbowing the belly and stomping on a foot.

I've run maybe six metres when the voice belonging to the 'ouch' registers, and I turn around.

'Mum,' I say, slapping a hand to my forehead. 'You scared the crap out of me!'

'Wow,' she says, clutching her stomach. 'You're strong.'

I shake my head. 'What are you doing?' I ask. 'And whose car is that?'

'Surprise!' she yells, throwing her hands into the air. 'It's yours!'

'What? I don't even have a licence.'

'Yet — but you'll get one.'

'I won't need one in Melbourne,' I point out.

'You'll need one here,' she says, folding her arms.

'I don't plan on returning,' I retort, folding my own. 'And now I want to walk.'

She looks defeated.

I sigh. 'Mum, we've been over this. I'm going to walk to school early from now on. You know why, I know why, Stan knows why. We don't need to go over it again. What we do need to go over is what exactly you were thinking when you decided to put on Ugg boots in this heatwave. And, more importantly, why you came out of the house in them. It's tacky.'

'My toes were cold,' she replies with a shrug. 'Come on, get in the car.'

I stay where I am, arms still folded, while she picks up my school bag.

'No,' I say, shaking my head. 'You've ruined my morning. I thought you were a stalker.'

My mother puts my bag on the backseat and looks at me sternly. 'I think you need to stop watching crime shows. They're really distorting your sense of reality.'

I scoff. 'Still doesn't explain why you were driving like a creep.'

'I got a phone call from Ellen. She started dating a new guy a month ago, and now he won't return her calls. I was trying to make sense of the situation, hence the slow driving.'

'Mum, those no-talking-while-driving rules we had in Melbourne apply in Sydney too, you know,' I point out. 'Except the cops are probably meaner and the fine is probably bigger. Just like how everything else is worse here.'

'Not this again, Charlie,' she says, exasperated. 'Get in the car. And I don't want to say it again.'

When her 'Dr Reynolds' voice comes out, I know it's time for me to listen.

———

Ten minutes later, we're sitting in the car in a McDonald's parking lot, eating sausage and egg McMuffins, hash browns and hotcakes. The car stinks of grease. I wind down the windows.

'You didn't have to bring the car to me, you know,' I say. 'I would have understood if you needed to stay at home with Stan, to …'

'To, you know?' she replies, a smirk on her face. 'This is our tradition, Chi. Not everything has to change now that we've moved.'

'The big things have,' I mumble.

'And therefore the small things don't matter, right?' she asks. 'That's where you're wrong, Charlie. The small things are always going to matter.'

She packs all the scraps in a paper bag and turns on the engine. We pull out of the parking lot.

'Why a car?' I ask. 'Is Stan trying to buy my love?'

'Not really,' she says. 'You liked him until we decided to move to Sydney.'

'That's true,' I admit. As stepfathers went, he was pretty good.

'Maybe it's the school?' she asks. 'He said he really wanted you to fit in.'

'I fit in at a public school,' I tell her. 'Not among entitled rich brats.'

'The education is good there,' she says, giving me a look. 'Plus he went there, and he's always wanted his kids to go there too.'

'I'm not his kid, Mum.'

She shakes her head. 'Don't break his heart, darl.'

I roll my eyes, but I know she's right. I should try to be nicer to Stan.

'I'd have loved a car at your age,' she says after a minute. 'One with a big red bow. This one had a red bow but I had to take it off before I drove it to you.'

'Again, you didn't need to bring it to me. And now it's christened in grease.'

'And, again, this is our tradition. I always give you a gift on your first day of the school year.'

'What happened to slogan shirts and novels?' I ask.

'My rich husband, apparently.'

She drops me off near school, kissing my cheek and promising to let me walk as much as I want for the rest of the year. I'm almost at the school gate when she winds down the window and yells out to me: 'Am I ever going to be forgiven?'

'I wouldn't hold my breath,' I yell back. And then I smile and wave her off, knowing I can never really hate her as much as I try to.

Mum's the only adult who gets me. She should be, I guess, considering she's a psychologist who's writing her PhD thesis on the struggles of and influences on the modern adolescent in Australia. I'm her favourite case study, which means she'll probably fail, because sometimes I'm seventeen going on thirty-seven.

So it sucks that we've been on such a sour note for a while now, but, hey, I didn't want to move. And the biggest betrayal of your life is not meant to come from your mother.

I had tried everything to convince her that the move from Melbourne would be a big mistake, but Stan really wanted to be back in his home town, and she was *in love*. My aunty Ellen, who considers herself nobody unless she has somebody, was extremely encouraging of the relationship and all that came with it. Even Mum's thesis, which she's doing at Melbourne Uni, was no hurdle, because her supervisor agreed to let her continue long-distance provided they had fortnightly meetings via Skype. As for work, she'd had her own practice for almost thirteen years, and had made quite a name for herself as a media commentator, so opening up a place in Sydney was not going to be a challenge.

And even if it were, Stan would fix it. He'd make sure that she wouldn't want for anything.

Stan. The man who changed everything. All my life, it was just me and Mum. She'd fallen pregnant with me when she was seventeen and, even though my birth father had skipped out on her, and everyone she knew (herself included) had been telling her not to go through with it, she'd decided to keep me. She always says that her life has been on the uphill since she heard my first cry.

But when I was thirteen, she introduced me to Stan. I didn't mind him at first. He was nice, hard-working, and knew I was Mum's number-one priority and didn't try to change that. They got married when I was fifteen, and she's been super happy ever since.

And me? Well, I stopped being super happy when I had to leave my friends, my school and everything I'd known since I was a kid. Now I'm stuck doing year 12 at some prestigious private school, which I hated the minute I saw it. But it had its perks — it always ranked highly in the HSC, and I needed to use that to my advantage. I was going to move back to Melbourne straight after school finished, and I needed good grades to apply to Monash University.

So my goals this year are to focus on my studies, and learn to survive without my mother. By the time I go back to Melbourne, she might have a baby in her arms, and she can play happy families with Stan. There'd be no room for a sulking teenager in the family portrait. And, in the meantime, I plan to hate on anything and everything for as long as I possibly can. This new school year included.

Matty

Matty Fullerton is listening to 'King' by Years and Years on Spotify.

Running against the clock looks really different in the movies. We see the action, but not the sweat; we feel the adrenalin, but not the painful breathlessness of untrained lungs; and don't get me started on the hair. The hair that always stays put and perfect. Unlike my own hair, which probably looks like a badly damaged mop just sitting on my head. And they wonder why I'm always in a hoodie.

I crouch down in the grass and shove my bag through the hole in the fence at the back of the school's quad, the escape route for the cool kids. They call it 'the blind spot' because none of the teachers know about it.

Until now. I'm halfway through the hole when I hear him clear his throat.

'Mr Fullerton,' Mr Broderick says in his signature smug tone. 'Leaving so soon?'

I sigh deeply and get to my feet, avoiding eye contact. 'Yes, sir,' I say, defeated.

'Remind me, lad,' he says, putting his hands behind his back and rocking on the spot, 'what did you and I agree on during our last interaction?'

'Three strikes and I'm out.'

'And, pray tell, what number is this?'

'Three, sir,' I mumble.

'Ah yes, third time *un*lucky,' he says. 'Unfortunate that. Now, please tidy yourself up and follow me into my office where we can further discuss your punishment.'

I give my bag a big kick, then slide to the ground, my back to the fence. So close. Ahead of me, Mr Broderick cocks his eyebrows at me and I roll my eyes, pick up my bag and follow him into his office. 'The dungeon of wrath', I've heard the other kids call it. And, lately, kind of like my second home.

Mr Broderick is Holy Family's deputy principal. Part of the furniture, he says, as though it will mask the irritation he feels at not having landed the top job after thirteen years in this role. I don't think the reason has occurred to him just yet: unlike our principal, Mrs Hendershott, AKA Mrs H — who nurtures as much as she disciplines — Mr Broderick likes dishing out punishment a little too much. Hence the office nickname.

Inside, he motions for me to take a seat, and walks over to the filing cabinet to get my file.

'I'm going to need a bigger folder soon,' he says. 'We're only two and a half weeks into the school year, and yet you've been in my office three times.'

I stare at him in silence.

'And still reluctant to speak, I might add.'

More staring.

Now it's his turn to sigh. He rises from his chair and walks over to the window that looks out on the school's manicured front lawn. 'We expect a certain level of appreciation from our scholarship students, Mr Fullerton,' he says, rubbing at a smudge on the window. 'I'm surprised that a student of your … background has not come to realise his good fortune and is willing to throw it all away for some reason that he won't discuss.'

He turns around and I bow my head, unable to look at him.

'Holy Family has a long history of awarding scholarships, Matthew,' he says. 'Once they're awarded, the recipients work tirelessly to prove they are worthy.'

He looks at me for emphasis.

'Education is a prized gift,' he says. Like I don't already know. 'Until recently, you seemed to understand that. Your grades were impeccable, we had no issues with your behaviour. In fact, you and I barely interacted during your first year here.'

'No, sir,' I say finally.

'But things have changed, and now I've found myself at a crossroad of sorts. You're not a good debater, are you, Matthew?'

'I don't believe I am, sir,' I admit.

'No, of course, I probably would have known if you were,' he says, giving me a fake smile. 'Maybe you would have argued yourself out of this mess. Are you athletic?' he asks, sizing me up.

'Well —'

'Mr Fullerton!'

I turn around and see Mrs H standing in the doorway, smiling.

'And this is the third time in what — two weeks?' she asks, looking at Mr Broderick.

'Something like that, Miss,' I reply.

She raises her eyebrows, then frowns.

'Would you mind stepping outside for a moment while I talk with Mr Broderick?' she asks. I look from her to him and then sigh, picking up my bag.

'Just wait out there,' she says, motioning to a seat in the hallway. 'I won't be long.'

I strain to hear their conversation, but only manage to catch bits of it. Him: 'Sneaking out again' and 'frustrating' and 'learn his lesson'. Her: 'proper way to learn', 'mature' and 'meet in the middle'.

I tiptoe to the door and lean in closer, trying to hear more.

'I thought we had agreed that the students would nominate themselves for that,' he tells her.

'We did,' she says. 'Only one has put her name down: Gillian Cummings. We do have a long list for the formal committee, though.'

'Well, yes, they all know how to party, don't they?'

They both chuckle.

'OK, well, if you think that's a sufficient punishment,' he tells her. 'But I am not —'

'Fabulous, it's settled then,' she says, opening the door. 'Sorry for taking your time, Matthew. You can go back inside now.'

I stand in front of Mr Broderick's desk, bag in my hands.

'It seems Mrs Hendershott is willing to give you another chance,' he says with his hands apart, as if he doesn't understand why. 'And in lieu of a punishment, she's going to make you work for your position here …'

My eyes widen.

'The school needs a yearbook. It's a long tradition dating back to the school's inception in 1932, and we've yet to miss a year besides 1944. War and all. You will be joining the yearbook committee.'

'But, sir …!'

'Would you prefer the debating team, or an athletics team of some sort?'

'I'd prefer to clean,' I mumble.

'Yes, well, we pay a company to do that,' he says.

'How am I supposed to —'

'You'll have help,' he says, as if that's an assurance. 'Mrs Hendershott will see to it. But if you want to be here, Mr Fullerton, you must prove it.'

I shake my head in frustration. He looks at me for a moment then gestures to the door.

'You may leave now.'

I rush out of there and run out of the school grounds just as the end-of-day bell sounds. I had begged for the earlier shift, and now I'm going to be late for it.

I arrive to work at the juice bar an hour late, and find my colleague Dionne in a bad mood.

'I'm so sorry,' I say, flustered. 'I got in trouble.'

'Matty,' she says, exasperated, 'you shouldn't ask for more shifts if you can't do them.'

'I can,' I say, putting on my apron. 'But sometimes things get in the way. Like school.'

'School's more important,' she points out. 'Are you that desperate for money?'

I ignore the look of concern on her face and shake my head.

'I'll be right,' I mumble. 'I'll work something out.'

She sighs and goes off to take her afternoon break.

'Where's all the fruit?' I ask her when she returns.

'Don't get me started,' she says, waving a hand in my face. 'The delivery was wrong. All morning I've been getting people to change their orders.'

'Again? It's the second time this month on late-night shopping day. Have you told head office?'

'I'll call 'em tomorrow,' she says. 'As you can probably tell, I've had a crazy day … working on my own and all.'

'I know,' I say. 'I'll make it up to you.'

'Well, I do need a favour,' she says. 'I'm going to the movies with a cute guy from uni tonight, and my legs are in dire need of a little waxing. Can I sneak out at, like, 8.30?'

I shrug. 'Just go whenever we get quiet.'

'Thanks so much,' she says. 'Let me ring the lady upstairs and see if she can squeeze me in. Otherwise I'll just have to shave in the bathroom.'

I shake my hand at her dismissively.

'OK, I know. Too much information.'

It's an hour before closing when Sammy, one of our regulars, comes up to the counter with seven dollars in assorted coins. I've known him long enough to know it's the entire contents of his moneybox, and I smile.

'One Berry Bravo?' I ask him.

He nods excitedly and I print the order for Dionne, placing it in front of her.

'Sammy, where's Elliott?' I ask him. Sammy has Down's syndrome and always comes in on Tuesday and Thursday mornings with his carer, but tonight the bloke's nowhere in sight. 'Are you alone?'

'Elliott's on holiday. Dad said to skip my juices this week, but I don't want to.'

'OK, we're making your drink,' I tell him, aware that any change in his day-to-day could cause a temper tantrum.

'We are out of strawberries,' Dionne whispers into my ear.

I turn around, eyes wide. This happened once before and the tantrum wasn't pretty. Though I'm less concerned about the attention than I am about upsetting him. The kid cried last time.

'What do I do?' she presses.

I look over to Sammy, who's smiling politely across the counter.

'He'd notice if we made it without,' I tell her, biting my lip. 'Go get some?'

She rushes out of the store while I try to distract him with his other favourite topic: rugby league.

A minute later, a woman comes over, looking flustered.

'Oh, thank God,' she says. 'You were supposed to stay outside the change room and not move.'

'Sorry, Mummy,' he says, looking defeated. 'I wanted my drink before they closed.'

'And I told you to wait, and come next week with Elliot.'

I busy myself tidying up the bags of popcorn on the counter, trying to avoid the conversation.

'But I always have it on Thursday,' he says, tears in his eyes.

'Fine,' she says, throwing her hand into her purse. 'Get him a large of whatever he wants,' she says to me.

'Ah, he's already paid,' I tell her.

'Then where's his drink?' she asks, looking at me like I'm stupid.

'Um, my colleague just went out to get strawberries because —'

'Oh, I don't have time for this,' she says, grabbing his arm. 'Come on, Sammy. We'll come back tomorrow.'

'No! Only Tuesday and Thursday!'

The mother glares at me and I feel stuck.

'Sammy, mate,' I say, 'I'm really sorry, but we're out of strawberries. Can we make you a Berry Bravo tomorrow?'

'No! No! No! Supposed to be on Tuesday and Thursday!'

By now, his voice has gotten louder and his mother looks even more frustrated.

'Oh God,' she says. 'People are looking.'

'My colleague'll only be a few minutes,' I tell her.

'She better be,' she snaps. 'What kind of juice bar doesn't have any fruit?'

I shrug helplessly and turn around to see Dionne running down to the store just as the tantrum reaches its peak.

She quickly washes the strawberries and makes his drink. I hand it to him.

He's immediately placated.

'That mum was some piece of work,' I tell her after they leave. 'She left him alone to try on clothes, and then she didn't want him to have his drink because she was in a rush.'

'Some people shouldn't have children,' she says scornfully.

When I get home, I see that nothing has changed. The lights are off and the curtains are still drawn. The TV blares from the living room, but she's not watching. I try not to think of the energy cost.

I switch on the kitchen lights and see there are two empty yoghurt tubs in the bin. At least she's eaten something.

I check the messages on the answering machine. There's one from her boss, asking if she's ready to come back. 'You've had a lot of time off,' the lady says cheerfully. 'We miss you.'

I make a mental note to think up another excuse. Meditation retreat in Bali?

Inside her room, Mum is in her usual spot, sitting on the bed, staring at the wall.

'I'm home,' I tell her.

'How was work?' she asks, not moving.

'Good,' I answer.

'Good,' she says, nodding. 'Good, good.'

I kiss her goodnight and go to bed.

But I don't sleep. Things are far from good.

Tammi

Tammi Kap is listening to 'Hard out Here' on Spotify.
#hardouthereforabitch #LilyAllen #Bestsongever
#girlpower #pressure #teen #girl

Lauren Pappas likes this.

Lauren Pappas Such a lil drama queen.

'Do you know what sucks?' my best friend, Lauren, asks from her seat at the table, her too-short skirt riding up her thighs. 'The HSC starts two days after my eighteenth. I'll probably rock up to the English exam hungover or still high, and I won't even have anyone to brag about it to because everyone will be paying attention to their stupid studies so they can get a stupidly good ATAR and get into a stupid university and live stupid successful lives.'

'Take a breath, ranty,' Ryan says, leaning over to grab a handful of her chips. 'And maybe buy a thesaurus. If I were you I'd be more worried about failing English because the only describing word you know is 'stupid'.'

'It's called an adjective, you moron,' she says, slapping his hand away as he reaches for more chips. 'I know stuff.'

He laughs and walks off.

'God, he's so hot,' she says to me. 'Why did we ever break up?'

'More like why'd you ever go out to begin with?' I ask, looking pointedly at her. 'You guys have nothing in common.'

'We have you and David,' she says, smiling. 'And our incredibly good looks.'

I roll my eyes at her and pull my lunch box out of my bag.

'Speak of the devil,' she says, winking at me, as my boyfriend, David, walks over. He bends down and kisses my collarbone.

'Hey, gorgeous,' he says, smiling. 'I have a surprise for you.'

'You're going to come watch my dance performance after all?' I ask hopefully.

'Eww, no,' he replies, laughing.

'Oh,' I say, pouting. 'Then what?'

'Hey, don't look so sad,' he says, rubbing my shoulder. 'I'm a soccer player. You know ballet's not my thing.'

'Yeah, but I watch all *your* games. This is a big performance. If I make state, I get to perform nationals at the Opera House.'

He sighs, looking away. 'I know, you've explained it before. But even if you beg me a hundred times, I still wouldn't wanna go.'

'Some boyfriend you are ...' Lauren says, giving him a dirty look.

'Don't you have somewhere to be, Pappas?' he asks, giving her a knowing look.

Her eyes widen for a moment and then narrow. She smirks at him.

'Oh, look, there's Mr Cheng,' she says, jumping up suddenly from her seat. 'I need to go ask him something about our Senior Science class.'

I watch her leave, wondering what that was all about.

'So …' he says after a bit, his face hopeful. 'It's Valentine's Day next Friday night, which is also the night that you, Tamara Kapsalis, turn the big one-eight. I thought it might be nice to get a hotel room with a view, steal some champagne from my dad and … just see where the night takes us …' He nuzzles my neck and plants a kiss in the same spot.

'Oh my gosh, David,' I say, shifting away from him slightly. 'We're in the quad, can you take the kissing down a notch? People are staring.'

I used to love our secret kisses in the hall in between classes. But the public displays of affection have been starting to freak me out, because the kisses have been going on for longer and his hands have started wandering into new territory.

'What?' he asks, moving away. 'It's not a big deal. The teachers don't give a damn.'

'It's just not polite,' I say, rolling my eyes. 'Plus we go to a Catholic school.'

I glare at his snort of laughter and he sighs.

'Fine, OK,' he says, gesturing to my lunch box. 'Can I have that banana if you're not going to eat it? I forgot to bring lunch and I don't have any cash on me.'

I smile and hand over the only thing I had planned to eat. At least that'll keep my calorie count down.

'So, what do you think?' he asks after taking a bite.

'Of your monkey-want-a-banana impression?' I ask. 'I think it's really great. The hairy Italian arms certainly help.'

He stifles a laugh. 'No, I meant about Friday.'

'Oh, right,' I say, putting my hand to my forehead. 'I might have something on with my 'rents. Can I get back to you?'

'Really?' he asks. 'Because you told me both your parents were working. And I already cleared it with Lauren, so I know you're not doing anything with the girls.'

'Who told you to clear it with Lauren?' I ask, suddenly frustrated. 'You're supposed to clear it with me, it's *my* birthday.'

'I wanted to surprise you,' he says, agitated. 'I was trying to be nice.'

I sigh. 'I'm sorry,' I say after a moment, but he's standing up to leave. 'Hey, come on, please let me apologise …'

He relents and lets me kiss his nose. 'I already paid a deposit, Tammi,' he says. 'I thought you'd be excited.'

'There's just so much happening this year already,' I tell him. 'I'm already under so much pressure to think about my future and uni preferences and what to do about dancing …'

'Yeah, but we've been going out since the year 10 formal,' he says. 'We need to move forwards.'

I nod, a lump forming in my throat. 'Yeah, you're right, I suppose,' I say, trying to smile.

'I'm putting in a lot of effort, you know,' he says. 'This is harder than you think. It's embarrassing, especially when the boys ask …'

'So you're more concerned with what the boys think of you than about what's right for me?'

'Of course you come first. I know, it's your body, blah, blah, but I'm a bloke. I have needs. I'm starting to feel like something's the matter with me.'

'There's nothing the matter with … Sorry, I have to go to the bathroom,' I say quickly, grabbing my bag and making a run for the toilets. Inside, I rush to the furthest cubicle and, a second later, I hurl into the toilet. The bell rings and I hear people walking to class, but I don't move. I just stand there, staring at the former contents of my stomach. Gosh, just the idea of sex with him is making me physically sick.

After a few minutes, I hear: 'Tammi?' It's Lauren.

'In here,' I croak.

'In where?' comes the response.

I open the cubicle door.

'Hey,' she says. 'Are you OK?'

I shrug. 'I don't know. I feel like I'm going to vomit. Again.'

'Well, you're not pregnant, that's for sure,' she says.

'Oh, come on, not you too,' I say. 'Why is he in such a rush?'

'Well … he's a guy, not a priest,' she says, shrugging. 'It's you I don't get — what *are* you waiting for? A husband?' she asks.

'No,' I say, my face reddening. 'And so what if I was?'

'"So what"?' she asks, looking at me like I've just grown an ear on my forehead. 'It's not normal, that's what. This is not 1932.'

I bow my head.

'Whatever,' she says, rolling her eyes. 'I don't get why you're holding on to it. It's just more teenage baggage that you don't need.'

'Is that supposed to make it easier?' I ask. 'Calling it baggage? Well, baggage can get lost and sent to the wrong place. It can get wrecked too.'

She scoffs. 'A room at the Four Seasons is not the wrong place, Tams. People lose their "baggage" in cars and back gardens and alleys outside parties. You think you'll find someone better than a guy that buys you Tiffany for your birthday and a Prada wallet for Christmas?'

'His parents paid for that stuff …'

'It doesn't matter who paid for it,' she hisses. 'The point is that most girls would kill for a guy like that. You've been spoilt. It's time to spoil him.'

'So he gives me gifts and I give him my body, right?' I ask, looking up. 'There's a word for that, you know.'

She glares at me.

'Fine, let's change the subject,' she says after a moment. 'I put your name down for the yearbook committee.'

'You did *what*?' I ask. 'I told you not to do that.'

I bury my head in my hands, wondering why my voice means nothing. To anyone in my life.

'Relax, it's no big deal, you go to a couple of meetings, write a couple of poems and you're done.'

'I don't even get the point of a yearbook. And I have enough going on in my life as it is.'

'Like what? You're an only child, your parents are loaded, you're passing all your exams … Why are you so stressed?'

I shake my head. 'Why don't you do it then?'

'Because I'm on the formal committee, remember? We can't both do it.'

'Yeah, but it will be so much work, and you know I'm busy with the clown job my 'rents don't know about.'

She shrugs. 'Come on, it's the only way I can have control over what goes in the yearbook,' she pleads.

'What does it matter? They just collect dust in boxes under people's beds anyway.'

'Yeah, but in twenty years' time I might wanna show my kids how awesome I was in high school,' she says, pulling her lip gloss out of her pocket and puckering her lips.

'You'll probably be awesome then too, so I'm sure they'll believe you,' I mumble.

'Hey, it's a lot of hard work staying on top,' she says.

I give her a face and walk out of the cubicle, shaking my head.

'Come on, just do it. That stupid cow Gillian Cummings is on the committee, and if I have no friends on it, who knows what she'll write about me.'

'So that's what this is about,' I say, walking over the mirror. 'Do you have any gum?'

She shakes her head and I turn to the sink. She stands there while I rinse my mouth out, then grabs some paper towel and hands it to me.

'Whoever's in there better make their way to class before I start waving detention forms,' Mr Broderick calls from outside. 'The bell rang ten minutes ago.'

'She probably won't write anything about you if you leave her alone,' I point out, picking up my bag.

'Maybe,' she says. 'But that's not any fun, is it?'

Gillian

Gillian Cummings 'All happy families are alike; each unhappy family is unhappy in its own way.' — Leo Tolstoy, *Anna Karenina*

Lauren Pappas You're not going to throw yourself in front of a train are you? #Didntthinkyoucouldgetmoretragic

The horn blares for the second time and I know my dad's starting to get worked up. Why did I decide to change my outfit at the last minute? Oh, I know, because Sammy decided Mum's spaghetti tasted like crap and hurled it at me when I tried to get him to finish it. Because, as usual, I was the only one taking care of him.

Sigh. I shouldn't get angry at Sammy. It's not his fault. It's not his fault we have to do these ridiculous photo shoots. And it's definitely not his fault that I have nothing to wear.

I hear the car engine turn off from my bedroom window and moments later my door swings open as I'm wrestling with a shirt.

'Aww, come on, Mum, can't you knock?' I ask, pulling the shirt up in front of my chest.

'Relax, Gill, it's not like I don't have boobs myself,' she says, exasperated. 'They just look completely different now.'

She admires her recent breast lift in the mirror, then shakes her head as if she's just remembering why she's there.

I turn away. Nothing I own seems classy enough for this stupid photo shoot for my father's campaign.

Seemingly reading my mind, Mum flicks through the sundresses, t-shirts and denim shorts in my closet. She shakes her head in frustration. 'Your clothes are more suited to concerts, not campaigns,' she says, walking away.

'Wait, don't go,' I plead. 'You know nothing I own is good enough.'

She sighs, and returns to the closet.

'Don't you have a black dress?' she asks. 'That one you wore to your Nanna Robertson's funeral?'

At first I have no idea what she's talking about, but then I remember it.

'Mum, that was three years ago. It's not going to fit me now.'

I'd got a little bit pudgier over the last two years. I was still smallish, but I didn't have the thigh circumference of a Victoria's Secret model, so by most standards I was borderline obese.

'You haven't put on *that* much weight, have you?' she asks, peering at me.

I look at the floor and wish I was three again, so I could be blissfully unaware of her expectations. I couldn't blame her, I suppose. When you were a former Miss World Australia and your husband the great-grandson of one of Australia's prime ministers, you'd want your kid to inherit some of your … something.

I, unfortunately, had nothing.

'Just put it on, we don't have a lot of time,' she says, digging it out of the back of the closet and handing it to me. 'Besides, I'm sure you don't want to wear anything out of my wardrobe.'

'That's an understatement if there ever was one,' I say, slipping on the dress and turning around so that Mum can zip it up. It takes a good few seconds, but when she finally does it, it feels like we've defied some scientific force.

'Try not to breathe and you'll be fine,' she says, smiling.

We make it to the car just before the third blast of the horn, but still have to sit through my father's frustration. Frustration that is probably made worse by the constant beeping of his phone (no doubt his staff are also frustrated by our lateness).

The photo shoot does nothing to diminish everyone's bad mood. His staff are annoyed that they have to work a weekend, my mother is irritated that she has to miss some socialite party or something and my father is antsy because his children are a let-down compared to those of his main opponent in the election. As if it's my fault I haven't single-handedly raised $20,000 for a cancer charity like the other dude's daughter (Dad neglects to acknowledge that the money was raised by sales of a lingerie calendar).

By the time we're done playing happy families for an hour in a Sydney park, I am dying of hunger.

'What's for dinner, Mum?' I ask.

'I'm not cooking today, honey. I just need some time for myself,' she says. Dad sighs heavily from the driver's seat.

'Well, can we get Oporto's on the way home then?' I ask.

'Sweetie, should you really be eating fast food right now? You saw how hard it was to get you in that dress today.'

I bite my tongue to stop the tears. Who needs magazines and pop culture to make you feel bad about yourself when you have parents like these?

When I get home, I turn on my computer, and see that my best friend, Sylvana, is on Skype.

'Heeeeey,' she answers excitedly. 'I am so glad the timings have aligned today and we can finally talk. Thankfully some good came out of today's shoot being cancelled.'

I laugh at her. 'You're so lucky you're beautiful,' I say. '"Timings have aligned" makes no sense.'

'Neither does not being able to talk to my best friend any time I want. How are you, Gill-star?'

'I'm OK. Nothing exciting on my end. Just school and Dad's political bull and what have you.'

'Awww, I'm sorry. Do you want to talk about it?'

'Not really,' I say truthfully. 'I'd rather hear about your adventures in the Big Apple.'

Sylvana and I have been best friends since year 5. She'd been doing a bit of modelling in her spare time, but right before we were due to start the school year, she got a call from a modelling agency in the US, who offered her work in New York. Since she was never the best student, she jumped at the chance.

'Things've been OK — apart from today's cancelled shoot, that is. My agent here seems really hopeful of catwalk stuff for bigger brands, but I think my agency back in Sydney wants me to relocate to Europe now.'

'Oh, what a tough life,' I say, rolling my eyes. 'Do you get to keep the clothes?'

'No!' she exclaims. 'Which sucks. Although some of them are so freakin' ugly, it's not funny.'

'Do you miss home?' I ask.

'I miss my parents, obviously,' she says. 'Even though they get on my nerves. Mum rings every two days to check what I'm eating and to make sure I'm still staying with the old lady she hired to take care of me. How she found her I'll never know.'

'Oh, she's just looking out for you,' I say. 'Trust me, you have it better than most of us. You're in New York!'

'Yeah, but models usually live together here,' she says, shrugging. 'So it's been hard to adjust. But just when I start feeling ungrateful, something happens. Like, last week, I saw Ryan Reynolds outside a pizza joint.'

'Oh my God, did you talk to him?' I ask. 'Was he with Blake?'

'No, I was actually more excited about my pizza,' she admits, laughing. 'The best pizzas I have ever had. And so cheap, only a dollar a slice.'

'So jealous,' I say. 'Although I think I need to lay off the carbs and cheese and whatever else. Even my mum is telling me I'm getting fat.'

'She said that?' she asks.

I nod, ashamed. Sylvana must notice my reaction because she changes the subject.

'Tell me about school,' she says. 'Is Lauren Pappas still being a bitch to you?'

'Honestly, I liked it better when I was invisible,' I admit. 'When I had you by my side.'

'Did you tell her you weren't the one who dobbed them in?' she asks.

I shrug. 'As if I'm gonna convince her,' I say. 'I'm more likely to find a cure for cancer.'

She giggles. 'Well, I'm guessing that having a best friend who lives in New York doesn't make you cool by association.'

'It does not,' I admit. 'Thank the Lord for the library.'

'Gill, you can't spend an entire year in the library,' she says, looking at me sternly. 'Make some new friends.'

'We'll see,' I say. 'I put my name down for the yearbook committee. Which you were supposed to join too.'

'Until the runway called,' she says, smiling. 'Trust me, I'm better at that. Who else is on it?'

'Mr Broderick put the new girl on it, so she gets to know everyone. That's all I know.'

'New girl?'

'Yeah, from Melbourne. I have no idea why they let her come in year 12. It's weird. Anyway, she seems OK. Dramatic, uses a lot of big words. Like, kind of a cross between snobby and antsy. Reeeaaeally down on the place.'

'Melbournians hate Sydney,' Sylvana says with authority. 'It's a known fact.'

'Whatever,' I tell her. 'Not my problem. I just have to finish school and leave.'

Sylvana looks down for a moment and reaches for something off-screen.

'Aww, I have to run,' she says. 'That was my phone — there's a casting downtown. Let's talk again soon, I miss you.'

I nod, trying not to show my disappointment. Our talks have been shorter and less frequent lately, and the wildly different time zones don't help.

'Go visit my parents, will you? Give them a hug for me?'

'Of course,' I promise her. 'Maybe I'll also get discovered selling cigarettes at a convenience store. Although I don't have your beautiful half-Czech, half-Jordanian colouring.'

'Aww, your luck will come. This year's going to be different for you. I can feel it in my bones.'

'Anyone can feel your bones, you skinny thing,' I say to her, laughing. 'Good luck at the casting.'

She blows a kiss, then the screen goes blank. And, suddenly, I'm back to being alone with my thoughts.

As much as I'm happy for her, it's really hard watching her life unfold while mine stays still.

But I only have to wait a year. As soon as this year is over, I'll be able to get out. Out of my school, out of my home, out into the real world, and on to the rest of my life.

RYAN

Ryan Fleming It burns.

The bell rings right as I look up at the clock for what seems like the millionth time. And just like that, I'm facing the moment I never wanted to face, never *thought* I'd face. I bury my head in my bag, pretending to pack my things to avoid the questions, remarks and looks of pity from my classmates.

But when I zip up my bag, no one's around. My accident is old news. To everyone except me.

I make my way to Mrs H's office, wondering what quote she will have for me today. Will it be comforting or motivational? It's not like it matters — whatever she says won't change anything. I belong on the field.

As I walk through the hallway, I pass two year 10 boys in their cricket gear, laughing and jostling with each other, tossing a ball between them. I think about putting my school-captain hat on and telling them they shouldn't be playing inside, but decide against it and walk by them in silence.

I'm still watching them over my shoulder when I walk straight into someone. It's a girl I don't know. She's dropped her phone, so I bend down to pick it up. I'm about to tell her off for wearing her school uniform today instead of her sports uniform, but she's quicker than I am.

'A perv and a klutz in one, just great,' she says, rolling her eyes.

'Huh?'

'A Neanderthal too,' she says, snatching her phone out of my hand and inspecting it. 'Even better. And now my phone cover is cracked.'

'What are you talking about? Who are you?' I ask, finding my voice.

'None of your business,' she says, slipping the phone into her pocket without looking at me.

'OK, fine, so that leaves what the hell you're talking about. Who's a perv?'

'Ah, that would be you,' she replies, looking at me if I were stupid. 'If you weren't too busy staring at jailbait over there changing in the hallway, you wouldn't have crashed into me.'

I turn around and for the first time notice two junior girls standing by a locker a few metres behind. One is attempting to shield the other as she slides a pair of shorts on underneath her netball skirt, but unfortunately (or fortunately, if you are a perv) you can still see everything.

'Oi,' I yell out across the hall. 'What the hell is wrong with you? Go to the bathroom.'

The girls burst into giggles.

'Sorry, Ryan,' they call out as they pick up their bags and head off. I shake my head and turn back to the girl.

'Thank Christ a teacher didn't walk past, it would have —'

'Hey, Ryan the perv-klutz-Neanderthal,' she interrupts, 'let me tell you what's wrong with girls like them: no concept of privacy. They've probably got dozens of pouty bathroom selfies in their underwear on Instagram. Being caught changing in the hallway is nothing.'

'Yuck, too much information,' I say.

She shrugs.

'OK, can't handle the truth,' she says. 'Anyway, I've just been to see Mrs H and she's sent me off to a Mr Broderick's office, but I think I'm lost. Whoever designed this school should be sterilised. Please tell me you're good with directions.'

'Not before I point out that I was looking at the guys tossing the cricket ball around,' I say, staring her down. 'I didn't even see the girls changing.'

'Yeah, sure, good cover,' she says, nodding absently.

I take a deep breath and sigh. 'I wasn't looking at the girls,' I say slowly. 'I was looking at the boys.'

'Boys, huh?' she says, shrugging. 'Well, whatever floats your boat, then. It's cool, I don't judge. Anyway, if you're not going to help me I should go find someone who will.'

I put my palm to my forehead in frustration as she walks away.

Then she calls out, 'You owe me a new phone cover.'

I whip around. 'I don't owe you anything,' I call back. 'You shouldn't be texting and walking in the hallway.'

'It would have cost you more if the phone broke,' she says in a sing-song voice, turning around and putting her hands out, as if she's trying to convince me what a good deal that is.

'You're getting nothing,' I yell.

'I like covers with polka dots,' she yells back as she disappears from view. 'And red's my favourite colour.'

Outside Mrs H's office, I wait on the couch and try not to make eye contact with the office lady who always updates me on her granddaughter who I don't know and don't care about.

After a few minutes, Mrs H calls me in and motions for me to sit on one of the chairs opposite her desk.

'And how has the new school year been so far, Ryan?' she asks. Mrs H always starts her first sentence with 'and'. It's weird, but it suits her, even though we'd get marked down if we did the same thing in English.

'It's been just fine,' I reply. 'But it's only the first week so it's probably all downhill from here.'

'Ryan,' she says, sitting on the edge of her desk, 'it's been a tough few months, I know that. But you're a strong, resilient boy. So maybe professional sports are not in your future, but look at your grades — you can do anything.'

'Yeah, well, soccer's everything to me,' I tell her. 'Always has been, always will be.'

She looks out the window at the buses driving off, taking their respective teams to sporting matches.

'It's not how far you fall, but how high you bounce that counts,' she says, turning back to me.

'Confucius?' I ask.

'Zig Ziglar,' she tells me. 'And he has a point. You were hurt, I get it. But stop looking at your injury as if it's a dead end as opposed to a detour. Something else on this earth can and will make you happy; you just have to get out there and pump some optimism back into your heart so that you're able to bounce beyond your hurt and find it.'

I sigh. Bounce?

'And if you don't find it this year, that's OK too,' she says, smiling. 'But, Ryan, stop sourpussing around. You're so much more than an athlete. Your academic record is excellent, you're loved by your peers, and I'm sure you're well aware that you're on the way to getting the St Jerome Medal, which could mean that financially your next step out of this school is set for three years.'

'But it's not going to be at a university in Europe where I can play football in front of professional scouts,' I say.

'No, it won't be,' she tells me. 'But that's no excuse to bum around for the rest of your life. And if you're going to be down and out on your schooling this year, you might as well leave now.'

I hang my head down in shame. The woman has a point.

'I'm giving you something to distract yourself until you find what it is you're looking for,' she says, handing me a file off her desk. 'Your first meeting is tomorrow, 3 p.m. in the computer lab. You'll collect the keys for the lab from the office at 2.55 and return them one hour later and not a minute after. The office ladies have homes to get to also.'

I glance at the folder and back up at her.

'The yearbook?' I ask. 'Oh, Miss, please don't make me do this. It's totally not my thing.'

'It's "totally" already decided,' she replies, giving me an evil little smile. '"Totes" decided even, as some of your classmates would say. You're in charge; don't let me down.'

'Mrs H, you don't understand,' I beg. 'A girl would do a much better job. They save photos. They keep journals. All my memories involve bats and balls.'

'Which is exactly why I chose you. Yin and yang — it's all about balance,' she says. 'And photos can be easily obtained. I'll make an announcement requesting that people provide materials.

You don't have to come up with it entirely on your own, you know.'

I don't answer.

'Oh Ryan, you're acting like I just asked you to clean toilets for the rest of the year! It's only a yearbook.'

I open my mouth to talk, but she's not finished.

'And need I remind you that if you still want to be in the running for the St Jerome Medal you need to be on top of your extra curriculars …'

'And without soccer I'm no longer on top of them?'

'Good golly, he's got it!' she says, smiling.

I pick up the file and my bag and stand up.

'Who else is on the committee?' I ask.

'Go to the meeting and you'll see.'

I pass through the front office on the way out of the school grounds and stop to stare at the plaques on the wall. Four years in a row we'd won the biggest soccer comp for private school students in Sydney. This year I would have had the chance to play interstate.

Now, everything was different. Life had changed, and I couldn't aim like I used to. Worse, I could no longer see the goal.

Charlie

Charlie Scanlon I miss Melbourne.

Pete Brady and **Katy Coolidge-Brown** like this.

Katy Coolidge-Brown #comehomecharlie

Charlie Scanlon I LOVE that I have my own hashtag Xx

Charlie Scanlon:
Kill. Me. Now.
Pete Brady:
That request is getting a little old.
Charlie Scanlon:
This time I'm serious. I've been asked to join the
YEARBOOK COMMITTEE!!!
Pete Brady:
Ew, sucked in! LOL! Don't they know you hate everything?
Charlie Scanlon:
Who's they? I've spoken to three people since I arrived: the

canteen lady, the deputy principal and the librarian who
won't let me watch TV shows inside the library.

Pete Brady:
So you haven't made any friends yet?

Charlie Scanlon:
You know my mantra. *No roots.*

Pete Brady:
Everyone needs friends …

Charlie Scanlon:
You should be on my side.

Pete Brady:
Or by your side, which is why you need to
#comehomecharlie

He sends me a winking-face emoji and I go warm and fuzzy
inside. The guy started a hashtag at my old school — how can I
not? Although there are a few issues with this:

1. I think I have a crush on my best friend.
2. He lives 877 kilometres away.
3. The situation is a bit chick–flick.
4. Chick flicks generalise. They never go beyond the
    happy ending.
5. If my happy ending is Pete, I won't complain about it.
6. Complaining is in my DNA. If I stop complaining, I
    have relinquished a part of myself to a man.
7. That's anti-feminist.

The bell's annoying ring disturbs the list-making in my head.
I glance at my watch and sigh. The committee meeting has come

despite my constant praying that it would get cancelled. And people wonder why I'm such a staunch atheist. I'm the victim here, shouldn't God be on my side?

I find my way to the computer lab, where the only other person is already seated and logged in to her school account.

I glance at the open, newish-looking notebook next to her. She has it open to a new page, and has written 'The Yearbook Committee — Minutes for March Meeting' at the top, and underlined it in red pen. I resist the urge to make fun of her with all my might, and feel like I've earned a sundae for my efforts.

'Hi,' she says, a little shyly. 'I'm Gillian. I'm in your Legal class. I like that your opinions give Mr Hess a run for his money. Do you like the school so far?'

'It could be worse,' I say, giving her a half-smile. 'No one's told me to wear pink on Wednesdays yet.'

'*Mean Girls* never gets old,' she says, smiling. 'But if they tell you to, maybe you should. Regina George has got nothing on the queen bee here.'

'You mean Lauren Pappas,' I say, nodding.

'Wow, you're fast,' she says. 'I've been going to school with these people for six years and I'm still learning things the hard way.'

I shrug. 'I'm good at reading people, I guess. I watch a lot of crime shows, if that explains it.'

She laughs, just as a scruffy-looking guy walks in, seeming even less enthusiastic than I feel. Something about him strikes me — there's something weirdly familiar about his eyes, his cheekbones, the way he seems both open and dismissive at once. I watch him take the seat in the furthest back corner, smack-bang against the wall, as if he hopes it will suck him in and transport him to a parallel universe. I decide to keep my eye on him — if it works, I definitely want in.

'Matty, do you really need to be wearing that hoodie right now?' a voice asks from the front of the room.

The voice belongs to Ryan the Perv, who tosses a file on the teacher's desk in the front and puts his hands on his hips, like he's trying to take charge.

'You take this school-captain thing too seriously,' Matty mutters.

'No, I mean it's hot. You know what, forget it.'

We sit in silence for several minutes, Ryan rubbing the back of his neck.

Ryan stops being so awkward when another girl, who I always see hovering around him and his mates, walks in.

'I see that she got to you,' he says to her, smiling.

'She always does,' she replies in a sing-song voice, taking the seat in the front row.

'Well, at least there's someone I know here,' he says.

Matty grunts from the back.

'Problem?' Ryan asks.

'You know, if you spoke to us, we would also be people that you knew,' he says quietly.

'Sorry, dude, not what I meant.'

The girl in the front rolls her eyes.

Ryan pulls a piece of paper from his pocket.

'Um, maybe we should just get started,' he says, looking at us all. 'Mrs H did say there would only be five people, so I guess it's just us.'

'Wow, the Neanderthal can count,' I say.

His eyes flash at me, but it's his friend who speaks.

'Who is this?' she asks, gesturing at me.

'Charlie Scanlon,' I say, giving her a small wave. 'Feminist killjoy. Currently pondering our generation's dumbing-down, and turns out the best case studies are right here at Holy Family.'

The room goes silent.

'I'm kidding,' I tell her, giving her a face. 'Well, except about the feminist killjoy part.'

She gives me a strange, confused look before turning back to Ryan. 'Seriously, you want *her* to work on the yearbook?'

'Well, actually —' he says, but I interject.

'Oh, I don't want to work on your stupid yearbook,' I explain. 'I was forced here. Apparently the best way to introduce new students to the school is to get them working on a project where they'll get to know the class through year 7 photos and those stupid profiles with dumb ambitions for the future and final quotes they found on the internet next to "news" items on the Kardashians.'

'Okaaayyy,' she says, turning her chair away from me slightly. I cheer inwardly, while Ryan looks on, dumbstruck.

'OK, so we've established you don't want to be here —' I open my mouth to say something else, but Ryan puts his hand out to stop me — 'on this committee or at this school. Trust me, I think I've got it.'

I lean back in my seat, smug.

'What about everyone else?' he asks. 'What can you bring?'

'I'm really excited to compile the best years of our high-school lives in one book we'll be able to treasure later,' Gillian says. 'Most of us are saying we can't wait to finish, but I bet we'll look back fondly on our memories in fifteen years' time.'

What a loser.

'Do you have any strengths that can help with the project?' Ryan asks her.

'Enthusiasm, clearly,' the other girl scoffs. Ryan suppresses a laugh, but Gillian misses the joke.

'Yep, very enthusiastic,' she says animatedly. 'I have loads of photos from all our excursions and camps, and I'm happy to ask around for more. I'll also record minutes of our meetings.'

'Ahh, I don't know if that's necessary ...' Ryan says, his voice trailing off.

She shrugs, unfazed. 'Maybe I'll just write them down for me then. I like keeping records of stuff. I can just send you action points. Of stuff we need to do.'

'Errr, OK,' he says uncertainly, looking a little out of his depth.

'Oh, and I can help with profiles too. You know — last words, favourite memories, and ambitions for the future,' she pipes up.

'Cool,' Ryan says. 'They'll probably be the hardest, there's always going to be lazy people we'll have to chase up.'

'So if they don't even care about the yearbook, why are we bothering?' Matty asks.

Ryan shrugs. 'I dunno,' he says simply. 'It's just the done thing.'

Matty raises his eyebrows, then puts his headphones on. I hear the faint chords of punk music behind me, and I'm jealous he has something to escape into. The room is awkwardly silent again.

Ryan and his friend start talking in hushed tones, and in front of me Gillian looks attentive, as if being on good behaviour will earn her a gold star. I shake my head.

'We should probably start something,' I say, my voice rising. 'None of us except her want to be here. Let's treat it like a Band-Aid and get it over with quick.'

'OK, where do we start?' Ryan asks. 'Mrs H put me in charge of this project and I have no idea what to do.'

'I was going to start with who made you boss anyway, but you've already cleared that up with the whole I'm-down-with-the-principal comment, so let's move on,' I tell him.

'Let's move on, *Ryan*,' he says slowly, pointing to himself.

'Ryan?' I ask. 'Hmmm, I liked you so much more as Pervert-from-the-Hallway.'

His friend's head swings up and she looks from him to me.

'She thinks she saw something that she didn't,' he explains.

'He was watching girls undress in the hallway,' I whisper to her knowingly, loud enough for everyone to hear.

'I didn't even see those girls,' he says, raising his voice. 'I WAS WATCHING THE BOYS WITH THE BALL.'

I bite my lip to stifle a laugh. I could heckle this guy forever.

'And she still doesn't believe me,' he says, putting his arms out then dropping them to his side. 'Not that it matters, so let's move on. Tammi, what can you bring to the yearbook?'

'I don't know,' she says. 'Ask Lauren.'

'Come on, Tams, anything,' he pleads.

She shrugs. 'I'll let you know,' she mutters.

'Why? Do you need to ask someone's permission?' I ask her.

'My best friend,' she says, not looking at me. 'She kind of made me do this. No bad pictures of her, favourable coverage, you know.'

Gillian scoffs and Tammi immediately turns around, narrowing her eyes at her.

'Problem?'

'She can't control everything,' Gillian says, her voice slightly trembling. 'It has to be fair.'

'Don't talk to me about fair,' Tammi replies, shaking her head.

'So we just have to ignore the fact that she's been a snob for six years?'

'You're not the only one on the team, Gill,' she snaps. 'We're all contributing. We all have a say.'

Gillian looks away. I almost feel sorry for her, but I don't want to say anything. I'm not here to make friends. *No roots.* I pull my phone out of my pocket and text my friend Katy — anything to make the time pass.

At ten minutes to four, we still haven't done anything besides clash. Ryan looks at us all from his perch on the teacher's desk. By now, Tammi has her head on the desk, Gillian has forgotten about her minutes and is looking out the window, I'm giving Ryan a blank stare and Matty is still lost in his music.

'Why do I have a feeling this is going to be more trouble than it's worth?' he asks as his phone alarm beeps. 'Meeting over,' he yells out. 'Next one in a month. Same time, same place. Bring friendlier attitudes.'

I'm all the way down the hall when I hear a door slam. I turn around to see Ryan, sunk down to the floor, back against the wall, head in his hands.

Matty

Matty Fullerton is sick of being bothered by the same old crap.

'The wheels on the bus go round and round, round and round, round and round ...'

For Christ's sake, I think, as the father and his three-year-old son in front of me go for it a third time. Couldn't they pick a less repetitive nursery rhyme? I sigh as loudly as I possibly can, hoping that they'll get the hint. But they don't, and with every bus stop that they don't get off at, it's looking more and more likely that I won't get home. Because I'll probably wind up punching Dad in the face and handing myself in to the police, because I'm a loser like that. A loser with a conscience.

Across the aisle, an old lady smiles at the performing duo and I realise that it's only me who's bothered by the sight of a father sharing a nice-yet-ordinary moment with his son. I wonder if there were similar moments between my own dad and me.

I strain my brain trying to remember something, anything — even the smallest fragment. An image of work boots in the hallway, a manly scent, the feel of stubble. But there's nothing. Instead, the reminder of my very blank past and my uncertain future sits in my backpack, waiting for action: another reminder of where I am (posh private school) and what I lack (a home environment worthy of being at one).

I get off the bus, pull the hoodie low over my face and start walking home. I'm checking the weather on my phone when I walk straight into a tall, hard body.

'Watch where you're going, dickhead,' the body's owner says.

I look up, and grin.

'Mo,' I say, clasping his arm. 'If your parents knew what your language was like …'

He laughs. 'How you been, Matt?'

I nod, smiling. 'Not bad, brother. And you?'

He shakes his head. 'Yeah, same old, same old.'

'Still loving those job sites?' I ask. 'Or are you sick of laying bricks?'

'Just you wait till I finish my TAFE certificate, man. Tradies make heaps of money. Your posh private school shoulda taught you that.'

'As if I'd listen anyway,' I tell him, smirking. 'How's Billy?'

'Still out, which is good. My dad watches him like a hawk.'

'You can't blame him,' I say. 'He put your parents through hell.'

'All of us, bro,' he says. 'We had to move from a nice house to a two-bedroom unit so my parents could pay his bail, you know? My sisters have nowhere to study, and Zeina's school captain. She's smart, she needs the space.'

'You don't need to tell me, man, I remember.'

'Want to come eat?' he asks. 'Mum made stuffed vine leaves today. I know you love 'em.'

I laugh. 'Tell your mum I miss her, I'll be round soon. I can't believe I haven't seen the new place. Been buried under homework and stuff.'

He shakes his head. 'Nothing to see anyway,' he tells me. 'We moved, but everything stayed the same.'

I pat his back. 'Some things do,' I agree. 'Catch you later.'

I continue walking. Back before I got the scholarship to Holy Family, Mohamed and I were best mates at Strathfield South High School. Now, his twin sister, Zeina, is the school captain, and his younger sister, Sarah — who put on her hijab at thirteen and didn't let her father's protests about discrimination change her decision — will probably be premier one day. And my best mate was making the kind of money I desperately needed, while I was stuck in a school where the people had about as much depth as a kiddie pool. Mo's home life — so traditional, so nuclear — was so different to my own. Their biggest problem was with elder brother Bilal's drug problem.

I duck into the corner store for a bag of pasta and a jar of sauce. If my life was like Mohamed's, I think, I wouldn't be cooking my own dinner. And I'd probably know something about my dad.

But it's not.

I didn't think that my attendance at Holy Family was going to improve my life in any way, but every time I doubted my presence there, I remembered Mo's parents' enthusiasm when I told them that I had got a scholarship. Those people were the biggest champions of education.

'We came from nothing,' his father would tell me. 'Bombs dropping on our homes all the time. Our own government used us as human shields. We couldn't trust them, couldn't trust the Israelis. We had no one. Here, my children have a life. They study, they get jobs. This country — Allah shower his blessings upon it — gives us so much. You get a scholarship at fancy school, you take it. My Sarah already talks about applying for uni scholarships, *Inshallah*.'

As if I could let the bloke down. So I took the scholarship. And not just for him, but for my mum too — I don't know if it was the grand building and immaculate gardens, or its rich history, but she was obsessed with the place. She once told me that when she was young she would walk past it every day on her walk to her own school, and see the girls in their blazers and hats, and dream of giving her children a better life than she got. A life that would start at this school, a life that would be filled with promise. Go figure.

I walk into our flat and the darkness is hard to adjust to after being outside.

'No miracles today, I see,' I say to the limp body on the couch. She sighs and I feel cruel, but I remember reading that you should try to maintain some normalcy, and this is the way we've always spoken to each other.

'Did you move at all today?' I press. 'Because I swear that was the position you were in when I left this morning and you were watching *The Today Show*.'

An empty bottle of cheap red wine is next to her, and a cockroach is feasting on some shards of chocolate that have fallen to the floor. She sees me eyeing it.

'I got hungry,' she mumbles, ashamed.

'You used to make proper food when you were hungry,' I tell her. 'What happened?'

There's a long pause. Then she says, 'Don't get frustrated at me.'

'Well, what do you expect? You won't even talk to someone. A professional, a friend. Me, even.'

I shake my head, then start towards my room.

'I just can't get up any more,' she says, quietly.

'Yeah, well, lucky I can get up for you,' I mumble.

I take my bag to my room and throw it against the wall, putting on Linkin Park's 'Numb' at full blast. A retro choice, I know, but a song that definitely sums up the situation.

I take the letter out of my bag and stare at it. Parent–teacher night. How would I get out of this one? Mum's obviously not in any condition to go, and if she didn't, Mr Broderick would come down on me. The guy was waiting for me to stuff up. Again.

Don't get me wrong, parent–teacher nights were fine at my old school. We fit in, Mum and me. I don't need to go into how different we are from the families at Holy Family, and parent–teacher nights are just a fraction of the reason. My classmates have the best lives: parties, the latest phones and tablets, promises of cars with good HSC results, plans for schoolies in Thailand and aspirations to move to London after a probably guaranteed university education that their parents paid for.

My mum couldn't even afford to pay her phone bill right now. And even without her current mental situation weighing her down, she would feel like crap next to all those glam mothers that are outside the gates every day.

I crumple the letter up and throw it against the wall, watching it fall into my garbage bin.

Later, while Mum sleeps, I walk through the flat and open the windows. The fresh air is nice, so I head outside to sit at the top of the stairs. We live in a unit block on the Hume Highway bordering Enfield and South Strathfield, and our flat has outside access. These buildings are red-brick, old, and usually filled with even older residents or housing commission bogans. Mum paid off the place with her inheritance when I was younger; looking at her now, it's hard to believe she once managed to support herself and a child and buy a place in the process.

I glance at the time on my phone and realise that it's late, and I haven't eaten yet, so I head back inside. I'm stirring pasta sauce while reading *Hamlet* when I hear her get up. She walks over slowly, and sits at the little kitchen table we got from a garage sale when I was six. I helped her paint it on the front lawn; seeing it every day reminds me that we're a team. So I decide to keep dinner diplomatic.

'What's my handsome little man doing?' she asks after a moment.

'I'm not a little man any more, Ma,' I say. *But I want to be. I want to be a kid again.*

'No, you're not, are you?' she replies, ruffling my hair as I place a plate before her. 'And you take such good care of me. My alpha and omega — my beginning and my end.'

I shrug at her affection and add some parmesan to her plate, then sit opposite her.

'Tastes nice, but this is more than I can eat,' she says.

'It's from a jar, it's certainly not as nice as your one with the real tomatoes and the fresh basil.'

She gives me a half-smile and continues eating her dinner, taking super small bites. After some minutes of quiet, she pushes her plate away.

'Sorry,' she says, looking at me. 'I don't have much of an appetite.'

'It's fine,' I reassure her. 'I'll just put it in the fridge. You should reheat it for lunch tomorrow.'

'Oh, I don't know if I —'

'Mum, it's better than chocolate and red wine.' I look at her pointedly and she purses her lips, like a chastised child.

Is this what my life has come to? I think, as I place the cutlery in the sink, realising more than ever that I need a father — someone — just so I don't feel so alone.

'Mum, there's parent–teacher night in two weeks, and I was wondering …'

'Matty, you know I'm not up to it right now,' she says, waving me away. 'I can't even go to work.'

'Actually, I was wondering … about maybe reaching out to my father.'

She widens her eyes. 'You've never asked about him before.'

I shrug. 'Well, I guess the time has come.'

She stands up from the table in a huff.

'No, Matthew,' she says, tossing her arm behind her as she walks out of the room. 'Take my word for it. We don't need him.'

I drape the teatowel over my shoulder, turn on the taps and sigh.

That's where you're wrong, Mum, I think, as I lean over the sink. *I need him.*

After I'm done tidying up, I sit at the table and try to do some homework, but my mood gets the better of me and I go to my room and hop online instead, checking out my favourite music blogs. Facebook pings a chat notification and I cringe.

Gillian Cummings:
I'm just about to send out the action points from the April meeting. You probably won't read them so I need to remind you about the camera. Charlie asked you about it and you left her hanging.

Matty Fullerton:
Who?
Gillian Cummings:
Charlie Scanlon, the new girl. She asked you to help her
with the school's camera and you went 'No sorry I'm
busy'.
Matty Fullerton:
Were you spying on me or something?
Gillian Cummings:
No, I just kinda overheard as you guys left the meeting.
It was a bit slack because she's new. And she needs that
camera for yearbook stuff.
Matty Fullerton:
This is the first time you've spoken to me on chat in the
18 months we've known each other and you're asking me
about some chick with an attitude problem?
Gillian Cummings:
We should all make her feel welcome.
Matty Fullerton:
I don't even feel welcome, how am I supposed to help her?
Plus I don't even care about that stupid yearbook.
Gillian Cummings:
It's just a camera.
Matty Fullerton:
You show her then, since you're so invested in the cause.
Gillian Cummings:
I don't know how to use it. You're always fiddling with it
at school functions. And you're the only student on the
committee doing ART, which means Mr Murdoch will give
it to you.

Matty Fullerton:
Why did you put art in capital letters? It's not an
abbreviation.
Gillian Cummings:
Oh, sorry. I'll fix that before I send the action points out.

Fed up with the conversation, I sign out, then crawl into bed
and turn out the light. But I can't sleep. My mind won't stop
wandering, so I get up and fish the letter about the parent–teacher
night out of the bin and stare at it for a moment.

My bedroom door is ajar, and I see blue light from the TV
flashing in the darkened living room down the corridor. I tiptoe
over and turn it off, being careful not to wake up Mum in the
process.

Back in my room, I sit on my bed and look at the letter once
again. I smooth out the wrinkles and then fiddle around for the
little box I keep under my bed, and place the letter inside.

Everything I've ever wanted to tell him and show him sits in
there, waiting for the day when he'll no longer be a mystery and
my life will be closer to 'complete'.

Or will it?

THE YEARBOOK COMMITTEE
Minutes for April Meeting

Recorded by: Gillian Cummings

Meeting Chair: Ryan Fleming (with occasional takeovers by Charlie Scanlon)

In attendance: Ryan Fleming, Charlie Scanlon, Matty Fullerton, Tammi Kapsalis, Gillian Cummings

NB: No March meeting minutes due to pretty crazy (and slightly unproductive) meeting.

Discussion:

* Another discussion on what everyone can contribute to the yearbook. Charlie says she can probably take pictures and write stuff, but she prefers writing. Tammi says she will look after people's profiles. Charlie makes comments about how the last words and ambitions listed in those profiles are going to give her a headache, because everyone is so 'shallow'. Ryan replies that she is giving him a headache.

* Matty sighs and asks if it is compulsory to attend meetings. He said this is the second one and he already feels like it is pointless. Ryan's facial expression says it all (and by 'all', I mean 'yes, it is compulsory'). Matty says his job is

really important to him right now, he needs the money. He proposes to put the entire yearbook together in his own time, if everyone else collects the content. No one argues, because he is a scholarship kid and we are 'advantaged'.

* But then Tammi says it's unfair, because she also has a job and she needs the money too. Ryan looks confused. She says she's saving up for uni and her parents don't want her to study off-campus, so she is relying on herself instead of them. Ryan asks if David knows. Tammi says that if he doesn't, it's because he wasn't listening. I hear her mutter that he never listens. (Note to self: Maybe life's not rosy for the popular kids. But maybe it's got nothing to do with popularity and everything to do with David being a jerk.)

* Tammi's mood means she is now giving Matty attitude. Matty retaliates. For a guy who is really quiet (we have never spoken) he can get quite icy. It suits the hoodie he is wearing. (Note to self: Maybe ask why he never gets in trouble for it. Like, I wore a pink wrap-around cuff to school once and got a recess detention.) On her way back to the desk Tammi looks at what I am writing. 'Those are not minutes,' she says. Apparently I am doing them wrong, to which Matty pointed out that if we don't really need them,

then it doesn't matter. She shrugged. (Note to self: I like them conversational.)
* Charlie tells Ryan that if he's going to be in charge, he needs to step up and stop this meeting being a waste of time. He says that he can't force people to get along. Then she says he's not the man for the job.
* The bell rings. No one listens as Ryan calls out the next meeting time. Including me. (Was trying to work up courage to ask Matty about hoodie. Decided against it.)

Action Points:
* Note to self: Bring snacks to next meeting. Food makes everyone happy.
* Remind Matty that, as the only ~~ART~~ art student, he needs to get the camera from Mr Murdoch and show Charlie how to use it. Charlie seems aware of this and is currently following him outside.

Tammi

Tammi Kap is listening to 'Girls Just Want to Have Fun'. When Cyndi Lauper talks about boys hiding beautiful girls away, I want to pump up the volume. Because I totes want to be a girl who walks in the sun.

Lauren Pappas Old school, I like it.

Manda Panda Love that song! We should watch the movie one night!

I hurry through the park, trying to make it back to the bus stop before the rain starts. Gosh, I can't believe I let that woman wrangle an extra half-hour out of me without paying me any extra cash.

I stop for a moment to catch my breath, then look at the time. Shit. I'm going to miss the bus. That means I'm going to have to wait an extra eighteen minutes for the next bus, in the rain, and I'll be home half an hour late, which means Mum and Dad will beat me home and I won't be able to sneak my gear upstairs without someone noticing.

I try to think of ways I can tell Dad about this job. I'd need to be tough about it, and for all the cons that would inevitably come from being honest, the one big pro would be that I would no longer need to lie. Maybe he'd even contribute something to my savings fund.

As if, I think, given that my father is the least supportive of my career aspirations.

I sit on the bus-stop bench and put my large canvas bag on my lap. Sixteen minutes until the bus arrives. Plenty of time to think up a plausible excuse for my tardiness, but a man arrives and decides to start a conversation, and suddenly my brainstorming has to wait.

'You got some change on ya, love?' he asks.

'Um, I'll have a look,' I reply, feeling sorry for him.

I turn myself slightly to the side and burrow through my bag for my wallet, but I don't have much change, not even a five-dollar note. I fish out what coins I have — a one-dollar coin and a few pieces of small silver — and hand them to him.

'That's all I can spare, sorry,' I explain apologetically.

'What about that tenner?' he asks, unashamed. I look at him blankly. Since when did people stop being thankful for any charity they got? Judging by his attitude, this man didn't need the money, he just wanted it. The woman from work's face comes back to me and I realise she had also taken advantage of me, even if her strategy was a bit more subtle.

I wish I could just disappear, if only to save myself from the stench of cigarettes and beer.

'You know what?' I say, standing up. 'I think I'll just ring a friend to come get me.'

I rifle through my bag for my phone and dial David's number.

'Hey, baby,' he answers drowsily. 'Whatcha doing?'

'Are you asleep?' I ask. 'It's 1 p.m.'

'Yeah, Ryan and I had a late night,' he explains.

'Are you busy?'

'Why, are you OK?'

'I'm fine,' I assure him. 'Just in Burwood. Hoping you could come pick me up, save me from waiting for the bus, which will take forever. I need to get back home before Mum and Dad, so I can hide the stuff in my room.'

'Ahh, I don't know, babe,' he says. 'It's no big deal, just tell them the truth. I'm sure they'll be fine with it eventually. '

'OK,' I say quietly.

'You're upset,' he says, sighing.

'Well, you know what I'm up against,' I explain. 'It wouldn't hurt for you be there for me when I need you.'

'I'm always there for you,' he says defensively. 'But this plan just keeps getting more and more complicated. I'm telling you, they'll come around.'

'So easy for you to say; your future's not riding on this.'

I hear him yawn and I look up at the sky, desperate. 'So you're not coming?' I ask again, hopefully.

'I can't now, I told you,' he says. 'Seriously, it'll be OK.'

'Sure, I guess,' I say, deflated.

'Hey — no harm done right?'

'Don't be silly,' I tell him. 'I'm a big girl. I'll be fine.'

I hang up and glance at the time again, wishing I had my driver's licence. And a car for that matter. I figure I might as well run or walk home — sure, it will be more hassle, but at least I won't have to sit next to the deadbeat at the bus stop who will probably rob me.

I cut through the park and quicken my pace, scratching at the remnants of face paint around my ears and hairline, and dodging parents with prams, pensioners taking walks and dogs on leashes.

I'm nearly on the other side when something smashes into the side of my head, knocking me over.

As I struggle to untangle myself from the two bags I'm carrying, the contents of which have scattered all over the path, the offending object — a football — is picked up and thrown to a horde of boys standing metres away by a devastatingly good-looking guy in a raglan tee and shorts.

'I'm so sorry,' he says. 'We boys lose our coordination when a girl walks past.'

I blush a little and he laughs.

'I meant the blonde chick over there,' he says, nodding his head in the direction of a tall woman running around the park in a crop top. 'Fred's got a thing for boobs.'

'Yeah, well, tell Fred he should try to get his fix at a time when he's not kicking footballs around, for the safety of us women without big boobs.'

He laughs again as I dust myself off.

'Here, let me help you,' he says, reaching down to grab my jumpsuit, shoes and red nose. 'Dress-up party?' he asks.

'Yeah, except I was the only one in a costume,' I tell him, taking my things and shoving them back into my canvas bag with ferocity. I'm ridiculously late now.

He looks at me blankly.

'Hired help,' I say, waving my bright-blue afro wig at him. 'I'm Tatty the Clown. I do kids' parties.'

'Your name is Tatty?'

'Tamara. But everyone calls me Tammi. Well, except the kids.'

'What, were you scared a bunch of six-year-olds would track you down if they knew your real name?'

I grin. 'You'd be surprised at what they're capable of.'

Something wet lands on my cheek and I look up. A raindrop. A second later, the clouds open up and it starts to pour, heavy and fast.

'I knew I should have taken the bus,' I mutter. 'I'm sorry, I have to go.'

'Wait —' he starts.

I quickly snatch my other bag off him. 'No, really, I have to run now.'

'You're walking? You have so much stuff, I can take it for you.'

I give him a quizzical look.

'What I mean is, I can take you. If we ride, it'll be much quicker.'

'Not allowed on motorbikes, sorry,' I say, a little weirded out. 'But thanks anyway.'

'Who said anything about a motor?'

He smiles and I'm shocked once again by how good-looking he is.

He points to a bike rack and I laugh. The rain has slowed slightly, but I'm already drenched.

'How are two people — and all this stuff — meant to travel on a push bike?' I ask.

He motions for me to follow him — and, against my better judgement, I do.

Without saying anything, he takes two of my bags and wraps one around each handlebar.

'Pegs,' he says, pointing.

'Huh?' I ask, wondering what the hell I'm doing.

'You put your feet there,' he says, gesturing to two steel bars poking out from each side of the back wheel. 'And then you hold on to my shoulders.'

I raise my eyebrows but do as he says.

'Directions?'

'Um, what about your friends?' I ask.

'They'll be here when I get back,' he reassures me. 'Hold on.'

I direct him to my street, asking him to drop me off at the nearest corner.

'Strict parents?' he says.

'Sort of. And you could be a creep.'

'I'm no creep, I'm Mike.'

'Well, Mike, you've certainly puzzled me enough for one day.'

'Here's hoping you think about me for the rest of the weekend,' he says, as he turns his bike around.

What a sleaze, I think, heading inside. But I can't help but smile.

The amusement vanishes as soon as I see my mother scowling.

'What?' I ask.

'Get in the kitchen,' she says, shaking her head.

I sigh and follow her inside. Dad's sitting at the breakfast bar, a NSW Police Academy brochure in front of him.

'You went through my mail?' I ask, horrified.

'Well, you are living under my roof,' he counters.

'I sent that to Yia Yia's place!' I exclaim.

'And I own your grandmother's place too.'

'Dad, that's a terrible abuse of my privacy.'

'And you have terribly abused my trust,' he says, frowning. 'Moonlighting as a clown while pretending to hang out with your friends? Deliberately applying for something I told you to forget about, and having the audacity to send it elsewhere so I stay in the dark? That's deceitful, Tammi.'

'What, do you have contacts at kids' parties now? Just in case the six-year-olds decide to rob a bank?'

He doesn't appreciate my sarcasm. 'It's up to me to know what's going on in my kid's life. What if some creep lured you over pretending he needed a clown. You couldn't go work in retail like other kids your age?'

'Well, what did you expect? You say no to everything.'

'I expect you to stick to what we discussed.'

'What *you* discussed, you mean,' I remind him. 'I never agreed to any of it.'

'Tammi, your father's just trying to look out for you,' Mum says, sighing. 'He's been in the force for twenty years. He knows what it's like. It's no place for a young woman.'

'Please, Mum,' I say, rolling my eyes. 'It's the twenty-first century. There's no such thing as "places for women" any more. We can go anywhere.'

'Just because you can, it doesn't mean you should,' he says. 'Being a cop is not safe, it's emotionally draining and sometimes your colleagues are as sleazy as the crooks. It's not an environment I want for you. You're going to find another career.'

'This is so frustrating!' I shout. 'This is all I want to do with my life. If I were a boy, you'd have no problem with it.'

'But you're not a boy, you're my only daughter, and just like I vowed to protect and serve the citizens of this state, I vowed to protect you and your mother the day you each came into my life.'

I roll my eyes.

'Seriously, Tammi,' he says slowly, 'haven't you heard my stories? Seen what I've gone through? What I've struggled with? Some if it haunts me every day.'

'And doing something that's not going to make me happy will haunt *me*,' I tell him. 'I want to be like you; please just accept that.'

'I don't have to accept anything,' he tells me, rising from his chair. 'I'm your father, and there's no way that I will support you in this. And if you're going to fight and threaten me, I'm going to remind you what you're dealing with.'

'What's that supposed to mean?' I ask.

'It means that the policing world is a small one. All it takes is the drop of a name to fast-track an application, or send it to the bottom of the pile.'

'You wouldn't do that,' I whisper, stunned. 'It goes against all your principles.'

'Every cop out there who has seen what I've seen will agree with me, Tamara,' he says. 'Even with their principles.'

I glare at him. 'I can't believe you would do this to me. I have no other options.'

'Yes, you do — lots of them,' he says. 'Just not policing.'

'Fine! I'll take up prostitution,' I yell, walking out of the room.

'Great,' he yells back. 'I can put you in touch with a few madams who own premises on my beat!'

I slam my bedroom door angrily, my eyes filling up with tears.

David, Lauren, Dad … Why do I keep letting everyone walk all over me? And why am I so powerless to stop them?

Gillian

Gillian Cummings When you see your best friend in a
shoot with Karlie Kloss on Insta #bowdown #SylvanaDarrar
#yougogirl

'I showed Charlie how to use the stupid camera,' Matty tells me
in Maths. 'Do you want to know what she said?'

I bite my lip, not sure if I'm supposed to answer.

'She said, "Great, now I have no excuse for getting out of this
crap." The chick's messed up.'

My face reddens.

He gives me a look that says 'I told you so', then opens up his
textbook.

I don't know what to say, so I open mine too and wonder why
algebra makes more sense than my own life.

I decide to corner Charlie at lunch. She's sitting under a tree, her
head buried in a laptop.

I stand in front of her for a few minutes, and she finally rolls her eyes, pulls her headphones out of her ears and gives me a look that is all attitude.

'Matty says he showed you how to use the camera,' I say.

She nods, then turns her laptop towards me. 'Do you mind? I really want to watch this.'

I fold my arms, purse my lips and try to match her, attitude for attitude.

'Nothing exciting happens. It goes into some convoluted storyline and someone comes back from the dead. In three more episodes you'll start to wonder why you're watching it.'

She death-stares me. 'Did you come here to ruin it for me?'

I shrug. 'No, I came to ask if you need help taking photos. I can go with you to events and stuff.'

'I don't need friends,' she says to me, as if she's doing me a favour by freeing up my time.

'This isn't about friendship; this is about our yearbook.'

She looks at me as if I'm the biggest loser that ever walked the earth. I start to feel like maybe I am.

'Why are you so keen to work on this stupid yearbook?' she asks. 'You heard Matty. No one else even cares.'

'I think I'll like it,' I admit. 'Maybe I'll remember the good times.'

'Can I give you some advice?' she says. 'You're at this school because you have to be. You didn't choose this. What comes after — that's what you choose, that's when the real good times will begin. This is all fake, forced ... for show.'

I swallow, and look across the playground.

She closes her laptop. 'Fine,' she says, after a moment. 'Maybe I could use some help. Next meeting we'll discuss what they want and you can come along for some of it.'

'And in the meantime you're just going to hang out under a

tree every lunch?'

'What do you want me to do? I told you, I don't need friends.'

'You could study,' I say.

'Haven't you heard? I don't need to.'

'I haven't heard anything,' I say. 'Look around. People don't talk to me.'

'And this worries you? Doesn't seem like they're worth talking to. Everyone here's so elitist.'

I put my hands on my hips and give her a knowing look. 'That's rich coming from you. You've been down on the place since you got here.'

'Well, my whole life has changed. All my friends are in an entirely different state. I don't need to explain myself to you.'

'Well, my best friend is on the other side of the world and I have to navigate time zones and work schedules to talk to her, so you're not the only one with problems.'

She opens her mouth to say something, just as something hard hits my head and splatters.

'Owwwww!' I yelp. I whip around and see them across the quad: Lauren, Tammi, David and a bunch of others, standing there, giggling.

My eyes narrow as Lauren gives me a pitying smile. Then she shrugs, turns back to her friends and laughs, her palm covering her mouth.

'They did that on purpose,' Charlie says, standing up.

I rub the back of my head and feel wet, chunky bits of apple through my fingers. 'Ewww!' I exclaim, shaking my hand and trying to see the back of my uniform. 'Did any of it get on my clothes?'

She glares at me. 'Are you just going to let that go? March up to her and tell her off.'

'No way! There's only five months left of school. After that, I won't see her again.'

'She threw fruit at you. What if it had broken your nose or something?'

'Well, it didn't, did it?' I say as I scurry away to the bathroom to clean myself up.

'What an idiot,' I hear her mumble, as the back of my head burns.

Later that afternoon, Charlie tries to talk to me about it again in my free period.

'Get over it,' I say, turning to the computer. 'I don't want to get into any fights.'

'Life is not just rainbows and butterflies.'

'I get it. But I also don't want to spend the rest of my school year cleaning myself up in the bathroom.'

'Whatever. What's "Diary of a Pollie's Kid"?' she says, peering over my shoulder.

I take a deep breath. 'It's my blog,' I tell her. 'I started it, like, two months ago.'

'Hmm,' she says, scanning the screen. 'Do many people read it?'

I shrug. 'I guess so,' I say. 'I have a Facebook page and an Instagram account for it, and my following is slowly growing. Every time I have to go to political events, I write about it.'

'What does your dad think?' she asks.

'He hasn't said anything,' I say. 'He has a whole PR team that sometimes makes me change stuff if they don't like the "tone" or the "angle". But mostly they leave me alone.'

She laughs at that. 'Is that why Lauren Pappas is bullying you? Because your blog's blowing up and she's trying to take you down a notch?'

'I don't know what you mean,' I say, logging out and packing my bag.

She looks at me for a moment, then turns away.

I send Sylvana a Facebook message while standing at the bus stop on my way home.

I got hit in the back of the head by a flying apple today. Are you sure you don't miss the school quad?

A few minutes later, I hear back.

I don't know. Tonight I wiped, like, 15 kilos of foundation off my face, tore off heaps of eyelashes when taking off my falsies, and there were reptiles in today's photo shoot.

I smile.

Yeah, but who was the shoot for? ;)

She doesn't write back.

I lean against the wall. There are so many students around me, but I'm the only one standing alone. I really am a loser.

I call Mum.

'Do you think Anton can do something about my hair soon?' I ask her when she answers. 'I need a change.'

'Yes, definitely, make an appointment!' I can hear the enthusiasm in her voice. 'What are you gonna do? Cut, colour?'

I start to make my way to the Westfield. 'I dunno, maybe both. I'll see what they say and when they have appointments.'

Inside, I make a booking for a hair assessment and style with a girl who looks like she stepped out of the pages of a magazine. As she pencils my name into the appointment book, I stare at my reflection in the full-length mirror. My plain, golden-red waves make me look like a child. And my knee-length skirt, smart blazer and little hat don't help either.

But maybe with a new hair style I'll look more mature. More in control.

She calls out to another girl — who looks just as glam as she does — and asks if her afternoon is free. The girl looks at me. 'Yeah, I'm free,' she says, her eyes scanning the length of my body.

'Hear that?' the first girl asks me. 'We can do it now.'

I sit at the basin while she washes my hair and massages my scalp, imagining myself lost somewhere — far away from the quad, my classmates, the yearbook that I really wanted to help produce but that no one else seemed invested in.

In the full-length mirror in front of me, I can see the hair stylist eyeing a wavy strand of my red hair. 'You should do a keratin treatment,' she says to my reflection. 'Much more grown-up than curls. You won't need to blowdry it, and it'll last three to six months.'

'How long does it take?' I ask.

She shrugs. 'Couple of hours.'

I nod and let her take the scissors to my hair, watching as she frames it around my face.

'Just trust me,' she says to my uncertain face, reflected in the mirror. 'I'm going to put a couple of foils here in the front too, brighten it up a little bit. It'll look hot.'

I swallow, nervous.

'So do you live in the area?' she asks.

'Croydon,' I say, nodding. 'My mum is friends with Anton.'

She smiles. 'Better take extra good care of you then,' she says.

A couple of hours later, I'm transformed. I eye myself in the mirror again, trying not to admire the girl staring back at me. I *do* look more mature. I wonder if it will change anything as I pay the girl and walk out, optimistic as always.

On my way out, I grab a tub of frozen yoghurt, looking forward to seeing Sammy's excitement. The bus ride home is a short five minutes and Sammy is on the front step when I arrive.

His eyes light up when he sees the yoghurt tub in my hand. He lunges forwards and grabs it, running inside excitedly calling about getting bowls and spoons.

'Don't hog it all!' I call out after him.

Mum emerges from the kitchen.

'Really, Gill?' she asks. 'You told me you wanted to do something about your hair; I thought you wanted to take your appearance seriously. Then you come home with frozen yoghurt?'

'Aww, come on, hun, it's just a snack,' my dad calls out after her. 'Nice hair, sweetie,' he says to me. 'Love it.'

'Yeah, but she has plenty of snacks,' she snaps. 'My trainer says if she continues grazing like that, she could balloon.'

I have a vision of cankles and plus-size stores and decide the yoghurt's not worth it.

'I'm not hungry anyway,' I mutter. 'Sammy will enjoy it more.'

I head upstairs and try to ignore my parents as Mum tries to defend her actions to Dad. I can't help but catch a few phrases, like 'size eight' and 'work for it', before the door of his office closes.

We've always been terrible problem-solvers. We just shut ourselves away instead, so nothing gets fixed. I always thought it was the worst thing, but now I can see it's an attitude that has seeped into my veins.

Which is why no matter what Lauren Pappas throws at me, she will always get away with it. Because I will always just shut myself away and let her.

And maybe because, deep down, I guess I deserve it.

RYAN

Ryan Fleming Planning the plays is definitely not the same as making them.

James Czalo Hang in there, mate. You'll get there.

I don't know why, but I'm going to soccer training. It's David's idea, of course; he's still trying to convince me of it as we walk over to the field.

'Dude, you need to quit feeling sorry for yourself and get off your arse,' he says. 'It sucks that you can't play, I know, but you're still part of the team. You can give us pointers, work out game plans, be our water boy …'

I shove him and he laughs, squirting me with his water bottle.

'I don't know how many sessions I can come to, though,' I say, not wanting to admit how much the joke had really stung. I didn't get this far to be a water boy. 'Especially now with the yearbook stuff happening.'

'Why don't you grow a pair and leave that frou-frou stuff to the girls?'

I laugh. 'I don't know how we're still friends, man,' I say, shaking my head.

'Seriously, though — the yearbook? Like, what the hell?'

'I can't let this accident screw up everything,' I say. 'It's messing with my headspace; I need a distraction. And Mrs H said doing it might help me win the St Jerome Medal.'

'You're still going for that?' he asks, looking at me incredulously. 'Why? What's the point without soccer?'

'Um, just because I can't play now doesn't mean I'll never play again, right?'

I know it's a mistake to look to him for reassurance, and my gut instinct seems to be right on track when he responds with silence. We may have been best mates for a while, but there's always been a little competition between us, and with me out of the picture David is the school's solo soccer star.

'Plus, there are other dreams. Just because I don't know what I want to do yet, it doesn't mean I shouldn't still chase a ticket. And the St Jerome Medal is the ultimate ticket. It'll pay for whatever I want to do next — at any uni.'

He shrugs with the indifference of someone who has his whole future filed into a box marked 'To be dealt with later'. Not to mention that whatever he wants to do, he'll have his super-wealthy parents to pay for it.

'Whatever you want, bro,' he says. 'You know I support you. Although that new chick from Melbourne — the one with the attitude — is super smart. She even corrects the teachers.'

'What, Charlie? She's going to give me a run for my money?' I ask, putting on his voice. 'Who does she think she is, bro?'

'She better not mess with the soccer lads,' he says, playing along with me.

'Damn straight,' I tell him.

He sits on a bench and laces up his soccer boots. Then he stands up and puts his hands on my shoulders.

'But, bro, I still can't get over it. The yearbook committee? You're cramping our style.'

'As far as you're concerned, Davo, your style's always cramped,' I point out, smiling. 'You're lucky Tammi stuck around.'

He laughs, tilting his head back, a guy with no worries whatsoever.

'I don't know. It could be good for me,' I say. 'Plus, you know Mrs H. I agreed to do it just to get out of her office.'

He shrugs and runs out to the coach.

I sit on the bench and watch him with the ball. He heads it, bounces it between each knee, pounds it with his chest, then repeats the process again. I'm struck by how natural he looks.

If it weren't for him, I might never have discovered the game. In some ways I owe a lot to him.

But he's also a big part of the reason why it's gone away.

Which is why, despite the friendly banter, things will never be the same between us again.

———

Later that afternoon, I take my laptop to our little courtyard out back and start Googling careers.

Lawyer? Nope — I'm a really bad liar.

Police officer? Nope — I want to get away from morons, not chase after them.

Teacher? No way — I've seen enough from my classmates to ensure I don't ever want to be a victim of behaviour like theirs.

Finance? Er, I hate numbers. And I can't even think of an actual job title of someone in finance.

No matter what I search for, all I can think about is soccer.

I close the laptop and lie back in the chair.

Moments later, Nanna comes out with a tray holding a jug of fresh lemonade and some glasses.

'Honey, why are you doing your work out here?' she asks. 'You'll be more comfortable at a table. Trust me, when your back goes —'

'— it goes. I know.'

She gives me a smile and shakes her head.

'I'm brainstorming careers,' I tell her.

'You'll find something, darling,' she says. 'Don't rush it.'

'You know, you're telling me the opposite of everyone else. I feel like I'm under so much pressure to discover my dream job right now.'

'Well, I'm the one who knows you best,' she says. 'You should listen to me.' She pours me a glass of lemonade. 'So tell me, what is that no-good friend of yours planning on doing?'

'Beats me,' I say, shrugging. 'Right now his sole focus is being the captain of the school soccer team.'

'He has a hide on him, I tell you,' she says. 'I can't believe his family didn't offer to help out with the costs of the physio after your surgery. It was all his fault you injured your knee, and they couldn't even send a card.'

'No one forced me to get on that four-wheeler, Nanna.'

'Yes, you keep saying that,' she says. 'But I know better. You do everything that he says just to avoid getting into an argument with him. And that time, his genius ideas got you more than just a detention.'

'Yep — a complete ban from the best thing in my life.'

'Until you find something else,' she says, patting my shoulder.

I down the glass of lemonade and hand it to her, and she carries the tray back inside.

Charlie Scanlon Just sitting here, repeating my mantra. #noroots

I find myself heading up the stairs into the library with Ryan Fleming by my side, and he nods a hello in my direction.

I ignore him. Seriously, how many ways can I say 'I don't want to associate with you' to these people?

We walk into the computer lab and I take the computer closest to the door. Everyone else is already here — Matty has his headphones on, Tammi is reading a magazine and Gillian is typing furiously into her phone.

At this rate, we'll be working on this yearbook well into our fifties.

'Guys,' Ryan calls out from the front of the room, 'can we start? We only have forty-five minutes.'

'Yes, but every month,' Matty says. 'Forty-five minutes *every month*.'

Gillian looks at him pointedly. 'Yes, and some of us would like to do something productive with that forty-five minutes.'

'Maybe you should do the whole thing yourself, since you're so enthusiastic,' Tammi says.

'It's because I actually chose to be here,' she snaps. 'I don't take orders from people who are supposed to be my friends.'

I make an approving sound and Tammi glares me.

'Not so tough when Lauren's not around, are we?' I mutter.

She gives me the finger and I smirk at her, just as Ryan clears his throat.

'Just come off it, all of you,' he says. 'Let's just do what we have to and get out of here.'

Silence descends on the room. Ryan has a point.

'The last meeting wasn't exactly successful, so I figured working with a little bit of direction might help us,' he says. 'I did some research and I read that magazines usually start with something called a flatplan, so I made one last night. I think.'

'What's a flatplan?' Tammi asks.

'It's a grid where we write what's going to go on each page,' he explains, fumbling with a clear plastic folder. He hands us all a copy of the flatplan. 'I hope it's OK, it took me hours. I want to make sure we have something to show Mrs H.'

'Oooh, dedication,' I say, rolling my eyes.

He gives me an icy stare. 'Can you just piss off? I don't want to deal with you right now.'

I mock-pout and say in a sing-song voice, 'Aww, you poor thing, you in your privileged school with your upper-middle-class upbringing. What could you possibly have been through that's so traumatic that you can't handle a little sarcasm?'

He looks at me for a moment, then shakes his head. 'Forget it. Empathy is obviously something you're unfamiliar with.'

'I just know who really needs it and who doesn't,' I mumble under my breath.

'Yeah, we get it, you know a lot of things,' he says. 'Can we move on now?'

'Actually, Ryan, I think this is really good,' Tammi says, looking up from the handout. 'Can we add more pages for photos if we need to?'

'I guess so,' he says. 'Depending on the budget.'

'Are our photos going to be in colour?' Gillian asks.

'I don't know, sorry.'

'It's OK,' Gillian says. 'How about I write down these questions so that when we meet with Mrs H, we can ask.'

'Great idea, Gill,' I say. 'How about we start with why Ryan has allocated six pages for boys' sport and only two pages for girls'?'

Ryan rubs the back of his head, while I smile up at him innocently.

'Did you go to some feminist school or something?' he asks.

'Yep,' I say with enthusiasm. 'It's located at the corner of Twenty-first Century Street and Get With The Program Avenue. Seriously, what is with this?'

'The girls' teams never win anything,' Tammi says.

I give her a death-stare.

'Look,' he says, 'there are only two girls' teams: soccer and netball. If you look further down there are two pages on dance comps, and another on really great Textiles projects that made it into the regional Visual Arts Display at the council.'

'Oh my God, I can't even begin to explain how wrong this all is,' I say, putting my hands on my head as if I'm trying to keep my brain from falling out from shock.

Everyone stares at me in silence.

Just great, I think. You try to teach them something and they look at you as if you have two heads.

'Dance competitions and Textiles projects? Is this what you want your daughters to look at in twenty years' time? A book that perpetuates the stereotype that women are good at home economics, but not competitive sport? Where's the equality? We've had a female prime minister, for heaven's sake.'

'Yeah, and look how well that turned out,' Matty mumbles.

'Doesn't mean you should stop pursuing equality,' I say. 'We need to highlight all the opportunities that the girls had here. If you keep this flatplan, then you're saying you agree with putting women in their boxes.'

'And this grid picture thing says all that?' Matty asks, confused.

Tammi opens her mouth to say something, but I cut her off.

'Don't tell me again about how the girl teams never win,' I warn her. 'Maybe if we supported one another more, we would win at something.'

'Don't lecture me,' Tammi says. 'I'm not the one with the attitude problem.'

I fold my arms. 'Yeah, but you *are* one of the ones who chuck things at innocent people's heads just for fun.'

'Please don't bring me into this,' Gillian calls out, waving her hands in front of her face.

'For God's sake, quit being a pansy,' I tell her. 'If you don't stand up to her, she'll never learn.'

'I didn't even do anything,' Tammi calls out angrily.

'Yeah, exactly,' I say. 'Your friend does the bullying and you don't do anything to stop her.'

The sound of a fist slamming against a table cuts through the argument. We all turn to look at Ryan.

'I've had enough of this shit,' he says. 'I'm telling Mrs H to either can the yearbook or get someone else to do it.'

He pauses for a moment, then shakes his head in frustration, picks up his school bag, and storms out.

The room goes silent. Everyone looks around at each other.

'Cool, I guess we can go then,' Matty says, shrugging and standing up.

'No, we can't,' Gill says. 'It'll break Mrs H's heart.'

He sighs loudly and slumps back into his seat.

'Well, what are we doing then?' I ask. 'Should I go out and find him?'

'Hell no,' Tammi says, looking at me like I'm an idiot. 'Your attitude is probably half the reason he left.'

'So what, we just hang around?' Matty mumbles.

'Yes, we do,' Tammi calls out, without turning around. 'He's not the type to bail. He'll come back — just give him a minute to calm down.'

———

Fifteen minutes later, Ryan returns, looking only a little calmer. He paces up and down the room.

'You know,' he says after a moment, 'I've debated the best teams in Sydney and won, I've captained our soccer team to three grand finals and won two of those, and I walked the Kokoda Track with my dad when I was fifteen — and all of that was cake compared to this stupid project.'

After a few minutes of silence he speaks up again.

'I'm giving you guys one more shot,' he says, putting his hand up. 'I know this flatplan thing is not perfect, but it's a start.'

'Well, how about you just add however many women's pages Run-the-World wants so we can move on from our sexism debate and actually get somewhere?' says Matty.

'Did you just reference Beyoncé?' Tammi asks, perplexed.

'Why are you surprised? I know I don't move in your popular circles, but I do live in the real world,' he says very slowly.

'Why are you talking to me like I'm stupid?'

'Because you just asked a stupid question,' he snaps.

Gillian lets out a snort of laughter and Tammi rolls her eyes.

'Seriously, why am I here?' she asks no one in particular, standing up. 'Gillian's right. I'm only here because of Lauren; if she's so desperate to have a say she can be here instead.'

Gillian's eyes flick to her in horror.

'If you leave me now, I'll tell David you're cheating,' Ryan warns.

The warning doesn't faze her. 'Tell him whatever you want,' she mutters, picking up her bag.

'Please don't leave,' Ryan says, stepping in front of her to block her exit.

'Come on, Ryan,' she says. 'Look around. Me and him have barely spoken more than three words to each other, this one hates our entire school, and this one is so enthusiastic she could burst. You need more of her and less of us.'

He stares at her. She sighs.

'Seriously,' she says, gesturing around the room, 'we're not a good fit.'

The alarm on Ryan's phone beeps. He silences it and shoves it back in his pocket, just as Matty, Tammi and Gillian and I all stand up.

'Sit back down,' he says, as we look at each other. 'Now.'

'I don't give a shit how much we hate each other,' he says. 'Mrs H has been good to us, so we owe it to her to finish the job. And yes, I know I am partially biased as the school captain, but there's no way in hell I am going to let this year be the only one not to have a yearbook.'

The whole room can hear Matty sigh.

'He has a point,' Gillian says.

'So, Charlie — can you please take the flatplan home and add your recommendations? Gillian, I'm going to rely on you to save all questions from future meetings, and Tammi, not only are you banned from leaving, but can you please set up a private Facebook group for us so we can communicate in between meetings? Gill can post the action points as a pinned post in the group, so we can all keep track of what we're supposed to be doing.'

'What do I do?' Matty grumbles.

'Easy,' he says. 'Make us a playlist for meetings. And let's take turns to bring snacks. We should try to forget all the stuff that happens out there' — he points at the window — 'and try to keep this part of the day free from everything else. Please.'

No one argues.

He gestures to the door. 'You can go home now.'

We all stand up to leave again. But just as Ryan reaches the door, he turns around.

'Oh my Lord, what now?' I say under my breath.

'Don't worry too much about boxes,' he tells me. 'Last year for International Day of the Girl, the boys' soccer team wore pink bands on the field and had a bake sale to raise funds for Girl Up. The future is not all doom and gloom.'

'*You* arranged it?' I ask, smirking.

'What can I say?' he says, shrugging. 'This is what a feminist looks like.'

He winks at me, then walks down the hall, whistling Beyoncé's 'Run the World (Girls)'.

THE YEARBOOK COMMITTEE
Minutes for May Meeting

Recorded by: Gillian Cummings
Meeting chair: Ryan Fleming (with occasional takeovers by
Charlie Scanlon)
In attendance: Everyone

The Snacks: I bought sugar-free, gluten-free cookies that I
baked out of this diet recipe book that Mum got me. Charlie
said they were fun-free and that I shouldn't be buying into
social pressure to lose weight. (I didn't disclose the pressure
was familial.) Ryan was polite enough to try to hide when
he spat his cookie into a napkin, but he is not very good at
hiding things. Charlie said she'll bring a couple of boxes of
crackers and some dip next time. Tammi said she will bring a
couple of blocks of Haigh's chocolate. Matty didn't know what
that was, and Charlie said it was snobby Australian-owned
chocolate and Cadbury's was just as good. Ryan waved his
hand dismissively and said that Haigh's Milk Honeycomb
chocolate was better than sex, and Charlie said he's probably
having sex with the wrong girls. It was the first time any of us
heard Matty laugh. It made him look kind of cute.

Discussion:

* It was resolved that Charlie and I will write about last month's ANZAC Day fundraiser.

* The matter of Matty's attendance at meetings was decided. He has to come, even if he has an after-school job that he 'needs' to go to. Matty used expletives in his reaction to this decision, which I shall not disclose here, in case Mr Broderick sees these minutes and gets offended. (I know they're for my eyes only, but you never know.)

* Charlie said recording minutes was a waste of time, and that I should spend the time listening and participating in meeting discussions instead of typing. Ryan agreed (!!!!) and said that the priority was just noting down the questions to ask Mrs H. Even though it freaked me out that those two were on the same page, I was firm in my resolve that it's good to keep records, even if I was keeping them just for me.

* Ryan and Charlie stopped being on the same page when he showed us his flatplan plan (?) which wasn't feminist enough for Charlie. (Note to self: clarify exact reason why.) (Was it really about sport?)

* Then a whole bunch of different ~~arguments~~ disagreements started taking place, which I could not keep track of.

(Note to self: learn to type faster, or download recorder app to record meetings.)

* Oh God. Tammi's at the door. Ryan is blocking her exit. She must be a good friend to do this for Lauren (who, if this is the case, does not deserve her). Ryan wins, Tammi stays.
* The progress made at this meeting: we agreed to stick around and try to make this thing happen.

Questions for Mrs H:
* Can she email Charlie everything she told Ryan about the template, because Ryan forgot it all?

Action points:
* Turn up to next meeting.
* Charlie to revise flatplan and send new one to everyone for section coverage.

Matty

Matty Fullerton He works hard for the money.

Mo Sharif Come to the job site, I'll show you hard work ;)

The fourth song winds down and I debate playing a fifth. I'm lying on the grass at Burwood Park, in the shadow of the big war memorial, taking a half-hour lunch break from work. Being outside on this autumn Saturday is so much better than being stuck inside that shopping centre serving little buggers who change their order three times while there's ten people waiting behind them.

My half hour is nearly up. I think about staying a little longer, but I'm on with a newish girl, Christa, and I don't want to risk her ratting me out — I need the money. So I decide against the fifth song, put my apron back on and walk back towards the centre.

My phone pings. It's a text message from Mo.

I thought you worked Saturdays? I come to visit you and you're not even here. So much for working hard.

I text back.

Hang on, be there in 2 mins.

Back at the juice bar, Christa is making a drink, but there's no one in line. Mo's nowhere to be seen.

'Did anyone ask for me?' I ask.

She shakes her head. 'Nah, sorry. Can I go on my break now?'

She heads off. The next half hour flies by and before I know it Christa's back.

She heads to the front of the stall and starts serving customers, while I stay in the back peeling fruit. A few minutes later, I hear a familiar voice and Christa giggling, and I smile.

'Mo, must you hit on everyone I work with?' I ask him, as I walk around to the front counter.

'Well, at least she's here, bro,' he says, clasping my hand. 'Every time I come, you're gone. Sweet-as job if you're making money without working. No wonder you won't leave.'

'What do you mean? I told you two minutes.'

'Yeah, and I waited seven,' he says. 'I timed it. You exaggerate so much, bro.'

'Yeah, I learnt from the masters,' I tease.

'*Shu,*' he says, exaggerating the Palestinian slang. 'Wanna go out tonight?'

'Sure. Where?'

'El Jannah in Punchbowl,' he says, his face lighting up.

'Mo, getting chicken sandwiches doesn't count as "going out".'

'We can watch the footy at your house after. That counts.'

'I can't, man, sorry,' I say. 'Mum's not well.'

'Still? Some virus, bro.'

'Yeah, I think it's more than just a vi—'

Christa clears her throat and looks pointedly at me, and I notice the long line of customers waiting for their drinks to be made.

'Sorry, man, I better get back to it. I'll call you.'

Mo waves as he leaves.

After we've closed, Christa tells me her car's on the other side of the park; she wanted to avoid paying for parking, which I can't blame her for.

'I'll walk you to your car,' I tell her. 'It's dark.'

'That's OK,' she says. 'I'll be fine by myself.'

The part of me that just wants to get home wants to believe her, but I know I'll feel guilty if I leave her to walk alone.

'Honestly, I'll feel more comfortable if I go with you,' I tell her.

'OK, thanks,' she says, looking relieved.

I'm walking back through the park afterwards when I notice a kid being flanked by two guys, who are gripping his arms. As I get closer, I realise it's Sammy.

'Oi,' I call out, 'what are you doing?'

'Mind your own business, dickhead,' the shorter guy says.

'Juice Man!' Sammy calls out. 'They won't let me stand here.'

'It's OK, buddy,' I tell him, approaching the three of them. 'Come on, guys, let him go.'

'Hey, man,' the taller one says, putting his hand up, 'we were just trying to, um, play a game of footy, and he wanted to stand in the goal.'

Sammy shakes his head violently from side to side. 'Nah,' he says, 'they don't even have a football.'

The shorter guy looks to his friend in panic, but his friend calms him down with a small gesture of his arm.

'Our mate's bringing the footy. The kid was just getting in the way, that's all. No harm done.'

I look at Sammy. 'Did they hurt you?'

Sammy looks frightened enough, but shakes his head.

'He shouldn't even be in the park at this time of night if he's ... sick,' the shorter one says.

'Yeah, we were just trying to help him,' the other says coolly. 'Seriously.'

I'm not buying it.

'It doesn't matter anyway, it's probably too dark to play,' the taller guy presses. 'But still, maybe you should take him home.'

I give him a suspicious look and it makes him want to try harder.

'I'm Mike,' he says, extending his hand. 'I gotta run. But like I said, no harm intended. Just wanted to make sure he was safe.'

They both head off, whispering loudly. I hear the shorter one asking whether the kid saw anything, but Mike just shrugs and says no one would believe 'someone like him'. I shake my head in disgust and turn back to Sammy.

'Why are you in the park all alone?' I ask. 'Come on, let's go call your parents.'

He shakes his head.

'No?' I ask. 'Well, you can't stay in the park on your own, buddy, it's dangerous. Does anyone know you're here?'

Another head shake.

I sigh and rub the back of my head. 'OK, how about we get an ice-cream, and we can come back and sit on the ledge there near the statue of the ANZAC soldier? That's my favourite spot in the whole park; it always makes me feel better.'

He nods and we cross the road, heading to the gelato shop. I buy him a kid's size chocolate and get myself a crème caramel in a waffle cone, and then we cross the road again. While we eat, he talks about video games and SpongeBob SquarePants and his carer, Elliott (who plays Xbox with him).

'Do you play Xbox?' Sammy asks.

'Yes, I play it with my best friend, Mo, at his house, because I don't have one. I play games on my computer at home, though.'

'I don't have a computer, but I have an iPad,' he says. 'And I have an Xbox. Can you come over and play with me one day?'

I smile and nod. 'Sure, and I'll bring you a Berry Bravo.'

He shakes his head as if I have insulted him. 'No, that's only on Tuesdays and Thursdays.'

I nod my head again, stifling a laugh. 'Of course, sorry, I forgot.'

He finishes the ice-cream and looks at me expectantly.

'So … do you want to tell me why you're out here by yourself?' I ask him.

Sammy starts blabbing about a sister who was supposed to take him out for an afternoon of shopping but who never showed, so he tried walking to the mall himself. Apparently, he cut through the park and that's when the 'bad men' started being 'mean'. *Poor kid*, I think, *his family sounds a bit messed up.*

'Do you have your sister's phone number?' I ask, pulling out my phone and praying I have credit.

He hands me a scrap of paper from a Superman wallet in his back pocket, and when I hear a dial tone, I'm thankful I remembered to pay my bill this month.

'Hello?' a frantic, weirdly familiar female voice answers.

'Hi, um, I'm here with Sammy at Burwood Park. He seems to be lost — is someone able to come pick him up?'

I hear the girl breathe a loud sigh of relief. 'Oh, thank God,' she says. 'I was so scared. I'm in Burwood now. Which part of the park?'

'We're near the big war memorial, the one that says —'

'— something about God and the victory. I know it.'

A few minutes later, a little hatchback parks across the road, its hazard lights on, and a girl runs out.

'Gillian?' I say. 'I thought I recognised the voice.'

'Oh, Matty, I thought so too! But then I saw a guy with his hood on and freaked out.'

'It's just a hood,' I tell her. 'You should be freaked out that your brother was in the park alone in the dark.'

'Gillie, I was scared,' Sammy says. 'I thought you forgot me.'

'Sammy, honey, I've been looking all over for you,' she explains slowly, throwing her arms around him. 'Sometimes there's traffic on the big road where Daddy's office is, and that makes me late. But you still have to wait for me to come pick you up. You can't come on your own.'

'But you were so long, and I was gonna miss SpongeBob.'

'There was a SpongeBob Squarepants show in the centre today,' she explains, her eyes flicking to me. 'I promised I'd bring him. The show is going to be there next week,' she says to Sammy. 'I'll leave a day free to bring you to see SpongeBob, no matter what.'

She grabs his hand and looks at me apologetically.

I give her a half-smile.

'Um, before you go,' I say, 'there were these guys that were hovering around him, youngish, like nineteen maybe. I don't think they did anything, but he seemed a little scared when I found him.'

'Well, thanks for staying with him.'

I shrug awkwardly.

'I promise to not go walking by myself again, Gillie,' Sammy says a moment later. 'But please don't tell Dad, I'll get in trouble.'

She swallows and shakes her head. 'I won't tell Dad, as long as you never do that again. You scared me.'

'Mean Mike scared *me*.'

I stifle a laugh. 'Well, now that you guys are reunited I should head home,' I tell her. 'My bus will be here soon.'

'No, wait, I'll give you a lift,' she says. 'Please, it's the least I can do.'

I rub the back of my neck.

'Come on, seriously,' she says. 'It's no big deal. Where do you live?'

'OK, thanks,' I say gratefully. 'I'm on the Hume Highway in South Strathfield.'

We clamber in the car and I take the back seat, trying to catch a glimpse of those guys from the park. Something about them made me uneasy.

After a few minutes, I notice that Sammy has fallen asleep.

'He's really tired,' Gillian says, looking at me in the rear-view mirror. 'He likes sameness and routines, and being alone in that park would've been hard on him.'

'I bet,' I say. 'He comes into the juice bar all the time, so I knew that he was out of his comfort zone as soon as I saw him.'

'It's so nice that you looked after him,' she says. 'I honestly feel so awful. How long was he with you for?'

'Twenty minutes or so,' I tell her. 'I had just finished work and walked a co-worker to her car, and when I cut through the park on the way to the bus stop I saw him with those guys.'

She stops at a red light, then rubs her temples.

'God, I was so panicked when he wasn't home,' she says. 'I didn't think he would try to walk to Burwood on his own. And I couldn't call my parents. I just started driving around in circles looking for him. Stupid Parramatta Road traffic.'

She says nothing for a while, and neither do I, but I can tell from her driving that she's tense.

Finally she says, 'I'm just scared they did something to him. What if they come for him again?'

'I don't think they will. They were trying to get him out of the park — that's what was suss. Just a couple of young guys "playing footy" in the dark. It was weird.'

I direct her to my building and she drops me off in the nearest side street, then performs a u-turn. She lowers her window just as she's about to drive off.

'Check out that poor lady in the bathrobe,' she tells me, pointing.

I look up and see my mum on the stairs, looking very much like a nutjob.

'I know, right?' I say, forcing a smirk. 'Some people …'

Tammi Kap Need. To. Focus. (Srsly, studying sucks.)

'I knew picking you for this assignment was a mistake,' I say, edging further down the bed.

'Not my fault you're hot,' David says, kissing my lips, my cheek, my ear. 'And that you never learn from past "study" sessions.'

'Come on,' I say gently, one hand on his chest shoving him away, and the other flipping through the pages of my textbook. 'I missed out on so much because of dancing so I really need to study now.'

'Mmmhmmm,' he says, wrapping his arms around me. 'Still sad that you didn't make nationals?'

I sigh in frustration and push his hands off me. 'No, I'm sad that I can't study and I really need to,' I say. 'Come on, we can't afford to screw around any more.'

He rolls his eyes. 'That's the problem, Tammi. We don't screw around at all.'

'Not this again,' I say. '*Please* just let it go.'

He pauses, then moves away, shaking his head.

'You know I like you,' he says. 'Love you, even. But I don't get it. We've been going out for ages — how long are you going to make me wait?'

'I don't know,' I say, suddenly angry. 'How long are you going to keep pressuring me about it?'

'Tam, I'm the laughing stock of the whole grade,' he says.

'What's the whole grade got to do with it?' I snap, standing up. 'Are you planning on telling everyone when it happens? Filming it maybe, so everyone can watch?'

'Why are you being so dramatic?' he asks.

'Because you're being so forceful!' I exclaim with a stomp of my foot. 'It's all you ever talk about.'

'If I wanted to force it, I wouldn't be discussing it!'

I rub my face in frustration as he gets up and paces the room.

After a moment of deep breathing — the kind he does on the soccer field when he's not happy with the game's direction — he takes my hand, changing tack.

'I thought you cared about me,' he says. 'I want you to know how I feel. I want to show you.'

I can feel my resolve failing. 'Look, I'm obviously not going to make you wait around forever,' I say finally, standing up to put my things in my bag. 'But there's so much happening now. You can't even commit to picking me up when I need you. How can I give you the biggest thing I possibly have to give?'

'Look, I told you I was sorry about that,' he said. 'But I stayed up late with some soccer guys.'

'You know, Ryan used to stay up late with you guys too,' I point out. 'But even if he only had three hours' sleep, he would still make time to meet up with Lauren when they were dating.'

'Yeah, well, look how long their relationship lasted,' he says.

'That's not the point!' I say. 'He made an effort for his girlfriend.'

He sighs. 'You girls are never happy with what you have. You're always comparing us to other guys.'

'It's not like I'm comparing you to some made-up guy,' I say, my mind wandering to the guy from the park.

'Yeah, I know, but I think I'd rather a made-up guy than Ryan,' he says. 'I'm so sick of being compared to Fleming. He's been off the soccer team for months and yet the coach still says "Fleming used to do this" and "Fleming once told me to try that".'

'Yeah, well, he's no threat to you now, is he?' I remind him, surprised at his selfishness. 'Now the scouts can recruit you and you might wind up playing in Europe.'

'And you'll still be a virgin,' he mutters under his breath.

I narrow my eyes at him as he rubs his forehead, wondering what I ever saw in him.

'Look, I should go home,' I say after a moment. 'I'm not going to concentrate here.'

'Aww, come on, the house is empty,' he says. 'Don't go.'

'But I'm so worked up now, and your mum could come home at any minute.'

'So?' he asks. 'I told her you were coming over to study.'

'What?' I exclaim. 'We had a deal. I told you I didn't want either of our parents knowing I come here when your 'rents aren't home.'

'What? Are you scared they'll think less of you?' he asks sarcastically. 'Trust me, the whole world knows you're an angel.'

'You're such an ass, you know that?'

He rolls his eyes. 'Stop overthinking everything and relax,' he says. 'You overthink your career, you overthink your family's reactions to that career choice, and you overthink sleeping with me because you're holding on to some old-fashioned ideas about God knows what.'

'I'm not holding on to anything that's old-fashioned, thanks very much,' I tell him, hitching my bag on my shoulder. 'If I was, then I would have told you from the start that I was waiting until I was engaged or married. But all I want is a bit of time till I feel ready. That's not too much to ask.'

He opens his mouth to say something but I continue.

'And I really hate it when you bring up the whole career thing in that petty tone,' I say. 'Is it that hard to be a little supportive? You know how much I want this. Dealing with my dad is hard enough; I don't need you to be a dick as well.'

'Well, maybe your dad has a point,' he says. 'Did you ever think about that? Like, maybe you have the type of personality that's just not cut out for that sort of job. Everything is a big deal to you. Look how crazy the thought of having sex makes you. As if you're going to be able to handle living on campus — where you can't earn any money — and waking up at five in the morning to do obstacle courses and seeing abused kids and dead bodies every day when you actually start working. Mentally, you won't be able to handle it.'

I scoff. 'Don't be a moron,' I tell him, standing at the door. 'I'll be fine living on my own — I've been saving my clown money for ages. I'm not the one who relies on my parents' money for everything.'

'Why does everyone always sound so jealous when they say that?' he asks.

'I'm not jealous,' I say. 'I just know what I want, and I want some credit.'

I turn on my heel and walk away.

I wait for him to follow me, but he doesn't. I guess he's too pig-headed to apologise. And tomorrow he'll call me like nothing happened, and I'll let him get away with it.

Like I always do.

———

Two hours later, my phone rings. It's not David, but I'm glad it's not — I haven't managed to absorb any of my study notes because of him.

'Hello,' I answer cheerfully, always happy to hear from my best friend.

'So when I was getting dressed today I realised that my hair is now long enough to drape over each breast if I ever wanted to do a modest topless shoot,' Lauren says.

'Ummm, okay,' I say, confused. 'Is that on your bucket list or something? You've never mentioned it before.'

'Oh, no,' she says, laughing, 'it's not something I'm planning on doing. I'm just saying it's good to know in case it ever comes up.'

'Uh huh,' I say, still confused, 'although maybe I should mention that there's no such thing as a "modest" topless shoot, in my opinion anyway.'

'Well, in *my* opinion, you're a prude,' she says.

'That line is getting a little old,' I say, smiling. 'Tell it to someone who cares. Anyway, what's up?'

'Just wanted to know if you want to meet me in Burwood for coffee later?'

'Sure, why not?' I reply. 'It's not like I'm gonna pass this Business test anyway.'

'Can't study?' she asks.

'Honestly, it's like some fairies crawled into my brain last night and built a fortress to prevent anything going in.'

'Eugh,' she replies. 'Sounds painful.'

'You think all study is painful.'

'Yeah, maybe I'll just make a sex tape and build a reality-TV empire instead.'

'I'm hanging up now,' I tell her.

She giggles. 'OK, see you soon!'

I arrive at our favourite cafe and get a seat outside. After ten minutes of sitting alone, I check my phone and find two missed calls and a text message.

Changed my mind. Meet me at the fro-yo shop?

I shake my head and try to sneak out of the cafe.

'Sorry,' I tell the waiter when she sees me, red-faced. 'My friend … can't come any more.'

'I'm going to kill you,' I tell Lauren when I get to the frozen yoghurt shop. 'I was sitting there for ages.'

She shrugs. 'Sorry, I had a craving.'

I shake my head. 'Where are we even gonna eat these? There's no tables here.'

'I don't know — stop getting antsy, I'll figure it out.'

We order the yoghurt (I pay, of course) and walk outside, the cold wind blowing our hair in all directions.

'I'm *really* going to kill you,' I tell her.

'Relax, it's not that bad,' she says.

'You have yoghurt in your hair!'

'Let's just sit here,' she says, gesturing to a table in front of the gelato shop. 'They won't be able to see us.'

I look at her guiltily.

'Just do it,' she says, sitting down. 'We'll be done in three minutes. If they tell us to go, we'll go.'

I take a seat across from her and start shovelling the yoghurt into my mouth so we can leave.

She looks at me and bursts out laughing.

'It's not a race, you know,' she says.

I grin at her. 'I don't want to get in trouble.'

'From the gelato-shop owner?' she asks, mocking me. 'Gosh, you overthink everything. *Relax*.'

Her words remind me of my earlier conversation with David, so I decide to ask for her opinion.

'Do you think I will be able to handle it in Goulburn?' I ask her. 'It's going to be a lot of hard work.'

'Do you want an honest answer?' she asks me.

I nod, biting my lip.

'I think you're a bit wussy,' she says. 'You don't have the backbone for it. I can't see you as a cop.'

'What can you see me as?' I ask.

She shrugs. 'I don't know, but policing … you have to be in control, strong. But you let the world get away with everything.'

I look down at my yoghurt. 'I think I'll be good at it,' I say quietly. 'Maybe I'm not assertive all the time. But I can do it in my work …'

'Yeah, 'cause clowning gives you so much experience in being assertive,' she says, rolling her eyes.

I look at her for a moment, but say nothing. Maybe she's right.

'My dad found the police academy pamphlets anyway,' I reveal. 'And someone told him about the clown stuff, which means I probably won't be doing it any more. I have one party left and then I think I'm done.'

'Good,' she says, smiling at me. 'You hated it.'

'That's not the point,' I say. 'I finally felt like I had my future in sight. Now I have to work on a new plan.'

'So do it,' she says dismissively.

I sigh inwardly, wishing I could talk to someone who got it.

'Is the pavlova flavour nice?' she asks a second later.

'Mmmhmmm, try it,' I say through a mouthful of yoghurt. I scoop some out with my spoon and move to hand the spoon to Lauren, but it falls out of my hand and into my lap.

'Aww, damn,' I say, wiping away at my pants. 'These are new.'

I'm still trying to deal with the mess when a voice behind me calls out my name. My stage name.

'Tatty? Tatty the Clown?'

Lauren nearly spits out her yoghurt in amusement. I look at Mike in shock, then stand up really quickly, knocking my bag off the table in the process and sending lip glosses, scraps of paper, loose change and tampons flying all over the pavement.

The first time I saw Mike, I was sweaty and had remnants of face paint all over me. Now there is a splodge of yoghurt on my jeans and my feminine paraphernalia is scattered everywhere. What is it about this guy that makes me so clumsy?

I force myself to stop staring at him and pick my stuff off the floor, all the while trying to work out how to deal with this situation. I hadn't mentioned him to Lauren, which meant her brain was currently working overtime reading into this.

'Hi, I'm Mike,' he says to her, extending a hand. 'Tammi and I met through … clown stuff, I guess.'

'Lauren,' she replies politely. 'You're too cute to be a clown.'

'So is Tatty, and yet she seems really into the kids.'

He's quick, I'll give him that.

'Mmmhmmm,' Lauren says, giving me a suspicious look. I pretend not to notice.

'Are you feeling rebellious today?' he asks me.

'Huh?'

'Yoghurt at the gelato store?'

'Ohh,' I say, wishing I were anywhere but here. 'Ha, yeah, something like that.'

'Well, you better not get into trouble,' he says. 'Or let one of those kids see you setting a bad example.'

'I don't think they'll recognise me,' I point out.

'That's too bad,' he says, smiling. 'Your costume doesn't do you justice.'

I blush and swallow hard, wishing Lauren wasn't here to see this.

'So Tatty, Tammi … whatever. Um, I haven't seen you around the park lately and I was hoping to run into you. A client wants me to do some extra work for these … events that she runs for charity, and I could really use some pointers.'

I look at him blankly. He's probably thinking I'm a dimwit.

'I don't know if you have my new mobile number, so I'll just write it down on this napkin for you and hopefully you can let me know.'

He scrawls his number on one of my napkins with the letter M underneath it and hands it to me coolly. I blush again, vaguely aware of Lauren watching this exchange with interest.

'Hang on,' she says a second later, 'didn't you say you were quitting the clown business?'

I swallow hard.

'Um, I'm meeting some friends for sushi so I better run,' he says, extending his hand to shake mine. 'Good to see you again, Tatty. I hope I hear from you.'

He walks off, leaving me with burning cheeks.

'Who was *that*?' Lauren asks.

I'm so busy staring off in his direction that it takes me a moment to register the question. 'You heard him,' I tell her. 'A clown guy.'

'Oh yeah? What's his work name?' she demands.

'Uh, Max. Max Laughs,' I say. 'I know, such a cliché. No wonder he needs my advice.'

'Uh huh,' she says, looking at me intently. 'Well, it sounded like he wanted more than just some advice, and seeing that you're in a relationship with our good buddy Davo, you really don't need this napkin.'

She watches my face intently as she starts to tear at the napkin. Then she seems to think better of it, and slips the napkin into her pocket.

'What?' she asks. 'You didn't want it, did you?'

I shake my head, unable to say anything.

'Good,' she says, smiling brightly. 'You do have a boyfriend after all, and you know I'm into the bad boys.'

I give her a dark look.

'What?' she asks. 'It's totally obvious — he has "bad boy" written all over him. And you say you want to be a cop. Pfftt.'

I shake my head and find myself jealous of her for the first time in a long time. She's so strong, so tough, so confident. And I'm just the weakling sitting next to her. Always have been.

I look down into my lap, where my hand lies. It's tingling where he touched it, like a little electric current is running through it.

There's something about him — a charismatic-stranger vibe that I find exciting, even though I also feel guilty for thinking so. But after all these years of sameness, he is something different.

And I am desperate to find out more.

Gillian

Gillian Cummings added a new photo.

Cristiana Lopez Love the new hair, Gill! Suits you.

Lauren Pappas So how many outfits did you try on before you got the perfect selfie?

Sylvana Darrar ∧ Moll. PS, SO sorry I haven't replied to your message. Things are crazy here. Will ttyl I promise xxx

'No, not that one,' I tell Matty. We're in the library choosing pictures for the yearbook. 'I look like a loser.'

'We all looked like losers in year 8,' he says, sighing. 'You should've seen me.'

'Lauren and Tammi didn't look like losers,' I point out.

He shakes his head.

'No, seriously, you weren't here. They had no —'

'For Pete's sake, you're wasting my time. Pick some pictures so I can get out of here before I'm old.'

'Fine, use this,' I say, picking an image off the screen.

He opens the file just as Lauren and Amanda emerge from one of the private study rooms.

'Oh, the school play in year eight,' Amanda says to me, peering at the screen. 'You were such a cute Sleeping Beauty.'

'Lucky we did it back when you were thinner,' Lauren scoffs. 'If we did that play now, you'd be waiting forever for someone to kiss you — even with your new try-hard hair.'

Amanda bursts out laughing, then bites her lip, feigning embarrassment, while Lauren just smirks at me.

'Leave me alone, Lauren. I'm busy,' I say, turning my back to her.

'Yes, Tammi told me how protective you are about your little "project",' she says, complete with air quotes. 'What was it that Gillian said to Tammi, Amanda? That I can't control everything?'

Amanda lets out another snort of laughter and Lauren looks pleased with herself.

My face reddens.

'Piss off, Lauren,' says Matty.

'Oh, cute,' she says. 'She protects the yearbook, and you protect her. Dregs and dregs. You two are made for each other.' She walks away, almost bumping into Charlie on the way out.

'No one has brought in any photos,' Charlie says, sitting on a chair next to us. 'I thought Ryan said Mrs H would make them do it.'

'As if she can make them do anything,' Matty says, turning back to the computer.

'We have so many blank pages,' she says, putting her face in her hands. 'I can't be bothered with this. I have a Legal assessment due in two days that I'm nowhere near finishing.'

'I've done mine,' I tell her. 'I can help you if you want.'

'Don't look so happy about it,' she says, giving me a look. 'Do you always cry when volunteering to help someone?'

'You're crying?' Matty says, turning to me. 'If you let her make you cry, then you're as stupid as she is.'

'Who? What? What are you talking about?' Charlie asks.

'Lauren,' he says. 'Who else.'

'Again?'

'I just had something in my eye,' I say, rubbing it for effect.

Matty grunts.

'OK, what is going on between you two?' Charlie asks.

I shrug, and start gathering my stuff up into a pile. She gives me a stern look.

'Matty?' she asks again, like a teacher who's caught out a student.

He shakes his head. 'Not my business,' he says.

'Or yours,' I tell her, walking out.

I go sit under the same tree I found Charlie under some weeks ago. We've spoken a lot since then, even hung out at lunch occasionally. But I wouldn't call us friends just yet.

Moments later, she emerges from the library with Matt in tow.

'Don't pretend that you're sleeping,' Charlie says, throwing her bag down on the ground next to me. 'We need to talk.'

'What, are you going to give me an empowerment speech from one of those feminist books you're always reading?'

She smiles. 'No, I just want to know why you let her do that to you.'

'Do what?'

'Don't play dumb with me, Gill,' she says, folding her arms.

'You fold your arms too much,' Matty says, looking at her.

'Usually when you think you're right. Which apparently is all the time.'

'Not helping,' she says, sliding a look at him.

He takes a deep breath and sits down on one of the logs that separate the concrete floor of the quad from the grassy area where I'm sitting, tossing his school bag between his legs.

'Well?' he says.

I sigh and close my eyes.

'I *really* don't want to talk about it,' I say.

The bell rings and I let out an internal thanks to the universe. *Saved by the bell.* But when I open my eyes, they're both still there.

'The bell rang,' I say.

'We heard,' she says.

'You should go to class,' I say.

'I make it a point to avoid things I *should* be doing,' she says, smirking. It was one of those looks that makes you just want to shove her face into a pie. Or, if you're Ryan Fleming, dog poo.

'You are irritating,' I say.

'I know, I love it.'

Matty smiles at us and I look from him to her.

'So, no class?' I ask.

'Guess not,' he says, shrugging.

'Want to go get some ice-cream?' I ask. 'I'll tell you all about what happened.'

We escape via the blind spot near the quad and catch the bus to Burwood, then on an impulse decide to hop on the train to Newtown, just to go somewhere different.

'Thank God I didn't bring my car,' Charlie says, when she sees the traffic on King Street. 'Sydney traffic sucks.'

'*You* have a car?' I say. 'Wow.'

'What?' she says. 'No big deal.'

Matty scoffs. 'You make out as if you're above all this privileged elite business, and turns out you're just like the rest of them.'

'It was a gift,' she says, offended.

He shakes his head. 'That's not a way to win this argument.'

Charlie declares that it's too cold for ice-cream despite my protestations, retaliating with her 'guest' status in our city.

'You don't even want to be here,' I point out. 'You can't use that argument.'

'Yes, I can,' she says. 'If I must suffer here, at least let me choose where to go.'

'OK,' I say defeated, even though I could eat ice-cream in sub-zero temperatures.

We end up at Doughbox Diner on Enmore Road, where they get a savoury crepe each and I get a sweet one.

'If my mum saw me eating this, she would die,' I say, wiping melted chocolate off my hands.

'You're making a mess,' Charlie says.

'Leave her alone; this is the happiest I've seen her,' Matty says.

'You softie,' she says, winking at him. He smiles and my heart melts a little.

'You guys, this is, like, real friendship!' I say, excited.

'Don't ruin it,' he says.

'But in the spirit of this alleged friendship, tell us what is going on with you and bitch face,' says Charlie.

'Honestly, I thought she'd be over it by now, because it was months ago, but I guess not,' I say.

Charlie looks at me expectantly. 'Go on, elaborate.'

'Well, when my best friend moved overseas last year, I started hanging out with them, you know? They were being nice to me and I didn't really have anyone else — it had always been just Syl and me. So we hung out for about three months in year 11 and then at the end of the year, when the year 12s had their muck-up day, they invited me out with them.'

'But why were year 11s at the muck-up?'

'It's tradition here,' I explain. 'In the olden days, the year that was leaving used to invite the year below to one of its final events as kind of like a hand-over. Anyway, I went with them one night. And they decided they were going to vandalise the main street of Croydon — The Strand — and blame the public school. They spilled garbage everywhere, sprayed a little graffiti, broke one or two shop windows — stuff like that. '

'And you didn't show?'

'No, I showed up,' I say. 'I just didn't know that I was being followed by a journalist.'

'Huh?' Matty says. 'So that's why you were on the news — not because someone saw you and dobbed you in?'

'Well … I don't know. Maybe someone was trying to get some dirt on my dad so they had someone watching the house. And when they saw me sneaking out at 3 a.m., they might have followed me. Or someone could have dobbed us in … either way, it ended up in the papers under the headline "MP daughter caught in school prank" or something. With photos.'

'Ahh,' Charlie says. 'So they all got busted?'

'Pretty much,' I say. 'One guy in year 12 even got arrested.' I look at their faces, trying to assess the damage. 'Really, it wasn't that bad — it only took the council, like, two hours to clean up the mess — but Lauren just can't get over it.'

'So who else was there?' Matty asks, finishing off my crepe.

'There was a bunch of us. Tammi, Amanda, David, Ryan —'

Charlie's head snaps up from her milkshake. 'Ryan?'

'Yeah, he's in with that crowd.'

'Yeah, but he's such a nerd,' she says, puzzled. 'I can't imagine his father-figure act would go down well during a school prank.'

'Well, he *is* the best one out of them,' I say, turning to Matty, who nods. 'He can still be snobby, though.'

'Yeah, but he acts so high and mighty, and it turns out he's a rebel,' she says.

'I think he just went 'cause Lauren made him,' I tell her. 'They used to go out.'

'WHAT?!'

Matty looks up from the doodle he's drawing on his arm. 'Why are you so shocked? The hot kids always go out with each other. It's, like, a law of nature.'

'Get back to your drawing, Picasso,' she says, giving him a dark look.

I laugh.

'Wow,' she says, exhaling. 'So she's a bitch to you because your dad was maybe being followed by someone who wanted the dirty on him, and gave the story to a newspaper. Was it even an important paper?'

'That's not the point,' I tell her. 'I got them in trouble.'

'No, you didn't,' she says. 'You didn't put a gun to her head and force her to go. I bet she kicked up so much of a stink that she didn't even get in trouble anyway.'

'Well … she did have to miss out on an Ed Sheeran concert because she got grounded. After she had boasted to everyone about getting tickets.'

'A fate worse than death,' Matty says, raising his eyebrows. 'The bloke is the bomb.'

'Yeah, he's pretty awesome,' Charlie says. 'And he would *not* tolerate her bullying.'

'Bullying is a strong word,' I say, biting my lip.

'It's bullying,' she says authoritatively. 'Since I've been here, I've seen Facebook comments, Instagram hashtags on your pictures, and —'

'— there was that time they put your school bag on the year 7 excursion bus and you got detention for not having your books,' Matty finishes.

'You knew about that?' I ask, thinking of that first prank they'd played on me after the muck-up day. I didn't say anything then — I thought it was fair payback.

'See?' Charlie says, folding her arms. 'Bullying.'

'Don't make me one of your case studies,' I warn her, looking down at my phone. 'Oh my God, it's almost six! Wednesday nights my mum goes out, I'm supposed to be home to watch Sammy.'

We bolt for the train, crashing into people entering bars and restaurants for their after-work catch-ups as we go, and squash ourselves into a packed carriage.

'She's going to kill me,' I say, banging my head against a pole.

'Relax, just tell her you had a meeting with yearbook people,' Charlie says, rubbing my back. 'It's not technically a lie.'

I look at her, frantic.

'Stop breathing like that, you're freaking me out!' she says. 'How old is Sammy anyway? Can't he look after himself for an hour or so?'

'He's got Down's syndrome,' I tell her. 'When he looks after himself it's a bloody disaster. Just ask Matty.'

'Which is why you shouldn't be in trouble,' he says to me. 'No offence, but I've seen how your mum is with him. She has no right to say anything to you.'

'I can call my mum and ask her to pick us up and drive you home if that will help,' Charlie suggests.

I nod, thankful for the offer.

We find Charlie's mum waiting for us across the road from Burwood station in the car that Charlie says was a gift. For some reason she seems to do a double-take when she sees Matty, but he doesn't notice — he's too busy checking out the car.

'You were *given* this?' Matty says, circling it. 'It's a Lexus hatch. My friend Mo would kill for it.'

Charlie shrugs and looks at her mum, who smiles.

'Are you sure we haven't met?' she asks Matty. 'You look so familiar to me. Doesn't he look familiar, Chi?'

Charlie shrugs. 'You know, I thought the same thing when I first met him,' she says. 'But I think it's just the hoodie.' She turns to me. 'When Mum had her psych practice in Melbourne she was always attracting these thug-type teenagers that thought they had problems, but really they just dressed like they did.'

Charlie's mum gives her an icy look. 'That's inappropriate,' she says. 'You don't know what those kids were going through.'

Matty suddenly looks uncomfortable.

'You know what, I forgot I have to do something. I better go,' he says.

'No, you jump in, Matty,' Charlie's mum says, smiling. 'I'll take you home too.'

But Matty insists that the bus is fine. 'I catch it every day,' he says. 'It's not a big deal.'

'OK, then text Charlie when you get home,' she resolves. 'Just so I know you're safe.'

A little snort of laughter — a reaction to the look on Matty's face — escapes me and I feel myself reddening with embarrassment.

On the way home, I revel in Charlie's mum's company. She's the opposite of her daughter — bright, bubbly and open.

'I can't believe you're related,' I whisper to Charlie.

We pull up in front of my house. While my mum would drive away in a hurry after dropping one of my friends off, Charlie's mum asks if she should come in and meet my parents, and when I politely decline, she waits until I'm safely inside before driving off with a beep of the horn and a wave out the window.

I think about her later as I'm stacking the dishwasher, having cooked and promptly demolished the single-serve frozen lasagne that Mum had left on the bench top. Sammy and I had shared it, even though I knew only one of us was meant to eat it.

When my mum arrives home, I don't bother apologising for my lateness, and she doesn't mention it. She probably doesn't want me to bring up the fact that she left her son with her trainer just so she wouldn't be late to dinner.

Instead I wipe the benchtop, grab the tub of ice-cream in the freezer and bring it out to the living room where my mum is sprawled on the couch. I hold it out to her, a kind of peace offering.

'Ice-cream at this hour? Really?' she asks, her eyes fixed on the TV.

I glance at my phone. It's 9.04.

'Come on, Mum,' I say, sighing. 'It's just dessert.'

'Have a banana,' she says. 'It's better for you. You're already a size 12.'

'Size 12 is average in Australia, Mum. Stop making out as if I'm fat.'

'Yeah, I know it's average,' she replies. '*For people my age*. Not yours. And *I* don't even look like that.'

'You have a personal trainer,' I point out. 'I don't have that luxury.'

'Sweetie, I love you, but you have to understand something,' she says, patting the couch next to her. 'I earned that luxury. I worked out and stayed beautiful and skinny and well-kept throughout my twenties, and sometimes I really did just want a Big Mac. But look at what I have now — my life is amazing. Don't you want that too?'

I look at her for a moment. Then I get up from the couch and shove the ice-cream back in the freezer, biting my lip to prevent myself from tearing up.

'Good girl,' she calls from the living room. 'Some time when I'm not watching *The Bachelor*, we'll have a chat with Daddy and see if he can get Greg to organise some sessions with you.'

'Or I can just train with you,' I say, stating the obvious. Not that I wanted to.

'Oh no, darl,' she says, amused. 'Those sessions are Mum's alone-time.'

I head upstairs to my room, feeling starved. If I had known my crepe was going to be a small entree to an even tinier main, I would have got one with a load of marshmallows.

I hear Sammy humming to himself in his bedroom and I tiptoe in for a cuddle.

'Gillie!' he says, his smile lighting up his face. 'Tomorrow's my smoothie day!'

'It is, it is,' I tell him, giving him a tickle. He squeals with laughter.

I lie next to him and pull the sheets over the two of us.

'You're so lucky, Sammy,' I whisper, as his eyes start to close. 'You don't have to put up with the crap that everyone drags me through.'

Later, I lie awake in my own bed, my mother's words ringing in my ears. *Look at what I have now — my life is amazing.* I wonder what it feels like to be so secure, to have everything you ever wanted. To wake up feeling like life is perfect. I was starved of those feelings, and on some level I guess my mum's ideas about what makes life amazing were part of the problem.

I go to sleep thinking about the future. Would I ever stop feeling like I just don't measure up?

RYAN

Ryan Fleming Friends: Holy Family is having their annual dance-a-thon soon! It's open to students in years 11 + 12 at all Catholic schools in Sydney. Come along for good food, great music and a great cause — raising money for the Cancer Council. DM for ticket info.

It's Monday of the third week back of term two, and I've been called to Mrs H's office. I eat my sandwich on the way, even though it's still another hour until lunch.

I knock on the partially open door and she motions for me to come in. I take the seat opposite her desk and try not to listen in on the phone conversation she's having as she hovers by her window. A minute or so later, she hangs up and sits down, folding her hands in front of her.

'How are you, Ryan?' she asks. 'Keeping well at home?'

'Yes, thanks,' I say.

'I'll keep it short, Ryan,' she says, shuffling some things around on her desk. 'Just want an update on how your yearbook project is coming along.'

'It's going OK,' I tell her. 'Slow, but OK.'

'Everyone is doing their fair share?'

'Um, I guess so,' I say. 'We're still mostly in planning stages, but so far no one has missed a meeting.'

'Good to hear,' she says, nodding. 'I've just looked over the list of names and I was a little surprised by it, I must admit. I knew Mr Broderick had chosen Charlie Scanlon and Matthew Fullerton, and Gillian Cummings seems to be that way inclined, but Tammi Kapsalis surprised me. I kind of picked her for the events committee. Is she doing OK with you?'

'Yeah, she is,' I say to her. 'She chose yearbook because Lauren Pappas was on events, so I guess she thought she'd do something different.'

'Oh, she did, did she?' she asks, smiling.

'Speaking of people on the committee, Mrs H, I was a little surprised about the decision to put Charlie there,' I say. 'I don't know how well it's going to work. Isn't it going to be hard for her to compile a book about memories of events she's never been involved with?'

'Not if she starts making headway on some new memories,' she points out. 'Plus you have the charity dance-a-thon coming up, and the school retreat next term. It's a good way for her to connect with you all, so she doesn't feel left out when the year wraps up.'

I shrug. 'Yeah, I suppose so,' I admit.

'Ryan,' she says, looking at me like my grandmother does when she's trying to teach me something, 'are you perhaps a little concerned because you've noticed that Charlie is — how should I put this — a bit of a threat to you, academically speaking? She certainly is very bright and that can be intimidating.'

I look on in disbelief. How does she know? My lack of a response says everything.

She smiles at me. It's a smile that's a mix of amusement and reassurance, and I can't help but go bright red.

'Not being on a field any more doesn't mean you need to give up on a little healthy competition, OK?'

'Yes, Miss,' I say, nodding.

I head back to the quad and find Lauren, David, Tammi, Amanda and a few others from our large group sitting around one of the tables, whispering excitedly.

'All right, what are you guys plotting?' I ask, plonking myself next to Amanda.

'We're not plotting,' Lauren says, smiling at me innocently.

'You plot so often you don't even know you're plotting,' I say.

'Why did we ever break up?' she asks. 'You know me so well.'

I shake my head. 'I asked my question first.'

'We're just looking at Gillian's latest Instagram posts,' she says, smirking. 'They're very … sophisticated. She probably thinks her new hair makes her look like some kind of fashion blogger.'

'And?'

'We were just discussing what to comment on some of them.'

Tammi gives me a worried look.

'Don't you think you've done enough?' I ask.

'Yeah, I think maybe we should —' starts Tammi.

'No one asked you, Tammi,' David says, cutting her off.

Her face reddens as the rest of them laugh.

'Seriously, you guys need to relax and take a joke,' Lauren says.

'Yeah, but your jokes tend to be pretty mean,' I say.

'Pfft,' she snorts. 'When did you get so sensitive? That accident knock your sense of humour out of you?'

'Really?' I ask, agitated. 'You went there?'

'Don't be so uptight, man, it's harmless fun,' David says, nudging Tammi, who gives a fake smile. 'Even Tammi's loosening up to the idea.'

'Yeah, loosening up to everything except you,' Lauren says, sneering.

David's face turns red. He snatches up his bag and leaves.

'Why'd you have to say that?' Tammi asks, her Greek side coming out in the expressions of her hands.

'Sorry,' Lauren says, rolling her eyes and looking anything but.

Tammi sighs and rubs her forehead. 'Now I have to go after him, which will just lead to another fight.'

'Then just break up already,' Lauren tells her. Everyone else looks on awkwardly.

'You just don't get it,' Tammi says, picking up her bag.

'It's OK, Tams,' I say. 'I'll go.'

I find David behind the school building, kicking a ball hard at the wall, catching it, then repeating the movements. *Everything he does is so predictable*, I think. An opposing team who studied his plays would smash him every time. But I don't tell him that. He has a hot-headed Sicilian temper, and if he goes off, it won't be pretty.

'Hey,' I say. 'So it's OK for you to troll someone you barely even know, but your friends can't tell you the truth?'

'I don't need a lecture,' he mumbles.

'And you don't need to listen to Lauren either,' I point out. 'How many times have you told me she's just a bored shit-stirrer?'

'She hit a soft spot.'

'She knows how to manipulate people and you know it,' I tell him. 'Don't give her ammo and she'll back off.'

'I'm not,' he says. 'I just came to practise.'

'OK,' I say, raising my eyebrows.

'I bet Tammi's pleased with herself,' he says after a moment.

'She's actually not,' I tell him. 'You know her.'

'Of course I know her. I know her better than you.'

I take a deep breath, reminding myself of that temper.

The bell rings and I give him a look that says it's time to go to class. He pauses for a moment, then shakes his head.

'I think I'm just gonna go home,' he tells me. 'I have a double study period anyway, so no difference. Can you take Tammi home? She sooks if she has to take the bus.'

I give him a half-smile. 'Girls, eh?' I say, trying to mend the awkwardness.

He grins. 'All so effing precious.'

———

In the car on the way home, Tammi's quiet. She won't stop fidgeting with the zips on her bag.

'Everything's different,' she tells me.

'What — you and David?'

'Everything, everything,' she says, looking at me. 'Me and David, you and David, me and Lauren, the whole yearbook thing, Gillian. Like, she's nice.'

I shrug. 'You didn't think she was?'

She shakes her head, as if that's not what she meant. 'Maybe I just see things differently now; putting other people down to stay popular feels dirty. It's turning me off Lauren — but I still love her.'

'Well, she has been your best friend for ages. You're probably just growing up a bit. She will too.'

'Maybe,' she mumbles, looking out the window.

'Tammi, I've gotta ask, are you stringing him along?'

'Oh, come on, Ryan,' she says, exasperated. 'Not you too. Since when do I have to explain my choices to everyone?'

'I didn't mean it like that,' I say. 'He's cut up about it.'

'Well, then, he should break it off with me,' she says. 'I still feel something for him, but I'm just so sick of being pushed into something I'm not ready for. Sex is everywhere. When my friends talk about it, it's like it's some big competition. It's on every TV show, in every RnB song lyric. It's so much pressure.'

'Did you ever think that maybe David's pressuring you because he feels the same way?' I ask. 'I mean, there's a lot of pressure for us guys too.'

'This is such an awkward conversation to have … with you of all people,' she says, sighing.

'I'm still your friend, Tammi,' I tell her. 'No matter what happens with David or Lauren or in yearbook meetings. And if you need someone to talk to and your other friends don't get it — well, I might not get it either, but I'll try.'

I turn off the car engine. Tammi moves to get out, but then she puts her bag back down in front of her and turns to face me.

'I saw on some TV programme one night that boys who are, like, twelve and thirteen are making their girlfriends *who are the same age as them* do it, because it's, you know, trendy. But, like, they don't actually know what they're doing. So they watch porn and stuff on the internet — and they think "Oh, that's what you're supposed to do".'

'Well, I get that most women don't like that pornographic stuff ...' I say. 'But do you really think that's what it's going to be like with David?'

'No,' she says. 'That's not my point. I'm just talking about the pressure to do it. It's almost like it's not your own decision any more.'

It's my turn to be awkward now, but I feel like I owe it to her to listen.

'I feel diseased because I want to wait — David makes me feel that way, and so does Lauren. I just want to not be scared or awkward about it when I do go through with it.'

'If it makes you feel any better,' I tell her, 'everyone is probably pretending to be fine with it anyway.'

She shrugs. 'In all honesty, Ryan, I couldn't care less what other people are doing, so long as they leave me alone. And right now, they're not, and it's driving me up the wall.'

My turn to shrug.

She shakes her head. 'I'm sorry,' she says. 'I feel awful, rattling on and on. Thanks so much for the advice. I hope David knows how lucky he is to be your friend.'

'The luck is all mine, apparently,' I tell her, scoffing. 'I go away with his family, get convinced by one of his crazy ideas, and come back with a broken knee and broken dreams.'

She looks at me sadly. 'And yet you're still trying to make *his* dreams happen.'

'I might as well live through his dream if I can't make my own happen. It sounds selfish ...'

'You're the opposite of selfish,' she tells me, getting out of the car and talking to me through the open window. 'Unlike David.'

'I've never heard you call him selfish before,' I tell her, looking at her pointedly.

'I've been too blind to see it,' she says.

'Love is blind,' I tell her, smiling.

She looks at me sadly before she responds. 'So what does it mean now that I can see?'

THE YEARBOOK COMMITTEE
Minutes for June Meeting

Recorded by: Gillian Cummings

Meeting Chair: Ryan Fleming

In attendance: Everyone

The Playlist: Matty kicked off the meeting with 'Eye of the Tiger' by Survivor, and we didn't need to enter into a discussion about what the subliminal message there was. Ryan gave Matty the thumbs-up, and we just got to work.

The Snacks: Tammi brought Haigh's Milk Honeycomb, which was a hit. Even Charlie had some. (At first I couldn't believe it was over ten bucks a block, but now I get it.) Ryan brought a bag of marshmallows and a packet of lime and black pepper chips, and we all pretended not to notice that Matty hogged them. Everyone else was relieved when I brought a packet of Arnott's Montes (I did learn from the sugar-free episode) and Charlie said she didn't feel like dip that morning, so she brought a batch of peanut-butter brownies that she baked (!!!). No one said anything in case it killed her feminist killjoy reputation, especially when Ryan put one in his bag for later. I don't know if it was the food, but it was the most successful meeting yet, and we only got into one fight (I don't even remember what it was about). (Note to Self: Pay more attention if you are going to insist on taking minutes.)

Agenda:
* Discussion on what has actually been collated so far: everyone was impressed with my coverage of the major school events from years 7 to 12, and the way that Matty had laid them out into our template. It turns out that we have so far completed about 36% of the yearbook. YAY!
* Discussion on remaining content: this time, we actually decided to, as Charlie called it, 'divide and conquer'. Ryan gave us each a task (see Action Points below). (He stopped for a moment to see if Charlie was going to argue, but she didn't, and everyone was really surprised.)

Questions for Mrs H:
* Is the yearbook going to be in colour?

Action points for next meeting:
* Charlie to interview teachers about their favourite memories of our grade. (She said that should please

Mr Broderick because it means she is getting to know the teachers. She said this with a very sarcastic tone that reminds me never to get on her bad side. I wonder if Mr Broderick, and Ryan, know not to get on her bad side also.)

* Ryan to write a reflection on our fundraising experiences over the last two years, and how we can keep a commitment to these causes going into the future. (That was his idea. It's kind of sweet.)

* Matty to be responsible for chasing up Ryan's reflection and Charlie's interviews for insertion into the template.

* Tammi is to be official camp reporter. (I offered to help her, because she can't be with all the groups at once, and she looked at me for a second to see if I was being serious, then said thanks, she would think about it. It was weird ...)

Postscript:

Tammi followed me after the meeting and apologised if she was cold. She just 'assumed' that I would not want to help her because of everything that's happened (is happening?). I told her that I don't hold grudges and that the yearbook was important to me, and that I want it to be great. She smiled and said she would appreciate the help, but could we keep it between us? I just rolled my eyes and walked off.

Charlie

Charlie Scanlon Reading *The Sex Myth* by Australian journalist Rachel Hills. Sooo good! #amreading #feminist #bibliophile

---

Katy Coolidge-Brown likes this.

Katy Coolidge-Brown Ohhh I have heard such good things about it.

I'm waiting on the stairs in front of the library one morning before school when Gillian calls.

'Hey! Where are you? I thought we were meant to meet up,' I say.

'I'm not coming to school today,' she tells me. 'I stayed up all night working on my English assignment and I'm so tired.'

'Damn you to hell, I wanted to tell you I booked my flight.'

'To Melbourne? That's awesome.'

'I know, first time back in six months, I'm so excited.'

'Yeah, it's home, why wouldn't you be? Oh, Sammy's here, he thinks I can play with him because I'm home! Gotta go.'

I open my laptop, excited to share the news with Pete. He's already online, and I take it as a sign from the universe that this is all meant to be.

Charlie Scanlon:
Booked this morning! Five weeks and counting.

Pete Brady:
The only exciting thing to ever happen on a Monday. So what are we going to do? Lord of the Fries, churros, tram to St Kilda for chats?

Charlie Scanlon:
Chips, churros, chats. How very us.

Pete Brady:
I know, we're super classy.

Charlie Scanlon:
OMG! Can't believe I forgot to tell you!!! I found a Lord of the Fries here!

Pete Brady:
Have you been yet?

Charlie Scanlon:
As if. I refuse to enter the premises in revolt.

Pete Brady:
That word is so sexy. I'll need to use it. So I'm thinking with LOTF there, maybe Sydney wants you to stay?

Charlie Scanlon:
And if it does?

Pete Brady:
I'd torch it in revolt. After rescuing you of course.

Charlie Scanlon:

Hmm, maybe skip the torching ...

Pete Brady:

Your mother's pregnant isn't she?

Charlie Scanlon:

Um, how did you know that?

Pete Brady:

Easy — you've never been this sensitive about Sydney.
How far along is she?

Charlie Scanlon:

4 months or so I think.

Pete Brady:

You never told me?

Charlie Scanlon:

I didn't know. There's a three-month rule.

Pete Brady says:

You're her daughter and you live in the same house.
Wouldn't you have heard her vomit?

Charlie Scanlon:

Not all women get morning sickness, you know. And the
house is palatial.

Pete Brady:

I don't know what that means but that's no excuse.

Charlie Scanlon:

Huge. It means huge.

Pete Brady:

I repeat — no excuse.

Charlie Scanlon:

OK, I knew. I just couldn't tell you.

Pete Brady:

I knew it! I'm gutted.

Charlie Scanlon:

Girls before fellas. OK, so I'm there Friday night, Saturday, Sunday. I have to be back at the airport at 4 p.m. on Sunday.

Pete Brady:

I'll make sure I keep all of Friday night and Saturday free.

Charlie Scanlon:

No Sunday? ☹

Pete Brady:

Sorry — I have something on.

Charlie Scanlon:

Yeah — what?

Pete Brady:

A thing.

Charlie Scanlon:

You know I'll keep pestering.

Pete Brady:

You'll laugh.

Charlie Scanlon:

Try me.

Pete Brady:

Um, I might be going to a church thing.

Charlie Scanlon:

ROFL. Seriously, what is it?

Pete Brady:

I knew you'd laugh.

Charlie Scanlon:

OMG — you're serious?

Pete Brady:

Yeah. There's like this youth BBQ on, and I'm going with a group.

Charlie Scanlon:

Wow. You're not even religious.

Pete Brady:

It's just a fun time out with some friends. I'm not becoming a priest, just going for the company and the sausage sizzle.

Charlie Scanlon:

I'll come for a sausage sizzle. There's wine at Catholic church too, right?

Pete Brady:

Lol, not for freeloading atheists like you.

Charlie Scanlon:

Me? I'm insulted. Seriously, I don't mind coming.

Pete Brady:

You'd hate it. You wouldn't fit in. You have a chin piercing for God's sake!!!

Charlie Scanlon:

So? You have tattoos! And I took my chin stud out when school started. We're not allowed to have them.

Pete Brady:

It's just a different crowd. Plus I'd feel weird bringing you when you don't know anyone. Sorry. Let's just stick to Saturday and Friday night for now. Think about what you want to do. Can't wait to hang out.

He signs out a second later and I find myself staring at his message, trying to read between the lines for some reason why things have changed between us. But I can't see it.

'Ouch, that's some fobbing,' a voice says behind me. I spin around and see Ryan sitting on a step behind me, smirking.

'How long have you been there?' I ask, giving him a dirty look.

'Long enough. So who's Pete?'

'No one you need to worry about.'

He shrugs. 'I'm not worried, but the guy sounds like a dick.'

'Well, he's not.'

'OK then, whatever.'

He walks past me and I quickly shove my laptop into my bag and hurry after him.

'Putting aside the fact that that was an invasion of privacy,' I say, falling in step alongside him, 'how much of that did you see?'

'Well, congratulations on your mum's pregnancy and your palatial house.'

I start to say something but he doesn't let me interrupt.

'I come from a long line of Catholics and should probably warn you that you're not allowed to drink the wine — which becomes the blood of Christ, by the way — unless you're actually a Catholic. And a Catholic who goes to confession for that matter, but even so, I find that the sausage sizzles at any communal event are a massive drawcard. Just look at Bunnings. As for the piercing comment, your friend Pete obviously doesn't know that the word "Catholic" means "universal", which means even people with three legs are welcome. God won't judge you for having a piercing.'

'Do you know people with three legs?' I ask.

'No, but I can understand why they'd want some Jesus in their life. The world is mean.'

'Starting with boys who read private messages,' I point out.

'You were blocking the way. And so was your school bag.'

'The phrase "excuse me" — you familiar with it?'

'Oh, that,' he says, shaking his head. 'I decided not to ask you to move in case you interpreted that as me declaring my superiority as a male.'

'Very funny,' I say, my eyes narrowed. 'So how come you were in the library? She wouldn't let me in, the cow.'

'She likes me,' he says. 'All the teachers do.'

'Yeah, I bet they're all gunning for you to win the St Gerard scholarship.'

He coughs, amused. 'Jerome. The St *Jerome* Medal.'

I fold my arms. 'Whatever it's called, it's gonna be mine.'

He smiles and nods his head. 'Well, best of luck then, Charlie. You probably deserve it more than me. Even if you're not very smart when it comes to choosing your friends.'

'What's that supposed to mean?' I ask.

'You'll see when you get to Melbourne,' he calls out, walking away.

I spend the rest of the morning thinking of Ryan's words and Pete's coldness, irritated that I let them both get to me when I had so much else on my mind: the yearbook was time-consuming, I had heaps of homework, and I actually wanted to make an effort with my mum and my new brother- or sister-to-be.

In fourth period, I get a text from Gillian, who asks if I want to come over after school while her mum's out. She must have texted Matty as well, because I hear him call out to me after homeroom, a bunch of papers in his hand.

'Did she ask for her homework?' I ask.

'No, but I think she'd like the distraction.'

'You're going to make some woman very happy one day,' I tell him. 'Such intuition.'

He shrugs, then tells me he'll catch up with me at Gill's.

By the time I have to leave for Gillian's, I'm too exhausted for her chirpy personality, but I don't have the heart to say I'm not coming any more. So it's especially irritating when she opens the door and seems utterly deflated that I'm alone.

'Is it just you?' she asks, looking over my shoulder.

'Great to see you too,' I reply.

'Sorry,' she says, smiling. 'I figured Matty would be here by now, but he's probably still working.'

'That's weird — he said earlier he'd meet me here. Why didn't he tell me he was working at the juice bar?'

'He isn't at his juice-bar job today. He also delivers junk mail in his area.'

I raise my eyebrows, but don't say anything. Why he would need all that extra cash? He did seem impressed with my car — is he saving up to buy one for himself? I'm making a mental note to ask him when Gillian puts some snacks on the breakfast bar in front of me.

'Carrots and cucumbers?' I say, grimacing.

'Blame my mum,' she says. 'She actually cut them up and everything.'

'Did it ruin her nails?' I ask sarcastically. She gives me an amused look and we both crack up laughing.

'So what time is she heading out tonight?' I ask.

'Six-ish usually,' she says, glancing at the big French clock in the living room across from us. 'They go out for dinner, and when she comes back she watches *Real Housewives* or *The Bachelor* episodes. It's her thing.'

Moments later, the doorbell rings. Gillian looks at the security screen.

'Sammy! Matty's at the door,' she calls. 'Can you go let him in please?'

I glance out into the hallway and see Sammy excitedly throw his arms around Matty. He drags him through the kitchen to the living area to show him a drawing he did. They play video games, and Gill and I chat while she prepares Sammy's dinner. Sammy chooses a DVD and takes his seat at the table, and the three of us head to the back verandah to escape the noise of the TV.

'Your house is nice,' Matty tells her, looking around.

She shrugs. 'Everything always seems nice on the outside.'

'What's going on?' I ask. 'Are you finally seeing through the staged pictures of Instagram?'

Matty rolls his eyes. 'Can't we talk about something easy so I don't have to concentrate?'

'What, your paper route dumbed you down?' I ask.

'Hey, it's junk mail, and I need the money. We're not all rich, you know.'

'Relax, I'm just mucking around,' I say, elbowing him.

'Well, can someone please tell Pappas to stop mucking around with *me*?' Gillian asks. I look at her quizzically and she hands me her phone. It's showing Gillian's Facebook page, where Lauren has uploaded a video of Gillian sitting down on a whoopie cushion in class.

'Woah,' I say, looking up at her. 'She tagged you in it and everything. That's nasty. When did this happen?'

'Yesterday.'

I clench my fists in frustration.

'She's *such* a moll,' she says. 'She won't leave me alone.'

'Can I see?' Matty asks, reaching for the phone. His eyes widen in surprise as he watches the video. Then he swipes through some of Gill's pictures.

'Wow,' he says, looking up at me. 'Look at all these backhanded compliments she's left on your other pictures.'

'Exactly,' she says, grabbing the phone back. 'And on my status updates too. She wants to appear innocent.'

'Read one,' I suggest.

'"You're lucky your boobs are small for your body shape. Otherwise you'd look a bit skanky in that outfit."'

Matty and I look at each other in silence.

'OK, don't be upset by what I'm about to say,' I warn her, 'but why do you have a public fan page? Switch to a private account and don't add her as a friend.'

'I don't want to,' she says. 'It's linked to my blog, which is doing surprisingly well. I just want to know why every post has to come with her commentary.'

'Because that's what you get when you have a public profile,' I point out. 'What did you expect?'

'The same treatment I experienced for the past five years, when they all just ignored me,' she replies. 'Why are they suddenly trying to ruin the first good thing that's happened to me in ages?'

'Because that's how they are,' I tell her.

'Yeah, well, they suck,' she says, folding her arms defiantly.

'Relax, no one cares what they think anyway,' Matty says.

'Actually, I do,' she tells him. 'The more followers I get, the better. People make money off their social media.'

'Well, there's your answer to why she's doing this,' I tell her. 'She makes you look bad, she wins.'

'I don't get it,' Matty says.

'Think about the one person whose popularity could be jeopardised by your success,' I explain to Gillian. 'Imagine if brands start sending you products and you go on trips, or you get a role on an Aussie TV show or something. It's not that far-fetched, and Lauren knows it.'

'Yeah, but there are a lot of other nasty comments here,' Matty says. 'It's clearly not just Lauren. No offence, Gill.'

'People are telling me they want to tie their HSC notes to my limbs and set me on fire, and you're worried I'll get offended at what *you* said?' she asks. 'It's the politician thing. People hate politicians. They all think that my achievements are because of who my dad is. Even though I built that blog up from nothing.'

'But our class has known about your dad for ages,' he points out. 'Why now?'

'You guys still don't get it, do you?' I ask, turning to Gillian. 'For six years you and your friend Svetlana —'

'Sylvana,' she interrupts.

'Whatever. For six years you were the nerds at school. No one looked at you. You were irrelevant. Then some modelling scout finds her, promises her some big career, and now your dad is hot ticket to be premier. So when you appear next to him on the news and Sylvana tags you in her pictures, people know who you are. Suddenly girls who were nothing throughout high school are becoming a kind of something, and Lauren's threatened by that.'

Gillian starts to say something but I continue.

'Somebody noticed Sylvana. And now they've noticed you too. And Lauren Pappas still has to apply to UAC and hope her parents' money is enough to get her into a Media and Communications degree, which she'll hate for the next four years anyway, because all she *really* wants to do is host a TV show or pash the hottie-of-the-month on *Home and Away*.'

'It's like you have a crystal ball at home,' Matty says, looking at me admiringly.

'Yeah,' Gillian agrees. 'You totally belong on the yearbook committee. Not only can you read everyone so well, but you're funny too. We need that.'

I shake my head. 'Honest and cynical, yes. Funny? I don't think so. But I will happily fake-read your future any day, my dear Matthew.'

'It's not so much my future that I'm concerned about as my past,' he says quietly.

'What?' I ask.

'Nothing,' he says, shrugging.

I give him a look.

'You talk about your stepdad a lot,' he says. 'Have you met your real dad?'

'My biological dad, you mean?'

He nods, as if the answer's obvious.

'Nope,' I say.

'And you've never wanted to?' Gillian asks.

'Honestly?' I pause to think about it. 'No, not really. I can't actually think of a time in my life where I've thought I needed to know about him.' As the words come out, I suddenly realise that's the first time I've said them out loud.

Matty nods his head slowly, looking down at the floor.

I bend down to face him. 'What's this about, Matty?'

'I've never met my dad,' he says simply. 'I don't know who he is, how my mother met him, if they were dating … if he wanted me. She could have been raped, for all I know.'

'Shush,' Gillian says, slapping his hand.

'What?' he asks. 'I mean it. I literally have no idea.'

'Hmm, my mum's told me what I need to know,' I say. 'Short relationship, he wanted her to have an abortion. She nearly did.'

'Thank God she didn't,' Gillian says.

'No, thank *her courage* she didn't,' I say. 'She was seventeen when she told him she was pregnant with me. She never saw him again after that.'

'How does that make you feel?' Gillian asks.

'Fine,' I say truthfully. 'I had such a happy childhood. But not all people are like me. Some of us need more.'

I meet Matty's eyes, but he doesn't say anything.

'It's OK to want to reach out to him, you know,' I tell him after a moment's silence.

'I don't know how,' he says.

'Well, can't you talk to your mum about it?' Gillian asks.

Matty looks out the window and shakes his head. 'She's … not in a good place right now.'

Gillian and I exchange glances. Matty stands up and pulls his hoodie over his head.

'I gotta go home,' he says. 'Say bye to Sammy for me, will you?'

He starts to walk off and I give Gillian a bewildered what-just-happened look.

We both get up and follow him out the front door. He's almost at the front gate when he turns around and looks at us.

'My best friend, Mo, told me I'd never make friends at Holy Family. "You'll be too different to them," he said.'

'Well, you're not,' I call out, looking at him intently.

'Big houses, flashy cars —' he starts.

'— mean nothing,' Gill continues. 'Come back inside.'

He shakes his head and turns around, grabbing the gate. But a second later, Gill's at his side, slamming it shut.

'I have a big house and fancy cars and parents with more status than they know what to do with,' she tells him. 'And when Sylvana moved, a big hole opened up in my heart. But lately it's started to fill.'

He gives her a half-smile.

'My friendship does that,' I say, folding my arms and smirking.

He takes a deep breath and looks at me intently. I suddenly feel guilty for making a joke.

'My mother's in a funk and I'm working two jobs trying to pay our bills. My house is dark and smelly and depressing. It's always been me and her, and now she's falling apart and I can't save her.'

'And you think your dad can?' Gill asks, confused.

'No,' he whispers quietly. 'But maybe he can save me.'

Matty

Matty Fullerton is listening to 'Steal my Sunshine' by Len on Spotify.

Mo Sharif Unusual song choice. Look forward to our run tomorrow.

'What's up, bro?' Mo asks, slowing down. 'You can't keep up with me any more.'

'Thought you loved beating me,' I say, panting and digging my hand into my side to try to relieve my stitch.

He jogs back to me and puts his hand on my back.

'Sit down,' he says. 'We might as well stop.'

'Sorry,' I mumble. 'I feel bad.'

'It's OK, I'll make up for it on the job site.'

We sit down on the footpath, warm sweat drying on our bodies.

'Go,' I tell him. 'Before your mum finds out you're out in the cold and starts screeching that you'll get slapped by the wind.'

'Best Arab saying ever,' he says, grinning.

I pull out my phone and try to capture the sun's morning colours rising into yesterday's darkness.

'It's so nice, isn't it,' he says. 'I love running before the world wakes up. I was surprised when you called me.'

'It has been a while,' I say. 'I've missed it.'

'School does that to you, bro,' he says. 'My sister's up all hours learning stuff for the HSC. *Alhumdulillah*, I got out.'

'It's not just school,' I tell him, honestly. 'My mum's sick.'

He looks at me, puzzled.

'Real sick, not the flu,' I explain. 'Depression or something. She does nothing all day. Barely even eats. It's been months.'

His eyes widen in surprise. 'Months? And you never told me? I could've brought you food. You know how much my mum cooks.'

'I thought it would go away,' I admit. 'But she won't even see a doctor.'

'You should have said something before,' he says, shaking his head. 'I'm your mate.'

'Yeah, I know, man, and I appreciate it. But you know me ...'

'The silent type, I know,' he says, giving me an amused look. 'What are you gonna do?'

I shrug. 'Dunno.'

We sit in silence for a few minutes longer.

'Do you remember in year 7 when you asked me why I didn't know who my dad was?' I ask.

'Nah, man, you know what my memory's like.'

'I told you I didn't really care who he is.'

He nods, waiting for the rest of the story.

'I think I want to find him now.'

He lets out a long, low whistle.

'I don't get you Aussies,' he says after a moment. 'It's like you guys spend your days searching for lost fathers and we just want ours to get lost.'

'At least they care about you,' I point out.

'It's care you'd want to run away from,' he says. 'They're always interfering.'

'We're never happy.'

'No, we're not.'

I think about this conversation in the shower as I'm getting ready for school. What if I was right about people never being happy? Would I regret reaching out to him? What happens if I learn something I don't want to know? I could never unlearn it — and then I would be miserable. Maybe there's a reason she never mentioned him.

I'm getting dressed when I hear the phone ring.

'Mum, can you get that?' I call out. But she doesn't move, and I bump my toe on the couch trying to scramble for it.

'Ouch,' I say out loud before putting the handset to my ear. 'Hello?'

'Matty? It's Cherry Nguyen.'

'Hey, Cherry,' I say, thinking how unnecessary the introduction was, I'd know her accent anywhere. 'No change yet, I'm sorry I forgot to call you.'

'Sorry, Matty,' she says, sighing. 'That's what I am calling about. I can't hold her position any more. Upstairs is hounding me.'

I feel bad for lying to her initially, telling her Mum was just taking a break. Maybe if I'd been more honest, she would have cut me some more slack.

'Please? Just one more month, she might get better …'

'If she doesn't see a professional, she won't change, love.'

'Please, I will speak to upstairs,' I beg.

'I'm sorry, it's terrible, but out of my control. If things get better, I will see what I can do, but we need to replace her formally.'

She hangs up. I can feel the anger rising like bile in the back of my throat. I hurl the phone at the wall, grab my school bag and leave, slamming the door behind me. My mother doesn't stir.

———

The day gets worse. Mr Broderick calls me to his office to question my lack of parental representation at the parent–teacher night.

'You've always had at least one guardian there, Mr Fullerton,' he says. 'But no one last night. I know there's a sense of finality to this year, but I must point out that you have not yet reached the end of the road.'

'My mum was out of town,' I lie. 'We don't have any other family in town.'

He leans back in his chair for a minute, and the way he looks at me makes me feel uneasy.

'It's funny you say that,' he says, rising from his seat. 'Because I called your mother this morning and she believes she never actually got a letter.'

I sigh. Now she's failing me at school, and she doesn't even know it.

'It's a little more complicated than that, sir.'

He scoffs, then sits on the edge of his desk and looks at me with utter disdain.

'I'd ask you to enlighten me, but I'm just not a fan of your attitude. So spare me the fake sincerity and go.'

I exhale and turn to leave.

'And I'll see you for after-school detention every day for the rest of the week,' he says.

I don't turn around. I know that if I do, I'll smash his face in.

———

'You got an after-school for that?' Charlie says, outraged, as she, Gillian and I are walking to class after recess. 'Far out. In public school, stabbing the principal would get you a lunch detention.'

Gill's eyes widen in surprise.

'I'm *joking*,' Charlie says, grabbing her arm. 'Honestly, Gill.'

'You have to tell him what's going on at home, Matty,' Gill says. 'Just be honest.'

'No way,' I say, shaking my head. 'Not him.'

'Mrs H then,' she says, as if it's as simple that. 'I'll go with you.'

'I'll see,' I say.

'We know what "I'll see" means,' Gill says, looking at me.

'Those parent–teacher nights are a waste of time anyway,' I say. 'What do they even talk about?'

'My dad told me they spoke about how our families can support us in our tough times of study,' Gill says, making a face.

'Some good that would do me,' I say. 'She can't even support me during the normal times.'

The girls exchange glances and I stop, just metres from our classroom.

'You know what?' I say, looking at them. 'I can't stay here. I have to go.'

I turn around and run down the stairs before they can stop me.

———

Two and a half hours later, they find me lying in the grass at Burwood Park.

'Have you been here the whole time?' Gillian asks, rubbing her hands up and down her arms.

'It's not so bad in the sun,' I say, sitting up and pulling my headphones off my ears. I don't tell her I'm freezing and my arse is wet, and that the damp in my hoodie feels like it's seeping into my bones.

Charlie folds her arms. 'You can't keep escaping into your music,' she tells me.

'You can't control everything,' I retaliate.

'I'm good at it,' she says.

Gillian smiles. I try to ignore them.

'You'll never get the medal if you keep wagging to chase after us, you know,' I tell Charlie after a minute of silence.

'What's the use of a free university education if I have no friends in whose faces I can rub it?' she asks, smirking.

I shake my head. She always knows what to say to break the tension.

'How did it start?' Gillian asks. 'Your mum's depression?'

'I don't know. We were fine. And then eight months ago she came to visit me at work, met Sammy and Elliot, told me she was going to go to the supermarket, and the next thing I know I get a call saying she'd fainted and I should go pick her up. One week later she was a whole other person.'

'Matty,' Charlie says, hesitantly, 'I know you're going through a tough time, and maybe in your head your dad can help … but how do you know he's not part of the problem?'

My head snaps up. 'I don't get it,' I say. 'She's never mentioned him, or seen him. How could he be the problem?'

'Her mum's a psych,' Gill says, piping up. 'She knows her stuff.' Charlie and I both narrow our eyes at her. 'Sorry,' she says, hands in front of her body.

'Some depressions — if it *is* depression, that is — are not just clinical,' Charlie explains. 'They could also be situational. She might have associated her relationship with your father, or some other thing, with a trigger, and that's what brought it on.'

'So Coles made my mum sick?' I ask.

'Don't do that,' she says. 'Don't mock me. It doesn't always make sense.'

I let out a grunt, and she looks frustrated. But she doesn't say anything more. We sit in silence for a few minutes.

'Can I ask you an ugly question?' she says, looking at me. 'Why now, all of a sudden? Are you only looking for him because your mum's out of it?'

'No,' I respond firmly. 'I don't think so anyway. It's just to learn some stuff ...'

'Stuff?' she asks.

I take a deep breath. 'You know how at school they're giving us all these talks about our future and where we're going and how to get there?'

They nod.

'Well,' I continue, 'how do I know where I'm going if I don't know where I'm from?'

Charlie and Gill look at each other, silenced.

'You should tell Mrs H,' Charlie says after a moment. 'She'll understand.'

I shake my head again. 'No, this is my problem.'

Gillian bites her lip. 'What if *I* talk to her?'

'No,' I say.

'You can't keep going to detentions and working overtime. What about your grades? What about uni?'

'I'll figure it out,' I tell her. She exhales, puts her head in her hands, looks around the park. That's one good thing about her — she doesn't argue. Though maybe if she argued more, her mum wouldn't be so awful to her — but who am I to talk?

'I want to work in music anyway,' I say after a moment. 'I don't need a degree for that.'

'But you're so smart,' she says. 'It'd be a waste.'

'I'm not at your school just because I'm smart,' I tell her. 'I worked my butt off to get in there because it was this goal my mum had set for me. It's all for her.'

'It's your school too, Matty,' she says, but I can't believe her. There's just too much of a gap between us.

'She grew up around here, you know, went to Burwood Girls,' I say. 'Her family wasn't well-off, and she told me that sometimes, when she was feeling down, she would come and sit on the grass across the road and watch the place. And daydream.'

'I get that,' Gillian says. 'It's pretty. It has history. And a reputation.'

'Exactly,' I say. 'She put it on a bloody pedestal. This school was her "out" from her ordinary life — she associated a successful, put-together, perfect life with it, and dreamed of sending her kids here so that they could escape whatever it was that she needed to escape from. Except when I finally came to this school, life didn't come together for me. It fell apart.'

Gillian looks at me sadly.

'Let's just change the subject,' Charlie says, looking at her.

We talk about homework and exams and yearbook stuff for a bit, and then they go home. But I stay until it's dark.

I thought that telling Mo, Charlie and Gillian would fix it, lighten the load on my mind. But I don't feel any better.

Across the way, I see Mike standing by a tree, chatting on his phone. Then he pulls out another one from his pocket, punches something in, and walks away. He doesn't seem to notice me.

'So suss,' I whisper to myself, gathering up my stuff to leave.

At home, I toss my clothes in the washing machine and get changed. I make Mum a cup of tea and bring it to her. She's in her usual spot on the couch in the darkened living room.

'You need some help,' I tell her, dusting biscuit crumbs off her robe. Her lips are dry; it's obvious she's dehydrated. 'We need a doctor.'

'I'll be fine,' she says. 'I just need more time.'

'I don't have any more time to give you,' I say, smoothing her hair. 'We're struggling.'

She's quiet.

'Mum, how come we never talk about my dad?'

'Because you don't have one,' she says.

'Everyone has one,' I tell her.

'DNA does not a father make.'

I shake my head. 'Maybe you have a reason for shutting him out,' I tell her. 'But if he's bad, I need to find out for myself.'

She ignores me.

'He's not a solution,' she says a minute later. 'Don't count on him.'

'I have no one else to count on,' I point out. 'My HSC is coming up — what am I going to do when they cut the power, or the phone line? What happens when I can't go to work because of exams? Who's going to buy food?'

'Things might be different by then.'

'Yes — if we do something about them now.'

'I told you, he's not a solution,' she says, turning away.

I exhale in frustration. 'Come on, Mum,' I plead. 'Tell me something about him — anything.'

Silence.

'Fine, I'll find him by myself, whether you like it or not.'

'He'll break your heart.'

'It's broken anyway,' I tell her honestly. 'So what does it matter?'

She scoffs. 'You think it doesn't, but it does. Sometimes you think other people can fix your brokenness, but usually they break you more.'

I sigh. 'You can't just tell me he's bad and leave me to deal with it.'

'I never said he was bad,' she says, closing her eyes. 'He was just a boy in a private-school uniform who lived a life so different to my own.'

I swallow. 'A Holy Family uniform?'

'Yes. Shiny and perfect and full of promise. I was the girl in the tattered clothes, sitting on a fence across the school, dreaming about my future.'

'And now your son is dreaming,' I say. 'Go figure.'

She shrugs and leans back into the cushions, holding her cup of tea close.

'What if I don't want to dream any more?' I ask. 'What if I just want a concrete answer?'

'Our love crossed a big divide,' she says quietly. 'And when it finished it was like our worlds had never collided. There's nothing left, Matty. Nothing.'

I sigh. 'So I definitely can't find him?'

'Or him you,' she says, staring off into the darkness. 'I made sure of that.'

I scoff. There's a coldness to her I have never seen before.

I walk out of the room without kissing her goodnight and slam my door, feeling like I'm at a worse dead end than before.

That night, I can't sleep. I have so many questions. How did it get like this? How did one supermarket visit turn everything to shit? I rack my brain for answers. But I have none. Just more questions. What is his name? Do I look like him? How long were they married for? Did he leave because of me? Are there any hereditary diseases I should know about? But mostly, does he ever think about me?

I reach out under my bed for the box, but as I do, I wonder what the point of it is. How would I even get it to him? Yet another question.

No answers, no opportunities, no future. I have no link whatsoever to this man who might be the only family I have left.

Tammi

Tammi Kap This sucks.

There are two awful things about being the only sober person at a party:

1. Hearing everyone's conversations at loud volume because they're so drunk they can't hear themselves, and
2. Wishing that you were also drunk just so you don't feel left out.

It's exactly how I feel tonight, as I'm sitting alone on the couch while David goes to get himself a drink. So far his drink-getting has taken thirty-six minutes, and already a girl from year 11 has thrown up at my feet and a guy from another school with really bad hair has asked me to dance. Twice.

It's a bigger party than usual. The soccer team has just finished its season and come away with a state trophy, which means they can finally set their sights on the interstate school comp for the first time ever. Not to mention one of the team-mates is turning eighteen. Needless to say, the party's pretty wild.

Lauren texts me from her grandma's seventy-fifth birthday party: *Anything happened yet?*

I ignore her, knowing the suspense will kill her. The soccer parties at Holy Family are the craziest ones, because boys from other teams often show up. Those who are in relationships bring their girlfriends, and those who aren't bring their charms. Lauren loves them — so she's probably cursing her grandma while everyone else is wishing the best for her.

My phone beeps again and I ignore it, looking down at my watch instead. 9.45. By most standards, it's still an early night, but I've already been here a lot longer than I wanted to be.

I must look extremely miserable, because Ryan detaches himself from a group of people he's dancing with and comes my way, stopping to get a can of Sprite from the tub by the door. He hands it to me and sits down.

'If you looked any happier, the world would explode,' he says as I move over to make room for him.

'And yet David still can't read the signals,' I say.

'Want me to go get him?'

'Don't be silly. He'll just resent me for wanting to leave early.'

'Then why'd you come?'

'I still don't know.'

He starts to laugh, but stops suddenly when Charlie walks through the door. She spots us on the couch and comes over.

'Hey,' she says, nodding to us both. 'Have you guys seen Matty and Gill?'

'Nope, sorry,' I tell her.

'I'm surprised you're here,' Ryan says to her. 'I didn't think this would be your scene.'

'Pffft, don't be ridiculous, Fleming,' she replies. 'I just came for the cake.'

As I laugh, she catches my eye, looking pleased.

I watch Ryan watching Charlie as she wanders outside. I just want to tell him to make his move, but it's none of my business and I can't be bothered getting into a D and M with him — the last one was awkward enough. We sit in an uncomfortable silence until someone calls Ryan over, and he heads outside too.

Still my boyfriend is nowhere to be found. I scratch at a scab on my shoulder and wonder what the hell I'm doing here.

Some time later, Matty and Gill arrive. They take a seat on either side of me.

'How's your night going, Tammi?' Matty asks.

'Let's just say I've been here a lot longer than I planned to be.'

'How long did you plan to be here?' he asks earnestly.

'Zero minutes,' I admit. He laughs and I feel glad that I've at least entertained someone tonight.

'Have you seen Charlie?' Gillian asks me. 'She told me she'd meet us here.'

'I think she's outside with Ryan,' I tell her.

She and Matty look at each other and smile, and I love the fact that their smiles don't hide their thoughts at all.

'Do you girls want a drink?' Matty asks, standing up.

I'm still drinking my Sprite so I decline, but Gillian requests a Coke with a dash of rum.

'How come you're sitting all alone?' she asks. 'Are you OK?'

I go quiet for a moment. If Lauren was here, she'd question

why I was even talking to Gillian. But tonight, for some reason, I don't care.

'David went to go and get a drink,' I tell her. 'He's been gone for about forty-five minutes now, and I'm wondering how long I'll have to keep being his doormat.'

She looks sadly at me. 'Don't be like that,' she says, putting her hand on my arm. 'He likes you a lot; it's so obvious.'

'No,' I admit. 'If he liked me he wouldn't leave me alone here. If he liked me he wouldn't ask for a "conditions apply" version of me, a version that suits him.'

'He's more stupid than I thought, then,' she says simply.

'And I guess that makes me stupid for going out with him,' I say testily.

'N-n-no,' she stutters. 'Sometimes we just deal with stuff that doesn't make us happy because we don't know any different, or because we don't want to make a crap situation worse.'

We sit in silence for a minute.

'I'm sorry about Lauren,' I say quietly. 'I get the backhanded compliments too.'

She shrugs and looks away.

'She's not so bad,' I tell her, wanting to believe it. 'She used to be really nice. She's always been there for me, more than anyone else.'

'Yeah, but conditions apply with her too, don't they?'

This time, I'm the one who shrugs.

'Conditions apply with everyone. I can never do what *I* want,' I reveal. 'That's how the world works.'

'I feel the same way,' she says. 'But I'm trying to do something about it.'

She gets up and leaves and suddenly I feel alone again. I look around, wondering again why I'm here. No one approaches me.

If Lauren were here, it would be different. Guys would be all over us — flirting, laughing, complimenting us. Well, her. And I'd just watch, knowing that everything that came out of her mouth was either a lie, or something that would come back to bite them. But, to them, five minutes in her glow would be worth it. Was it still worth it for me?

The DJ calls out that he has a special request and I roll my eyes when Katy Perry's 'Unconditionally' starts blaring through the party. *Relationships in high school are all show*, I want to call out. But I don't, and a second later, Gillian and Matty are standing in front of me.

'Come on!' Gillian says, putting out her hand. 'One day you'll find a guy who's going to love you unconditionally, so stop wasting yourself on that douche.'

I take her hand.

We dance hysterically and crazily, in a way that I would never dance if Lauren or David were around. And it's so invigorating that I feel high enough to laugh and hug them when the song finishes, and then liberated enough to just admit that it's time to go home. If David doesn't give a damn about me, then why should I wait around for him?

'Want a lift?' Matty asks, nudging me out of my thoughts. 'I have my mum's car. I'm taking Gill too, so I can drop you off first.'

I nod and grab my bag from underneath a cushion on the couch, and the three of us make our way to the front door.

Outside, a bunch of guys are smoking weed and I'm not surprised to find David among them.

'Hey, hey, hey,' he calls out to me. 'Just where do you think you're going?'

'Home,' I say bluntly. 'Where else?'

'But the party's just getting started,' he tells me. 'I was going to take you home.'

'Yeah, right,' I tell him. 'You said you weren't gonna drink tonight. Why would I go home with you if you've been drinking?'

'Yeah, bro, did you forget what her dad does?' one of David's mates chimes in.

'Shut up, Sanders. Come on, stay a little longer,' he says, turning back to me, and tugging at the waistband of my pants. 'I'll be inside in a few minutes. I'll even dance with you.'

'Your "few minutes" is an hour at least,' I tell him, moving his hand away. 'I know this because I've spent half my night sitting on the couch alone.'

'That's your fault,' he hisses. 'No one told you to be such a deadbeat. If you let loose a little, you'd have a little fun.'

'If letting loose gives me a licence to treat everyone around me like shit, I'd rather remain uptight, thanks.'

'What's your problem?' he says. 'Why are you so moody?'

'I'm not,' I say, sighing. 'I just want to go home.'

'And you're not going to let me drive you?'

'David!' I snap. 'I know I let you get away with a lot. But it's definitely not OK for you to think I'm so worthless that I don't have a right to be driven home by someone who is at least sober.'

'Huh?'

'You don't see my worth,' I tell him. 'I'm nothing to you.'

'That's not true,' he protests. 'I take care of you.'

I shake my head. 'I take better care of myself,' I say quietly. He looks at me intently, then notices Matty and Gillian in the distance.

'*They're* your lift home?' he scoffs. 'Listen, I don't want you to be a loser by association so how about you stay a little longer, and I'll get my mother to pick us up.'

'No,' I say, hitching my bag over my shoulder.

He grabs my hand, and Matty is over in an instant. Suddenly the hoodie makes him look sinister.

'Is everything OK?' he asks. 'Ready to leave, Tammi?'

'Oh right, you guys know each other from the yearbook!' David says. 'I was wondering when my girl started associating with losers. Especially Scummy Cummings over there.'

'Watch. Your. Mouth.' Matty says, gritting his teeth. But David is never one to shy away from a fight and comes up a little closer to him.

'Or what?' he asks.

'You know what? I'd rather beat you when you're sober. This is just too easy.'

Gillian and I look at each other, surprised. I've never seen this side of Matty.

David looks him up and down and sniffs, but, to his credit, Matty just smirks and walks away, Gillian and me trailing behind him.

'Go ahead, take her off my hands,' he calls out after us. 'She doesn't put out anyway.'

Matty's eyes widen at Gillian, who turns and gives David the bird with both hands. *Don't turn around*, I tell myself, *no matter how good you used to have it, how much you used to like him, how sweet he used to be.* I keep walking towards Matty's car, tears welling up in my eyes.

On either side of me, Gillian and Matty reach out and grab a hand each, like guardian angels. And the tears give way to a smile, because I finally feel my worth for the first time in ages.

THE YEARBOOK COMMITTEE
Minutes for July Meeting

Recorded by: Gillian Cummings
Meeting Chair: Ryan Fleming
In attendance: Everyone

The Playlist: Two songs today! We wanted to get our minds off our upcoming trials and also remind ourselves that we're halfway through the biggest school year, so we asked Matty for something upbeat. Matty chose 'Sing' by Ed Sheeran and 'Happy' by Pharrell Williams. And instead of spending a few minutes discussing subliminal messages, we danced in our seats. And it was FUN. Tammi shook her head and said that Lauren would kick her arse if she knew what she was doing. And Charlie said that we would all help Tammi kick Lauren's arse right back. It was the first time we had a team moment, and it was nice.

The Snacks: Doughnuts! Tammi brought them. Charlie didn't bake anything this time, but she did bring these two amazing cheeses. Ryan brought crackers and dried apricots and grapes, as per Charlie's request, and she made this really nice platter on two sheets of A3 paper that she got out of the photocopier drawer. And she wonders why the librarian can't stand her. I brought two packets of chips with me, and I gave one entire one to Matty and we shared the other bag. And Matty brought a bag of fun-size Mars Bars, and Charlie ate three, then made him hide them. He did not argue.

Agenda:
* Progress report by Matty. He reckons he's doing OK inserting everything in, and that it looks really good. Go us!
* Decide on how we are going to lay out the profiles — will each student get an individual page? Charlie says no. Ryan agrees. Tammi says less work for us if we keep them short and have a few on a page.

Questions for Mrs H:
* Does Mrs H want to pen a letter or note to put in the yearbook?
* Is school photo day anytime soon? We haven't received any letters/notices, and we want to make sure we have enough time to use the photos for profile pages.

Action points for next meeting:
* Everyone to brainstorm ideas of other things to include.

Gillian

Gillian Cummings is more than a little sick of numbers and percentages. And not just because of my upcoming Maths test.

Tonight, we're actually eating dinner in the dining room. There are no mobile phones in sight, Dad is participating in the conversation and the TV has been off since he came home. In our family, this could only mean one thing: he's doing well in the polls.

I don't monitor the polls like I used to — Dad pays more attention to them than he does to me. And I don't like feeling inferior to percentages. Fathers are supposed to get angry over missed curfews, seedy boys and skirts that are too short; my dad loses his cool over news reports.

But tonight, things are different. Dad is relaxed, Mum is not being her usual 'darling' self — it's like we're a normal family.

'So, Gillian, did the UAC book arrive?' Dad asks. 'Have you had a look through it?'

I nod. 'Yeah, but I still don't know …'

He shakes his head. 'I knew from a very young age —'

'— that you wanted to be the premier of New South Wales,' I finish. 'I know. I just need more time.'

'You don't have that much longer,' he points out.

I sigh. 'I'll figure it out. There's a careers day at Sydney Uni on Saturday. I might ask my friend Matty if he wants to come.'

I wait for him to ask about Matty, but he doesn't. Neither does my mum, because she already established he's 'just a friend'.

'That sounds like a fun idea,' Mum says, taking a sip of wine. 'As long as it's not on a Wednesday.'

'Nope, it'll be on a weekend.'

'I want to own a juice bar,' Sammy says wistfully. 'Maybe Matty could work at mine.'

I smile at him affectionately and Dad nods in approval.

'A business man,' he says. 'A fine choice for a fine sir.'

Sammy giggles excitedly, then starts making pictures with his peas, while my mum makes worried faces.

'Told you the chairs would be a mistake,' Dad tells her. 'Who gets white dining chairs?'

'It's the latest style!' she says, as if he should know better.

'I'm supposed to represent the average Joe,' he tells her for what seems like the hundredth time, as if he really believes it. 'I don't need the latest style.'

'You don't need a fancy car either, but it's OK to have one of those,' she says.

I look from her to him in amusement — I've heard the same banter over and over again. I decide to change the subject.

'I was thinking Teaching,' I say, plucking a career out of my head just to make conversation. 'Or Childcare?'

'Do you want to come home smelling like baby poo and

vomit?' Mum asks, looking at me like I'm an idiot. 'Gosh, I could barely hack it with you lot.'

'She got a nanny,' Dad says, looking at her with bemusement. 'Even though she didn't have a job.'

'Now you look here, Peter Cummings,' she says, pointing a fork at him. 'Everything you achieved was with me by your side. Being an attractive wife is a full-time job. All those blowdries and charity events; having to make small talk with boring politicians at those stupid functions you drag me to …'

'I could do Law!' I pipe up, wondering how I got them here.

'Oh, don't be ridiculous, Gillian, you have no backbone,' Mum says, sculling her glass of wine. 'Hmm, I'd say we're done here.'

'Well, I guess I just put her in a mood,' Dad says, as she gets up to collect the plates.

He pulls out his phone and goes to his office to spend time with percentages instead.

When I grow up, I think, *I just want to be at peace.*

————

On Saturday, Matty and I go to the careers day at Sydney University as planned, and we meet at Burwood Station in the morning and catch the train to Redfern. We're quiet as we make our way to the university through the suburban streets, absorbed in our surroundings. The buildings around here are old — older than the ones in Croydon — and they have plenty of character.

'I could be an Aboriginal and I wouldn't even know it,' he says.

'I guess the dad issue is still on your mind, then,' I say.

'As if it wouldn't be,' he says. 'You don't get it — your family is right there, you know them.'

'Yeah, though sometimes I wish I didn't,' I say.

'Things will get better after the election,' he says. 'I'm sure of it.'

I just shrug — I'm not so sure. My mum would still be selfish, and my father would still just be wrapped up in something else, something other than his kids.

'Could you maybe do a little digging?' I ask, changing the subject. 'Look for old letters, legal papers?'

'I've never gone through her stuff behind her back,' he says, looking conflicted. 'It would feel weird.'

'Well, it's either that, or go on without knowing.'

'That's true,' he says, exhaling. 'What a screwed-up position to be in.'

We spend the next hour walking among stalls, checking out the facilities and peeking inside study halls.

'There are so many clubs,' he says, peering at all the signs. 'Charlie would love some of these.'

'Too bad she's still set on Monash,' I say shrugging. 'Though I'm sure they have feminist clubs there too.'

'Probably,' he says. 'Hey … did you know that the school soccer team is in Melbourne this weekend?'

I whip around, fast. '*What?!*'

He nods conspiratorially. 'Ryan and Charlie could run into each other,' he says.

'No way,' I say. 'She's probably hanging out with Pete and her other Melbourne friends. She wouldn't be near a soccer field … It's a big city.'

He shrugs, but doesn't say anything. We just look at each other for a moment.

'Just quietly, though,' he says, leaning over, 'don't tell her I knew.'

'As if,' I say. 'She wouldn't have changed her plans anyway.' I walk off, signalling for him to follow me.

I see him mulling over my words, then he comes after me, as if he understands.

Later, we sit in the sun in the quadrangle, eating hot chips with gravy and drinking cans of Coke.

'Thanks so much for coming with me today,' I say to him. 'I know you only came because I was scared to come alone. Though I'm glad you at least took a pamphlet.'

'Hey, it's no big deal,' he says, swallowing a mouthful of chips. 'If it helps you decide, it's worth it.'

'I think I like the idea of some of the Media courses,' I tell him, flicking through brochures I've collected. 'It would be good for my blog. That chick I told you about — the one who sends me outfits — she said she's willing to pay if I make sure I'm pictured wearing her clothes next to my dad in the papers.'

His eyes widen in amusement. 'Are you gonna do it?'

'I don't know,' I say, wrinkling my nose. 'What if there's a contract? You know, one that says photos must appear or whatever. And then no photos show up in the newspapers ... I suppose I could put them on Insta and Snapchat but what if it's not enough? I need, like, a manager ...'

'Study Business — then you can do it all yourself.'

I shrug. 'Maybe,' I say. 'I really don't know.' I eat a forkful of chips, knowing I'll regret it later.

'This place is massive,' he says between mouthfuls. 'You're never going to be able to find your classes.'

I shove him. 'My sense of direction is not *that* bad,' I say. He giggles and takes another chip.

'It's really nice here, though,' he says. 'It suits you.'

I smile in agreement, taking a sip of my Coke. 'I think so too,' I say. 'But … Lauren wants to come here.'

'And?' he asks, looking me in the eye. 'What difference does that make?'

'I want school to be the end of my interactions with her,' I say.

'So let it be,' he says simply. 'Reinvent yourself. Pretend you don't know her.'

'Do you think she'll be popular at uni too?' I ask.

He shakes his head. 'I don't think uni works that way,' he says. 'Plus, that depends on whether or not she gets in. Doesn't she need an ATAR of, like, 96 or something?'

'Yeah, it was 95.5 last year,' I say. 'But she's probably just going to pay her way in anyway.'

'Money talks,' he says, closing the empty chip carton and standing up. He extends his hand to me. 'Shall we do some more exploring?'

We decide to explore the quadrangle then sneak in to one of the upstairs areas, where the offices are quiet and rows of pictures line the walls.

'This campus has so much history,' he says, looking around. 'We should have done the tour.'

'It would have taken us eight minutes to get lost,' I point out.

He nods, then stops to lean against a window and look out below.

'Awesome view,' he says. 'If you decide to come here, I'll definitely come visit.'

I smile. 'I have no idea what I want to do, though.'

'You're loving the yearbook,' he says. 'Why not publishing? Or something in the care industry — you're good with Sammy, and you're kind of like the affectionate one on the yearbook committee.'

I laugh. 'Yeah, compared to Charlie and Tammi,' I say. 'That doesn't mean anything — everyone is more affectionate than those two. Although Charlie's control does border on care ...'

'Who are you kidding?' he asks, turning back to the window.

'Woah,' I say, spotting an old picture on the wall. 'I found your '80s doppelganger!'

He comes up behind me. 'Where?' he says, his breath on my neck.

'Here, look,' I say, pointing. '"The USYD Business School's Entrepreneurs Club 1986."'

'Sounds nerdy,' he says. He peers more closely at the picture, then stands up and scrunches his face at me.

'Don't you think he looks exactly like you?' I ask.

He stoops down again. 'I don't see it,' he says finally. 'Come on, let's go.'

We're making our way downstairs when he feels his pockets and declares he's lost his phone. 'It probably fell out of my pocket upstairs,' he says. 'Wait here; I'll run up.'

I don't buy it. I give him a head start, then quietly sneak up behind him. I hover at the entryway to the hallway and peek around the corner.

Matty is standing in front of the picture again, staring at it. After a few seconds, he pulls out his phone and snaps a picture. I jerk myself away and try to make my way down the stairs quickly and quietly.

'Find it?' I ask, when he comes back outside a few minutes later.

He holds up his phone.

'Cool,' I say. 'Home time?'

We don't talk much on the train ride. He listens to his music, and I play on my phone. Well, I pretend to.

I want to know if he too feels that picture could mean something, and that's why he's not talking to me.

We say goodbye at the station. As soon as I know I'm out of his sight, I punch in the name that I memorised, wondering if I have spelt it correctly.

Stanislav Reyznoliksi

Just another name from the past? Or a firm clue to the future?

RYAN

Ryan Fleming is stoked to have kicked another a goal. Well, not literally, but it still counts.

David DeLooka PAAARRRRTYYYY.

James Czalo ^ This one is here for all the wrong reasons.

Patrick Anzilierio What did you expect Jimbo? Esp after that plane ride #neveragain #butwestillneedtoflyhome #allthelols

'That'll be three-fifty, thank you,' the girl at the kiosk says to David.

'Three-fifty for water?' he asks incredulously. 'Jeez, that's steep.'

I sigh and make an awkward, apologetic face at her as he counts the silver in his hand.

'Not your fault, obviously, but what a rip,' he says, as he hands over his money.

She just gives him a polite half-smile.

We head off, but after about five metres, he stops again.

'Dude, come on, you can drink it on the bus. I can barely see the team any more.'

'Relax, *dude*, it's Melbourne, not Malaysia,' he says nonchalantly. 'We'll find them.'

I sigh again, keeping my eye on the trail of school jerseys off in the distance.

'That chick was cute,' he says after we start walking again. 'Think I should go back and get her number?'

'After you told her off? Really?'

He shrugs. 'It's not *her* shop.'

'You don't know that,' I point out. 'Anyway, that doesn't change the fact that you made a pretty bad first impression.'

'Blah,' he says. 'I just got here. There's probably hotter chicks around.'

Even though I know David's always been all talk, I think of Tammi. How did she put up with him for so long?

We catch up with the rest of the team and board the shuttle that will take us into the city.

'Ok, boys, listen up, because I'm only going to say this once,' Coach says, in his signature loud voice. 'This is the first year that we've qualified for the Australian Interstate Interschool Soccer Cup, and I'd like it if weren't our last. We played hard, and we deserve it. Special mention to Fleming — a real sport doesn't abandon his team even if he can't play and I know he'll be an invaluable asset as we plan our plays. Please take some time this weekend to thank him for his off-field support.' He pauses for the collective cheers and pats on my back, then continues. 'That's it from me. If you need anything, come find me or Mr Sheppard. And don't make me regret bringing you.'

He sits back down and we all get talking again. Before we know it, we've arrived at the hotel.

'Stop taking up the entire footpath,' Coach bellows as we hover around the bus, trying to collect our bags.

'Hey, isn't that that chick from school with the pole up her ass?' David says to me, gesturing across the street. I look where he's pointing and see Charlie.

'Yeah,' I say, waving. She waves back and makes her way over.

'Aww, man, why'd you do that? Now we have to talk to her,' he grumbles.

'*You* don't have to do anything,' I point out.

She crosses the street and smiles. 'I was hoping I could walk by without you seeing me,' she says honestly.

'Hello to you too,' I tell her. 'What are you doing here?'

She shrugs. 'My mum and I made a deal that I could come down during school holidays.'

'Your mum is so cool,' I say stupidly, cursing myself for not thinking of anything better.

'What a great conversation,' David says, sarcastically. 'Such a shame I need to go and unpack.'

'He's such a dickhead,' she says, scowling after him.

'Yeah, well, he's not so crazy about you either.'

'I didn't know you guys were coming this weekend.'

'Yeah, sorry I didn't mention it, I didn't think you'd care.'

She shrugs. 'Meh. It wouldn't have made a difference,' she says. 'I was coming anyway. And who would've thought we'd run into each other?'

I look away, unsure of what to say.

'So this is where you're staying?' she asks.

'Yeah. You?'

'Just around the corner. Oaks on Collins.'

'On your own? I figured you'd stay with friends or family.'

'I don't have much family, and my friends love an excuse to come to the city. Plus I prefer being on my own.'

'Is it safe, though?'

She looks amused. 'Same as everywhere else really. I'm going to be moving here in a few months; I better get used to it.'

'So you're not even giving Sydney a chance?' I ask.

'It's just not my cup of tea.'

'Well, Melbourne's not mine, then.'

'Gee, I hope I'm never on your debating team.'

'The feeling's mutual,' I tell her. 'Actually, it's not. I'd never want to be on an opposing team to yours.'

'Wise choice,' she says, looking at her phone. She slips it back into her pocket and gives me a sincere smile.

'You should check out the city if you have free time,' she says. 'It's pretty awesome.'

'I have a ton of stuff to do — team bonding, helping Coach out with plays, stuff like that,' I say. 'Speaking of team bonding, want to work on the yearbook since we're both down here? We're a little behind … Monthly meetings were a big mistake.'

She rolls her eyes, pulling a Sharpie out of her bag. 'Forget the work and go exploring. It will be worth your while. Buzz if you need some tips.'

I look at the scribbled digits on my forearm, as Charlie walks away.

'Fine, don't say bye,' I call out after her.

'Well, I didn't say hi either,' she calls back without turning around.

She has a point, I think, heading through the doors of the hotel.

Inside, the rooms are decent and spacious, with a basic kitchenette and a sizable bathroom. David has already spilled the contents of his bag on the floor. He emerges from the bathroom in a robe.

I laugh. 'You look like a douche.'

'Best part of a hotel stay,' he says. 'Feel it, it's like magic.'

'I'm not feeling the robe.'

'There's another one. You should wear it,' he whispers. 'We can be robe buddies.'

'Yeah, because that doesn't sound seedy.'

He laughs and hurls himself at the bed by the window, his robe flying up.

'Aww, man, wear something underneath it at least,' I say, grimacing.

'So when are you gonna bone that chick and get it over with?' he says.

I whip around. 'Don't ever say that in front of her,' I warn him. 'She'll go on a never-ending feminist rant.'

He shakes his head. 'Chicks like that just need a good, hard —'

Thankfully, a knock at the door interrupts him.

'Boys, meeting in the lobby in ten minutes. Don't be late,' Coach says.

'Looks like you're gonna have to get dressed again,' I say to David.

'How much slack will I get from Coach if I go down like this?' he asks mischievously. 'It'll be funny, yeah?'

'Yeah — and it'll be even more hilarious when he bans you from playing the first game,' I point out. 'Don't be an idiot; the team needs you.'

'Yeah, especially because you're so wussy about your leg and won't get on with it.'

I turn away so he doesn't see the murderous look on my face. 'I've told you, man,' I say. 'Doctor's orders.'

'Then why come down?' he calls out from the bathroom, where he's putting on his pants.

'Because I haven't stopped being part of the team,' I tell him. 'And I don't need to remind you why it is I can't play.'

'Here we go again,' he mumbles as we walk out the door. 'How many times do I need to say sorry?'

However many times it takes to mean it, I think, following him down the hall.

He walks nonchalantly before me into the lift. I take a deep breath and count to three, just like Nanna had told me to, as I press the button for the ground floor.

Next to me, David snaps a selfie in the mirror, oblivious to the chaos he leaves in his wake.

The bitterness builds up inside me, and I clench and release my fists, trying not to let it get to me.

'One day, it could spill over,' Nanna warned me once. 'And David shouldn't be around when it does.'

———

'Dude, wake up, you've been asleep for hours.'

I wake up to find David standing above me, dressed in a collared shirt with sleeves rolled up to his elbows, and chinos.

'Have you really taken off that robe, or am I dreaming?'

He chuckles. 'Get dressed. We're going out.'

'Now?' I yawn. 'What's the time?'

'7.30, and Melbourne is waiting for havoc,' he says, rubbing his hands together and smiling, a twinkle in his eye.

'I don't think I have the energy to get out of bed, let alone wreak havoc,' I tell him. 'We've had a big few days.'

'Exactly,' he says. 'We earned it.'

I get up from my nap, stretching. 'Where are we going and who with?' I ask.

'Probably the casino, if everyone else is eighteen too,' he says, shrugging. 'And pretty much the whole team.'

'Cool,' I say, pulling on my jeans. 'Winning a big trophy is definitely cause for a night out.'

'Yeah, buddy,' he says. 'And Johnno managed to get some drinks so we can start the party here.'

'What? What if Coach sees?'

'He's gone out, man, relax.'

'You boys can be so focused when you want to be,' I say, smiling. I button up my shirt, grab my room key and follow him down the hall.

David knocks on Johnno's door — one knock, a pause, then three fast knocks — and then says, 'Liege.'

I give him a strange look.

He smiles and raises his eyebrows, like he's really proud of himself.

'Don't look at me like that,' I tell him as we walk inside. 'That was the dumbest code knock ever.'

Inside, the boys are smoking and getting wasted.

'Open the balcony door before someone smells it,' James Czalo calls out, brushing past me. I catch him rolling his eyes, and we smile. James was always one of the more mature ones — together, we are like the fathers of the group — but he still knew how to have fun.

I take a shot and welcome the break in seriousness after the few days of solid focus on soccer and nothing else. Even though I've just had a nap, I'm looking forward to sleeping in tomorrow.

'Hey, it's 8 o'clock,' someone calls out some time later. 'Shall we head?'

Jackets are put on and cigarette stubs are wrapped in paper, then shoved in plastic bags and chocolate wrappers — more elaborate scheming from boys used to flouting the rules.

We exit the lift into the lobby and head out onto the street, the boys jostling and talking loudly over the top of each other.

'We're never going to get in anywhere,' I say to James. 'Not if we're already this rowdy.'

'We'll see,' he says, shrugging. 'We'll probably split up anyway. Not everyone's eighteen.'

'Let them sort it out,' I say. 'We deserve to have fun too.'

'Amen,' he says, grinning. 'Hey, look, it's Charlie Scanlon.'

She's outside her hotel, huddling in the cold, wearing a black dress, a long cardigan and heels. I've never seen her in heels.

'Wow, you look amazing,' I blurt out to her.

She ignores the comment. 'You'd think I'd remember how cold it can get,' she says, smiling.

'Are you OK?' James asks.

'Yeah, just waiting for my friend.'

'Oh right, I forgot you used to live here,' he says.

'How could you forget?' I ask him, recovering from my compliment going unacknowledged. 'She never shuts up about it.'

She gives us a half-smile. 'He's right on that one. Where are you guys off to?'

'Boys' night out, don't know where yet,' James says.

'Fun,' she says. 'If you're all over eighteen, you should check out Madame Brussels. Used to be a brothel. It's pretty cool.'

'Please don't say brothel in front of these clowns,' James says, laughing.

'So how were the games?' she asks. 'Ryan didn't post any whingey status updates on Facebook, which must mean you probably won them all.'

James laughs while I scowl at her.

'Something like that,' he says, putting his hands in his pocket. He peers down the street. 'Ah man, we've already lost the others. And in record time. Shall we go?'

'We'll find them soon enough,' I reply. Then to Charlie, 'Are you sure you're OK waiting here on your own?'

She nods. 'All good, he'll be here any second.'

I realise I'm dawdling. I want to meet this Pete of hers. This guy she can't stop talking about.

'Well,' James says, looking at me pointedly. 'We better get going. Have a good night, Charlie.'

We start walking down the street and I start playing guessing games with the guys we pass. The muscular guy with a shaved head; the one who's a cross between a hipster and a nerd; the redhead with a heavily tattooed arm — could any of them be Pete?

'Do you think maybe we should make sure he arrives?' James says, seeming to reading my mind. 'I don't like the thought of her out by herself at night.'

'Good idea,' I say, thankful that it wasn't me who said it.

We go back and find her arguing with the redhead. She reminds me of David's Nonna — there are a lot of hand gestures and pointing at phones. Then the redhead walks off in a huff.

We're just about to turn around when she sees us. She swallows her pride and walks over. 'Something came up,' she says, slipping her phone into her jacket pocket. 'I might just grab some dinner somewhere and call it an early night.'

I'm about to say something, but she cuts me off.

'And no, I don't want to tag along with you guys, before you ask me.'

'Wasn't gonna,' I say, shrugging.

We stand there in silence, confused about what to do next.

'I better get going,' she says finally.

'Are you sure?' I ask. James is giving me a look I can't decipher. She opens her mouth to speak, but James gets in first.

'Look, I'm gonna go catch up with the boys. David has my … um, thing. Ryan, why don't you and Charlie get something to eat, and you can catch up with us later if … your headache gets better, that is.'

Huh?

'You know, you were worried that it would get worse if you came out with the boys, but I convinced you anyway?'

I nod slowly, finally starting to understand. Sort of.

He leaves. Charlie and I stand there in silence for the second time that night.

My phone beeps. A text from James.

Sorry, I'm a crap wingman, but I did my best. Enjoy your night.

'So what now?' I ask Charlie.

She shrugs. 'I don't need you to babysit me. You can go.'

I shake my head. 'You heard the guy, my headache will get worse if I'm around those boys.'

She shivers and rubs her hands up and down her arms.

'Do you want my —'

'No, I don't want your jacket,' she snaps. Then, in a softer tone, 'But thanks for asking.'

'So maybe now you can show me why Melbourne is so awesome,' I say.

She looks at me curiously. 'Maybe,' she says, folding her arms.

I give her a pointed look and she rolls her eyes.

'Fine,' she says, turning her face so I won't see her smiling.

'Lead the way,' I say.

She walks ahead of me, and I hang back for a moment and watch her. It's a much better view than when she's in her school uniform.

We do a lot of walking that night. She's in her element — the crowds don't faze her, and she has an air of confidence and familiarity that's different to the guardedness she has at school. At one point, a seedy-looking guy bumps into her and I panic, thinking he's going to take her bag. But she just yells out some profanity and keeps going.

We have dinner in Chinatown, then she takes me to The Paperback Bookshop on Bourke Street, which she tells me she's always loved, because it stays open late.

'I could spend ages in here,' she says.

I want to spend ages in there myself, and I barely even read.

We walk over to Federation Square, watch a little bit of sport on the big screen and just absorb our surroundings. Someone whizzes past on a skateboard a bit too closely and her body slams into mine. For a second she just stays there in my arms, looking up at me. Then she starts talking about sweet cravings, and the moment — if there was one (maybe I just imagined it?) — disappears. So we grab some warm churros and hang out at Southbank, looking out on the river.

We talk about school and the yearbook and the future and the past. About soccer and Melbourne and family and Sydney. Her hair blows in all directions in the wind, and she laughs. She licks chocolate off her fingers and bobs her head to the rhythm of music that I can't hear.

The girl sitting next to me is different to the one I know at school, and I'm stuck between awe and fear. Awe because she's amazing, and fear because I don't want to feel this way about a girl. Not at eighteen, and certainly not a girl like this. I find myself being withdrawn, quiet.

'Ryan,' she says, breaking the heavy silence, 'I think I'll take that jacket now.'

I shrug out of my jacket and slip it over her shoulders. She looks out at the water.

'It smells like you,' she says.

'Is that bad?' I ask.

She smiles. 'No,' she says, breathing in the scent. 'It's actually kind of nice.'

Charlie

Charlie Scanlon Being a high-school student is like seeing a real-life film clip of Pink's 'Stupid Girls' all day. Why dream of being president when you can grind against some guy every day?

Katy Coolidge-Brown likes this.

Katy Coolidge-Brown That's totally your song, Charlie! I miss you. Hope I get to see you in Melbourne again soon xx

'So how was your weekend?' Tessa Zanetic asks as we're working out a formula in Chemistry one afternoon. 'Get up to anything exciting?'

'Not really,' I shrug. 'Went out for yum cha on Saturday morning with my stepdad, hung out at Gleebooks in Glebe, studied. Oh, and I looked at apartments in Melbourne.'

'Wow, you are really considering moving?' she asks, wide-eyed. 'I mean, I know you've spoken about it heaps, but I always figured that when the time came you might …'

'Discover that I'm really a Sydney person at heart?' I ask, smirking. 'Not gonna happen.'

She laughs. 'I just thought you might panic and change your mind,' she says. 'Like, I still need my mum. I couldn't possibly live on my own yet. And I don't think she'd let me.'

'Well, I'll be studying there, I hope,' I say, scrawling in my notebook's margin. 'Plus it's always going to be home. There's no connection for me here.'

'So a school in Sydney gives you a scholarship and you use it to move?' she quips.

I look up from my notebook. 'Don't do that, Tess,' I warn. 'Don't just assume that I'm going to get that medal. I'm sick of hearing about it.'

She shrugs. 'Sorry, it's just that …'

'Come on, Tess, let's just work this stupid formula out.'

She looks back down at her notebook, chastened, and I feel guilty. But I'm not quite sure why. It's not like I have a say in winning the medal. My only out would be doing badly on purpose, and I just didn't want to do that. Law was hard enough to get into as it is, and I really wanted to study at Monash.

But if I did win, Ryan would miss out on another thing that he had hoped for in his after-school life. And I wasn't sure I wanted to be the one who took it away, even if I wasn't doing it on purpose.

We work a little bit more in silence before I drop my pencil on my notebook and look at her.

'Just quietly … do you really think I might get it?' I ask.

'I'd say it's definitely between you, Ryan and Jane, but everyone knows that,' she says. 'Jane always gets dux at the end-of-year awards, but she's a bit slack when it comes to non-academic things. Ryan's smart, and he's kind of an all-rounder, like you. Teachers love all-rounders, you know.'

'I'm not an all-rounder,' I point out.

'Yeah, you are,' she says. 'Compared to me anyway. You're on the yearbook committee.'

'I was forced onto it.'

'Yeah, but you weren't forced to organise that fundraiser for ovarian cancer research,' she says. 'Plus you convinced Mrs H that we need to do something for International Women's Day.'

'Yeah, I just don't get why that wasn't celebrated here,' I tell her. 'Female causes should be top priority if we really want to break the cycle …'

Tessa's eyes start glazing over, and I remind myself that the majority of my classmates don't care about my speeches.

Just then, Ms Richards tells us she's stepping out for a few minutes.

'Just keep working on whatever you're doing, and if anyone asks I've gone to the bathroom,' she calls out as she closes the door behind her.

'Does she take us for idiots or something?' I mumble. 'Everyone knows she's going to the bathroom to smoke. One day soon a student will get blamed for it.'

Tessa shrugs. 'And when they do, she won't own up to it,' she says. 'It's just not fair that someone so young is teaching HSC Chemistry. If you think about it, she was in our shoes five years ago. She hasn't even seen enough exams to tell us what to expect.'

'She's not even in the classroom long enough for us to learn,' I counter.

'Good point,' she says, flipping between the two pages she's been working on. 'OK, well, I think I have the formula figured out, but I could be wrong. What's yours looking like?'

'Hmmm, doable, I think,' I reply. 'How about if you get two lots of everything and we each test our own out?'

'Yep, I'm down with that,' she says. 'I'll just go get the stuff.'

She returns a moment later and I busy myself prepping the material. A moment later, Ryan sits down on the stool next to me. I try to ignore him, but I can't. I thought we had a moment — well, a few actually — the weekend before last in Melbourne, but since then he's gone back to normal and I don't know why.

'Your formula's wrong,' he says, peering at my notes.

'How would you know?' I ask. 'You're walking around talking to people while those two girls over there do your work.'

'Relax, they're just checking it,' he says, smirking. We exchange a look that is only ours, as if we're privy to something that the rest of the world is oblivious to. So maybe he hasn't forgotten Melbourne? I feel flutters in my stomach and I put my hand on it, trying to steady myself. *Don't lose your shit over a guy, Charlie. No roots, remember?*

'Your formula is still wrong, though,' he says, nodding at my book again.

'Stop trying to distract me,' I tell him, as I put my goggles on and start to tip liquids into a beaker. 'I know what I'm doing.'

'Are you sure about that?' he asks, tilting his head to the side to peer at my work station again. 'I can help you if you want.'

'Yeah, help me fail. Ms Richards already has it in for me.'

'It doesn't help that you give her attitude when she gets things wrong.'

'She gets a lot wrong for someone who's teaching year 12,' I say in frustration, thinking of Tessa's comment earlier.

'Yeah, but you don't let anything go,' he points out.

'Is this about me taking control in meetings? The yearbook flatplan set a bad —'

'Charlieeee,' Tessa interrupts.

'Tessa, hold on,' I reply, putting my hand out but keeping my eyes on Ryan.

He shakes his head. 'No, it's about you being so highly strung,' he says. 'You don't let anyone stuff up.'

'I am not highly strung!' I exclaim.

'Oh no,' he says, his eyes on the bench behind me.

'What?' I say, whipping around, only to be hit in the face with a warm liquid and bits of glass from my beaker. There's a big blob on the ceiling of the science lab, and everyone is staring at me.

'Ouch,' he says. 'Lucky you're wearing goggles.'

'Oh no,' Tessa says. 'She's always going on about the bloody beakers. We're dead.'

Ryan peers up at the ceiling. 'I think the beakers are the least of your concerns,' he says, as a drop of liquid falls down onto his forehead.

'This is all your fault,' I tell him furiously.

He has the audacity to look shocked. 'Wait, what?' he asks, wiping his face down with a hanky. The guy has a hanky. Is he for real?

I bury my face in my hands. 'Seriously, what do I do?' I ask no one in particular.

'Look, we'll clean up the mess before she gets back,' he says. 'Trust me she won't even —'

'What is going on in here?' Mr Griggs, the History teacher, asks, the lab door shutting behind him. 'And who is supposed to be taking this class today?'

'I'm sorry,' Ryan says. We're seated outside Mrs H's office.

'Not as sorry as Ms Richards is …' I say, the dread in my voice clearly audible. 'I just know she's going to take it out on me.'

He shakes his head. 'I can't believe Mr Griggs heard from across the hallway. He's got supersonic hearing or something.'

'Well, the blob did make a noise when it exploded,' I admit.

'Yeah, but it's a Chemistry class,' he points out. 'It can't be completely quiet all the time.'

We're silent for a few minutes. I open my mouth again to speak, but Ryan cuts me off.

'Shhh,' he says, motioning to the door with his head.

We creep up and press our ears to the door. Mrs H is telling Ms Richards that she's at risk of losing her job.

'Shit,' I whisper to him. 'She's on probation? She's teaching year 12 and she's on probation?!'

'Well, our Chem teacher did abruptly leave at the end of term four,' he says. 'Maybe they just hired the first person who applied.'

'Some fancy education,' I say, rolling my eyes.

He shrugs. 'Especially if you need it,' he snickers. 'I'm smart enough to figure stuff out on my own, but you —'

My elbow makes contact with his ribs.

'Oww,' he says, making a pained face at me. 'OK, maybe I deserved that.'

We hurry back to our seats. The door opens a second later. When Ms Richards walks out I'm thankful that looks can't kill.

Mrs H calls my name from the door and I head inside.

'You've called my mother in?' I ask, after she's sufficiently chastised me.

'Yes, she should be here soon. I'd like to explain to her that it's not normal policy for teachers to be allowed smoking breaks during their classes.'

'Well, I'm sure she knows —'

'Be that as it may, our school hasn't stood here for over a hundred and fifty years because we didn't do things properly,' she says. 'Your parents deserve to know that we take our students seriously. And that it won't happen again.'

'She's learned her lesson then?' my mum asks, as the secretary ushers her in. Even though she sometimes acts like a bimbo, my mother is headstrong when it comes to the rights and responsibilities of students and teachers.

'Mrs Reynolds, please, have a seat.'

I tune out, the image of the blob on the ceiling hovering around in my head, while Mrs H and Mum discuss Ms Richards' future as a year 12 teacher.

Eventually, it's time to leave and I stand up, giving Mrs H a half-smile.

'It's good to see you getting along with Ryan, Charlie,' she says, smiling. 'With the two of you on the team, I know you're going to produce a real winner of a yearbook.'

My mother gives me an amused look then walks out. I follow her, eager to explain.

Ryan stands awkwardly to attention as Mrs H calls his name.

'That's the guy who distracted you?' my mum says loud enough for both of them to hear. 'He's *cute*. If he was in my class, I would have burnt down the entire science lab.'

I pinch her arm menacingly, and try not to think of the smug look that's sure to be on Ryan's face.

It's Friday night. I'm at the school charity dance-a-thon, which Gillian has somehow managed to convince me to attend. It takes me about forty-six seconds to realise that these people suck in a 'nightclub' setting even more than they do in a school one. Maybe one day I can pen a bestselling book or an award-winning TV series based on the pitfalls of my generation.

'And I suppose there's some new-age feminist problem with dancing,' Ryan says, sitting down next to me. 'Or maybe it's the music. Or the charity we're raising money for ...'

'Shut up, Ryan,' I say, in a sing-song voice. 'And the feminist movement is measured in waves. First-wave, second-wave —'

'OK, I get it,' he says loudly. 'Why aren't you dancing?'

'I'm allergic to teenage losers,' I say, smirking.

'Like you can talk.'

'Your school has tainted me.'

He laughs. It transforms his face, and unfortunately I find myself smiling too. *God, if you exist,* I plead silently, *don't make me like this guy.*

He stands up, and for a second I think he's going to leave.

'Dance?' he asks, as Walk the Moon's 'Shut Up and Dance' comes on.

I shake my head.

'Why? Your mum would approve.'

He winks at me and I chuckle. And then I surprise myself by standing up.

'You're lucky I like this song,' I say, smiling.

We make our way to the middle of the dance floor and join in on a circle of students performing stupidly exaggerated dance moves, and I actually laugh. Ryan's a terrible dancer, and he knows it. But he doesn't care — he moves into the circle and pulls people into the centre with him, applauding as they too humiliate themselves. And they all seem to enjoy the attention — not just because he's popular, I suddenly realise, but because he's the kind of bloke that you would want as your best mate, the guy everyone can count on. Across the circle, he smiles that smile again and for a second I wonder what it would be like to have known him for more than just a few months. And to know him for a little longer than the few months I have left with him before school is finished and my life here is over.

Suddenly I start feeling flushed. I need to breathe, need some fresh air, need some space. I fan my hands in front of my face, but he shakes his head, and I think, *Shit, can he see right through me?*

It's enough to make me want to get out of there. I hurry outside the hall and to the side of the building, where I lean against the wall, hoping to hide in the darkness until I stop feeling so flustered.

But a couple of minutes later, he's there, standing in front of me, as though my awkwardness is some sort of lighthouse that has drawn him to me.

'Are you OK?' he asks.

I look down at my shoes, the floor, anywhere but his face. And those kind, earnest eyes that are also insanely beautiful.

He tilts my head up with his index finger.

'I didn't mean to make you uncomfortable,' he says. 'Come back inside — I won't make you dance if you don't want to.'

I get a grip on myself and smile. 'I don't think you should make *yourself* dance,' I say, folding my arms.

He laughs and rubs the back of his neck. 'I'm that bad, huh?'

I check my phone for the time, and suddenly notice the date.

'There's exactly four months till graduation,' I say, holding my phone up. 'I have a countdown.'

'Of course you do,' he says, raising his eyebrows. 'Well, that's not long at all. Before you know it, you'll be back in Melbourne and Pete won't be able to lie to you as easily as he does now.'

'Hey, don't be like that,' I say. 'He was honest afterwards.'

'Yeah, after he made sure that you weren't going to come and ruin his prospects with whatever you said her name was,' he retorts. 'What — he couldn't just tell you he was going to a church youth group to hang out with some chick who invited him? Does he like having you hung up on him while he chases other girls?'

'It's not like that,' I mumble. 'And don't worry, I sorted him out on the phone the next day.'

'I bet you did,' he says. 'You should come with a warning.'

'Hey, what's that supposed to mean?' I ask, punching his shoulder. Oww. The guy obviously works out.

'It just means … you're not afraid to stand up for yourself,' he says, slowly.

I smile.

'Was he at least sorry?' he asks a moment later. 'He bailed on you twice in one weekend.'

'Ryan,' I say quietly, 'do you really want to talk about another guy right now?'

He shakes his head and takes a step forwards, placing one hand on the wall by my head. So close … and yet I don't move.

'I'm not normally like this around most girls,' he says, swallowing.

'I'm not most girls,' I say.

He exhales, and his seriousness freaks me out. So at odds with the guy I just saw on the dance floor. I think back to that night in Melbourne — the effortless ease with which we fell in line together as we wandered the city, how hours passed without me realising, the way his jacket smelt when I shrugged it over my shoulders. And how I didn't shower that night, because I wanted to fall asleep with that scent against my skin.

God, I was in denial. But this guy — I mean, come on, the cool jock? He's such a cliché.

I look up at him and falter.

OK, yes, maybe a part of me, deep down, wants to render the most popular guy in this dumb school helpless. I know this, because when he finally works up the courage to kiss me, I don't give him shit for it.

'I wanted to do that in Melbourne,' he says, pulling away.

'I would have let you,' I whisper.

'Ryan?' a voice to our left says.

He looks up and sees Lauren and Amanda, and takes a huge step backwards.

'I thought you needed a break from girls this year,' says Lauren. 'That's why you broke up with me, remember?'

Ryan puts his palm to his forehead and exhales. Then, because I am so good at picking them, he runs after a crying Lauren Pappas and leaves me standing alone in the dark, leaning against a wall, heart broken.

Matty

Matty Fullerton Even the music can't fix it.

'I still don't get it,' Gillian says, slamming her head down into her textbook. 'Can't I just write the answers in my calculator?'

I give her a dark look.

'I know,' she says. 'Even if there was no risk of getting caught I still wouldn't do it.'

It's recess, and we're inside a classroom prepping for our Maths trial exam, which is in a couple of days. She's complaining that her brain is all over the place, and I just want to shake her and say *How do you think I feel? I'm convinced that a guy I saw in a picture has the answers to my future.*

But I can't say that. It just doesn't make sense. People don't randomly find their fathers in old photos hanging on university walls.

I've looked at the picture every night since I snapped it. I wanted to show it to Mum, but Charlie's words kept echoing in my ears: *How do you know he's not part of the problem?*

I need to talk to her.

'Where's Charlie?' I ask Gillian. She looks like she had really been concentrating, and for a moment I feel guilty.

'She's coming in late today,' she says, looking at her watch. 'She went to the ultrasound with her mum. She should be here by fourth period.'

Damn. I consider sending her text instead, but Gillian suddenly has a conspiratorial look on her face. She leans towards me.

'Ryan kissed her on Friday night,' she says, her voice lowered.

'Really?' I ask.

'Don't get too excited. Lauren lost her shit straight after it happened,' she says. 'She burst into tears, and everyone gathered around her, and she kept going on and on about how insensitive it was because she and Ryan only just broke up —'

'Like, ten months ago,' I point out. 'How long is he supposed to mourn her for? I would have danced on tables the same day.'

'Duh — obviously it was all for show.'

I shrug. 'So what's the big deal?'

She rolls her eyes. 'For a smart guy, you can be really dense sometimes.'

I just stare at her, confused.

'Ryan is a nice guy, sensitive, you know?' she says, a serious look on her face. 'So now he would be feeling really guilty about how he made Lauren cry and will probably slow down on things with Charlie. Guys aren't good at seeing through antics like that.'

I purse my lips. I want to argue, but I think she's right.

I can't find Charlie in the quad at lunchtime, and neither can Gillian. Then our phones beep.

I can't be bothered coming downstairs. It's cold. I'm in B3.

We head upstairs. Charlie's sitting at a desk with her laptop open, eating sushi rolls.

'I bought you guys some too,' she says, gesturing to the plastic boxes next to her.

'BEST,' I say enthusiastically, digging in.

Gillian just looks at her.

'I don't want to talk about it,' Charlie says sternly.

'But —' Gillian starts.

'What did I say, Gill?'

Gillian sighs loudly. 'OK.'

Charlie shows us the ultrasound picture of the baby.

'Wow, that's pretty cool. So what's the ultrasound for anyway?' I ask.

'They check that the baby is doing OK, that there are no major abnormalities. You can also do a test for things like Down's syndrome.'

'They can see that?' I ask, surprised.

She gives a small shrug. 'Yeah, they see all sorts of stuff. You don't have to do the test, but you can if you want to ... you know ...'

'Abort?' Gillian whispers.

Charlie nods reluctantly. It gets a little awkward.

'I don't know if the test was around when your mum was pregnant with Sammy,' Charlie says, putting her hand on Gillian's arm. 'But do you think that it would have made a difference?'

'I don't know,' she says honestly. 'It might have. But she does love Sammy.'

'Yeah, she does. You all — we all do.'

The end-of-day bell goes. The three of us walk out together.

Ryan is in front of us with a couple of his mates. He keeps sneaking looks back at us.

'His face is red,' Gillian whispers to Charlie. 'He's nervous!'

Charlie rolls her eyes and slides her hands into her pockets.

'He's an idiot,' she says. 'And I'm an idiot if I let him get to me.'

Ryan waves goodbye to his mates at the school gate, and Gillian hurries off, wanting to make an early bus. Ryan turns to us as we approach. It's as if he's doing some sort of awkward solo slow dance — he shuffles, unsure of what to do. But Charlie pretends not to notice and doesn't slow down as we pass him.

'I shouldn't have let Lauren get to me,' he calls out after us.

'But you did let her get to you,' she calls back, without turning around. 'And like always, her manipulative plan worked out perfectly.'

I turn to sneak a glimpse at him. He just sighs and walks away.

'You're cold,' I say to her.

'I need to take care of myself.'

'Yeah, I get that,' I tell her. 'But you also need to feel.'

She loops her arm in mine.

'Can I come over?' I ask. 'I don't have work today.'

'Hell yeah,' she says. 'My mum loves you.'

'At least someone's mum does,' I say, smiling. 'Well, at least she shows it.'

———

'Wow, your house is huge,' I tell her, as we walk through the door. The decoration is tasteful — it's not like one of those over-the-top rich-people homes.

Her mum is in the kitchen, standing at the stove.

'Pancakes, Mum?' Charlie says. 'The doctor said you need to be careful because of the gestational diabetes.'

'That doctor is ageist,' she says.

'No, he's a professional.'

'But I really felt like them,' she says in a whiny voice.

'You're being embarrassing,' Charlie says, glaring at her.

'No, she's not,' I say, extending my hand. 'It's good to see you again, Mrs Reynolds.'

'Pleasure is all mine, Matty,' she says as she takes my hand, an open smile lighting up her whole face. 'Want some?'

I nod eagerly. Charlie shakes her head and goes upstairs to change. When she comes back down, we've polished off the whole batch.

'Hogs!' Charlie calls out, sitting on the stool.

'So how was school today?' her mum asks. They chat in a familiar, jokey way that makes me miss my mum — the way she used to be, not the empty shell at home. Afterwards, Charlie stacks the dishwasher while her mum sits on the couch with her feet up, rubbing her belly.

'If I fall asleep, I'm sorry,' she says to me. 'Being pregnant is exhausting! It's so nice to have you over though. Charlie never has anyone over. She keeps going on about her "no roots" philosophy.'

I look over at Charlie, who goes red in the face.

Later we try to study, but neither of us can concentrate. I ask how her stepfather has managed to fit into the dynamic that she and her mother had — how do you just add someone else into an already-established story?

She shrugs. 'You find a way,' she says. 'He's nice, and he works all the time anyway. Sometimes it doesn't feel any different, except that we're no longer in a two-bedroom townhouse in Melbourne.'

'Do you miss it? Being in Melbourne?' I ask.

'I did miss it a lot,' she says. 'Then things started changing, and I started to miss it less. You and Gill. Ryan. But now I'm really missing it again.'

'You should give him another chance.'

She exhales. 'There was nothing really solid there anyway,' she says. 'Plus, I'm still planning on going back. I don't belong here.'

I nod my head slowly, and check my phone for the time. 'I think I better go home now. Mum probably hasn't eaten anything all day.'

'You shouldn't be doing this, Matt,' she says, standing up. 'You deserve to be looked after. My mother is a psychologist and I spend an hour every single week with her trying to analyse what the hell is going on in people's heads. It can be useful to talk to someone.'

'But who can I talk to?' I ask. 'There's no one.'

'What about Mrs H? This is a big year and —'

'And what? Mrs H will fix my problems for me?'

'She deserves to know — at least so you don't keep getting detentions left, right and —'

'No,' I say, more firmly. 'I will figure it out.'

She walks me to the front door and holds it open while I stand on the front step, looking out onto the street.

'We're your friends,' she says. 'You should let us help you.'

'I wouldn't want to mess up your "no roots" philosophy,' I tell her, walking away.

She calls my name, but I don't turn around. She makes no effort to follow me.

———

It's late at night, and I've just spent ages working on a mock essay for my Modern History exam. Finally finished, I tiptoe out into the lounge room. Mum is asleep on the couch.

I look at the time — 11.05. I don't want to wake her up, so I go into her bedroom to get a blanket. But when I'm in there, I pause, thinking about what Gillian had suggested at the careers day. Could the answers to my questions be here somewhere?

There's nothing underneath the bed or in her closet. I go through her chest of drawers, hoping to find something — anything — that would give me a clue into her past ... and my past. When I go to pull out the bottom drawer, it catches.

I slide the drawer out completely, and shine the flashlight from my phone into the cabinet. There's a little cardboard box. Slowly and quietly, I pull it out.

There are a few things inside. A plaited friendship bracelet, a birthday card from her sweet sixteenth, a New Year's Eve 1990 party hat. There's a picture of the two of us on my first day of preschool. I'm wearing a Thomas the Tank Engine jumper, and Mum is holding me in her lap, kissing my cheek.

There's also a picture of a couple on their wedding day. I flip it over. There's a caption in scrawled handwriting that reads 'Mr & Mrs Fullerton 1970'. I'm struck by how much Mum looks like her mother.

At the bottom of the box, there's a white envelope. It's sealed, but the glue is old and I'm able to gently ease it open without leaving any obvious marks. Inside, there's a yellow-gold wedding band, and two pictures. One is of my mother with some guy's arms around her. Their backs are to the camera, but she's looking over her shoulder, laughing.

The other one is an ultrasound picture, like the one Charlie showed me today, except this one is older, and the baby is smaller. 'Baby Jellybean', it says on the back.

I run my fingers over the image. I get what people mean when they talk about life being a miracle.

I look at the text underneath and try to decipher it. It says 'eight weeks gestation', some numbers I don't understand, the date. I put it back in the envelope, but something strikes me and I look at the date again.

'No way,' I say out loud.

This image was taken in 1996, some one-and-a-half years before I was born.

Mum often told me I was her alpha and her omega — her beginning and her end.

But judging by this picture, I wasn't the real beginning.

Someone had come before me.

THE YEARBOOK COMMITTEE
Minutes for August meeting

Recorded by: Gillian Cummings

Meeting Chair: Ryan Fleming

In attendance: Everyone

The Playlist: We started off with 'Counting Stars' by OneRepublic. Matty said it was because we were at the tail end of our trials, and we were probably losing sleep and that we should keep our eyes on the end game because we only had a few months left before the future unfolded, and that was going to determine whether we were going to count stars ... or something. It was a long explanation, and I got bored. But it was the first time he has been this passionate, which was kind of cute.

The Snacks: Pizza! We ordered pizza, and they delivered it to us at the school gate as everyone was coming out of homeroom, and everyone looked at us. (Secretly, I think we all felt pretty smug walking through the quad with it.)

Agenda:

* Yearbook progress made during trials: This turned into a thirteen-minute session about the trials and answers that we got wrong/got right/left out, so Ryan canned any mention of trials.

* Profiles: We agreed that the profiles would be short. To be fair, we would use the school photos (because there's more of an even terrain, Charlie said, in terms of how we look) so each student would only have to fill in a form that she would create, with Name/Ambition/Last Words/Thing they'll miss most. Tammi offered to distribute it, because she's popular, and Charlie is not.

* Funnies: This was Matty's idea, and it's a good one. He said that we should try to make a list of all the funny things that students and teachers have said over the years. We resolved to let Ryan be in charge of that, because Matty and Charlie have not been here long enough, I have already done heaps of photo and event stuff, and Tammi's going to collate the profiles. Charlie suggested we create a Facebook group so people could just write their funny memories in it, and it would be less work for us because then we could just cut and paste into the yearbook

template. Ryan called her a genius, but she ignored him.
I guess that means she is still mad.

* Art: Matty put forward ANOTHER idea on and suggested
  that maybe our yearbook Facebook group should have
  some creative stuff in there too, like a song about our
  grade, or one of those maps of the school that shows
  where all the cliques hang out. Everyone — oh, Mr
  Broderick has just walked in. He is exchanging words with
  Ryan who looks confused. Charlie is butting in. Mr Broderick
  is talking about fairness and his hands being tied, and Ryan
  is getting angry. Mr Broderick walks out, Ryan kicks the desk
  and yells out, 'This is crap!' Tammi is shaking her head in
  anger, saying she isn't surprised. I am going to stop writing
  now, so I can find out what's going on —

Postscript:
Apparently some 'students' (ahem, Lauren for sure)
complained that we have 'extra access' to the Library after
hours. This is apparently unfair because it gives us an 'edge',
like extra time to access resources ('She can access those
resources at lunchtime,' Tammi says, rolling her eyes) and
extra time around teachers (like we ever talk to them). Matty
is mad because it's easy to just turn up to meetings when
they're on school grounds, but now there is going to be

extra time spent travelling to meeting locations, and we don't want to give up our lunchtimes either (just in case anyone suggests that). Charlie is wondering if this has anything to do with Ryan and her and The Thing That Happened At The Dance-A-Thon that we are not allowed to discuss.

Questions for Mrs H:
* Where are we supposed to work now?!

Action points for next meeting:
* Find a place to meet.
* Remember: t's us against the world. Even if Ryan and Charlie have gone ten steps back.

Tammi

Tammi Kap Fun night in with Mum, the TV and Thai take-away. I love Fridays.

Lauren Pappas Can't wait for our hang out tomorrow! #lovethewholeweekend

'I told you I don't want to talk about it,' I tell Lauren and Amanda. We're having dinner at a cafe on Burwood Road. We started coming here when we were about thirteen, for milkshakes and chats about boys. Now we're seventeen, drinking coffees, ordering main meals that could fill up a rugby player and planning our futures — and it's still our favourite place.

'Who cares? It's not like it's some big secret,' Amanda says.

'Tell me about it,' Lauren says. 'We're all going to read it anyway.'

'Yeah, the whole class is going to read it, which is why no one gets a sneak preview,' I remind them. 'Mrs H's orders.'

'Yeah, but how will she know?' Lauren says mischievously. 'Just slip us a few pages so we can give you some feedback.'

Lately it's like my bullshit detector has had a much-needed upgrade; it seems to go off constantly when I am around her. My father used to warn me about how manipulative she was, but I never saw it until recently. Now I can finally see her for what she is. I smile, thinking about how it will make his day when I tell him he was right.

'She's smiling! I knew it!' Lauren is saying. 'So there is something about that time I skinny-dipped in the lake at year 10 camp. Oh no.' She's feigning embarrassment, but I've known her long enough to know she's actually ecstatic about the prospect. Ladies and gentlemen, my attention-seeking best friend.

'Relax, there's nothing about that,' I say. 'That much I can tell you.'

'Then why were you smiling?' she asks quizzically.

'Because I was thinking about my food,' I say, as the waiter comes over. I rub my hands in anticipation of the crisp chips and mushroom sauce, the perfect sidekicks to my chicken schnitzel.

'So you really mean it?' Amanda asks. 'No sneak preview?' She takes a forkful of her caesar salad and shoves it in her mouth.

I giggle. 'There's dressing all over your face.'

'Seriously, what was the point of you even being on the committee?' Lauren asks. 'Remember we discussed that you'd do yearbook and I'd do formal planning, and that way we can debrief and warn each other about, you know, a bunch of stuff.'

'Yeah, but I think we both know I got the raw end of the deal,' I tell her.

'Relax,' she says, scoffing. 'How hard is it to scan a few pictures? Mrs H is making us all contribute stuff anyway.'

'Well, when you see the yearbook and how few contributions have actually been made, maybe you'll understand.'

'Maybe the group is crap,' Amanda says. I swear she's just waiting for my friendship with Lauren to fall apart so she can be chief best friend.

Lauren nods. 'The team is made up of losers and lame-asses — except you and Ryan, of course.'

'Come on, Loz, that's slack ...' Amanda says.

'Seriously,' Lauren says, laughing. 'As if "Funkerton" even knows anything worth remembering. He's spent the last two years with his head in a hoodie, and headphones on his ears.'

'I know!' Amanda exclaims. 'And nothing would have got through to him with those headphones always on his head.'

'That's what I meant, you tosser,' Lauren says, shaking her head and smirking at me.

'Oh,' Amanda says.

'And then,' Lauren continues, 'you have that snob, Charlie, who's been here for three minutes — like, what does she know? — and dopey, happy Gillian who probably wants to write about rainbows and butterflies, and make us all look like sissy kids who don't have lives.'

'Like her, you mean?' Amanda says.

They crack up laughing and I sit there awkwardly.

'She's not so bad, you guys,' I say quietly.

'Come off it, Tams,' Lauren says. 'You're always defending her these days.'

'Yeah, because you're making fun of her over nothing,' I say.

'Not over nothing,' she grumbles.

'OK, I'm sorry, not nothing,' I counter. 'Just one little thing that wasn't even her fault.'

'It was totally her fault!' Lauren exclaims. 'I got grounded for six weeks because of that.'

It goes silent. They're both watching me, and I feel my cheeks go warm.

'Did you do it?' I ask, quietly. 'Did you delete those pictures you got?'

'Not yet,' she says, flicking her hair. 'But I will.'

I look at her, pleading with my eyes.

'I only just got them yesterday,' she says in a huff.

'Yeah, from who? And how?'

She shrugs. 'I don't have to tell you,' she says. 'You won't even talk to me about the yearbook.'

'That's different,' I say, feeling like I am talking to a child.

'What are you accusing me of?' she asks. 'Snitches get what they deserve. She shouldn't walk around half-dressed.'

'She was in her room!' I cry.

She shrugs.

I'm looking in her eyes, searching for clues that I know I won't find. But she never betrays herself. 'No guilt whatsoever,' I observe.

'Guilt is a strong word,' she says. 'Besides, no one outside school has them.'

'You did PM them to us on Facebook,' Amanda says quietly.

'*What?!*' I ask, burying my head in my hands. 'Who's us? You told me when you got them that you were gonna delete them. Now you've put them up online?'

'Relax,' Lauren says dismissively. 'I only sent them to our group. It's not like they're on my wall.'

I shake my head.

'This is too much,' I say. 'Don't you think you've gone too far?'

'Hey, you seemed fine with payback a year ago when you got in trouble too,' Lauren says.

'I didn't think you'd go overboard,' I argue. 'Don't you get it? She was forced into a situation none of us would want to be in. She can't help who her father is. She can't help that journalists will want to use her to attack him. We were there, we broke the rules, we deserved what we got.'

'And someone else got to see Ed,' she says, pursing her lips. She slides her plate away from herself and sighs. 'I've, like, totally lost my appetite.'

Amanda looks at me wide-eyed. I decide to wait out the tantrum and look out onto the street instead.

There's an Asian girl sitting alone at a table outside the cafe, poring over a textbook. Across the road, a guy is leaning against a wall in front of the bank, next to the bus stop. Three buses come and go, but he doesn't move.

The girl stands up, puts her book in her satchel and walks into the cafe, leaving her satchel on the floor next to her table.

Nonchalantly, the guy crosses the road, hands in his pockets. Then he drops his hand and picks up the satchel.

'That guy just stole her bag,' I whisper to no one in particular.

'What?' Amanda asks, oblivious.

I stand up quickly, watching him walk quickly up the road — just as the girl exits the cafe and realises her bag is no longer under her chair.

I don't know how it happens, but my legs take on a life of their own and the next thing I feel is adrenalin pumping through me as I'm sprinting down Burwood Road, chasing a thief with a stranger's bag. I'm fighting the hair that's flying into my face, the acid build-up in my lungs, and my brain, which is telling me to stop, over and over again.

The thief has now started running, but the gap between us is getting smaller and smaller. Then I hear a car rev its engine and see it speeding down the road ahead of me. It screeches to a stop near where the thief now is, and two guys get out.

The thief tosses the satchel to the floor and turns down a side street, just as the two guys and I meet at the corner.

'He's disappeared,' one of them says, looking down the street. 'Probably hiding out in someone's front yard.'

I'm breathless, vaguely aware that the stickiness on the back of my shirt means I must be sweating profusely. How glam.

'Well, at least you've got your bag back,' the other guy says, bending down to pick it up for me. 'You were going for it pretty fast.'

'Yeah,' I say, panting. There's no need to explain the scenario to him. What would I even say?

'Is everything in there?' the first guy asks.

I try to catch my breath. 'Yeah,' I say, nodding. 'Thanks so much for helping.'

'No worries,' they both say, heading back to their car.

I place my hand on the wall to steady myself, looking back up towards the cafe. I can't see the girl. By the time I make it back there, she's on the phone to the cops.

'Oh, thank you so much!' she squeals when she sees me with the satchel in hand. 'It has my uni USB in there, I was dying!'

'Maybe don't leave it on the floor unattended next time,' I say.

'Trust me, I know that now,' she replies. 'It happened so fast, I can't believe it.'

'These things do,' I explain, as if I know first-hand.

'I saw you running when I came out, but didn't even see why,' she says, laughing. 'Are you a cop?'

'More and more each day,' I reply, smiling.

'Busted,' Dad says from the darkened kitchen as I am tiptoeing downstairs in my pyjamas. 'Sneaking out?'

'Dad, you scared the hell out of me!' I shriek, turning on the light. 'And now I've stubbed my toe.'

'Poor baby, let me kiss it for you,' he says, taking off his boots.

'Eww, no,' I say, recoiling.

'Yeah, they're probably not as cute as they used to be anyway,' he says, shrugging. 'So what brings you downstairs at this hour?'

'Midnight snack,' I tell him. 'I've been trying to sleep for an hour, but my stomach keeps growling.'

He looks at his watch. 'Your mum was eating at 8.30 when I called,' he says. 'Are you hungry already?'

I laugh. 'No, I ate out. And then I guess I kinda burnt it off … studying.'

He looks at me, puzzled.

'Why are you guys making so much noise?' Mum asks, walking into the kitchen.

'Aww, sorry, Mum,' I say, making an apologetic face. 'I got a little hungry.'

'Yeah, serves you right for not finishing off that cheese with me,' she says, going over to hug my dad. 'I had to finish it all by myself — it's going to go straight to my thighs.'

'And they'll still be gorgeous,' Dad says, smiling.

'Oh, gross,' I say, shaking my head. 'Do you guys want to take it upstairs so I can eat in peace?'

'No way, I'm starving,' Dad says. 'I've just come home from a twelve-hour shift — think I've earned myself a frozen pizza.'

'You might as well have picked up a real one on the way,' Mum says, turning on the oven and shaking her head. 'They're just as bad for you.'

He grabs a frozen pizza and a beer out of the fridge, and hands Mum the pizza. I sit at the breakfast bar and decide to come out with it, in the hope that it will help make my case for going to police academy.

'I've earned some of that pizza too, you know,' I tell him. 'Doing the same sort of thing.'

He swallows a sip of his beer and puts it down on the bench between two hands. 'Oh yeah?' he asks.

'Well, I was having dinner with Lauren and Amanda ...'

'Because that always starts off a great story ...'

'Dad, please! This is serious.'

Mum smacks him lightly on the arm. 'Go ahead, sweetie.'

'Anyway, I noticed this guy at the bus stop next to the bank. He was hovering, and it just looked weird. So I just kinda kept my eye on him. Then I saw this girl accidentally leave her bag on the floor outside, and as soon as she did, he, like, crossed the road in this really subtle way and just grabbed the bag and kept walking. And I don't think that anyone else saw because no one did anything ...'

'And?' Dad asks, looking at me curiously.

'Well, I don't know what came over me, but I just started chasing him.'

'You *what?*'

'I started running after him, for real,' I explain. 'Like, this adrenalin took hold of me and I bolted after him I don't know how many blocks, but it felt like a lot even though it wasn't that many. It just happened so f—'

'Tamara, stop,' he says, holding his hands up. 'Do you mean to tell me that you chased after a guy who you didn't know, who could have been dangerous, to retrieve some irresponsible person's backpack?'

'Well, it was a satchel and we don't know that she was irr—'

'She has to be if she left it on the floor,' Mum says.

'That's beside the point,' I say. 'The point is that I wasn't even scared to do it. It was instinctive.'

'Instinctively stupid,' Dad grunts. 'I can't believe you're pleased with yourself.'

'Why wouldn't I be?' I ask, confused. 'Someone broke the law and I —'

'— should have left it to the people whose job it is to enforce it,' Dad says.

'Why? So those same cops can call the girl — and I quote — "irresponsible"?' I ask.

'Yes, if it's going to teach her a lesson,' Dad replies. 'Come on, Tammi, that wasn't safe.'

I sigh and shake my head.

'Honey,' my mum says, sliding a look at him. 'Your dad's proud of you I'm sure, but he's just concerned for your welfare. The guy could have been on drugs, he could have been mentally unstable — what were you planning to do when you reached him?'

'Taser him with her lip gloss, apparently,' Dad says hotly.

'Niko, you're not helping,' she says.

He sighs.

'I had back-up,' I say, quietly this time. 'Two guys stopped their car and everything. It felt good.'

'A lot of feel-good situations can end badly, Tammi,' he points out. 'Drugs, joy-riding, sex with strangers …'

'I know that,' I say, rubbing my temples. 'I'm just trying to tell you that if I didn't panic about it, then maybe there's something in this for me. Please. I'm trying to talk to you about it rationally. I need you to take me seriously.'

'Well, I'm sorry, but I can't,' he exclaims. 'How will you tell Yia Yia that you're going to go live in a dorm on your own for six months and then fight crime for a living? She'll say no Greek boy will marry you.'

'Dad, don't bring Yia Yia into this,' I tell him. 'And can I point out that you didn't marry a Greek girl?'

'Yeah, and he still has to hear about it twenty years later,' Mum mutters. 'Not to mention that the *Xena* Aussie wife only wanted one kid.'

'We're getting sidetracked,' I say, opening the oven. 'Today was like the best work-experience day ever. It's like God gave me a glimpse into my future. And you know what? I liked what I saw.'

My parents look at each other and shake their heads. I look back at them for a moment then shrug.

'I'm just gonna eat this upstairs,' I say, putting a slice of pizza on a plate. 'Good night.'

As I walk up the stairs, I can hear them whispering.

'She knows how to put up a fight,' Mum says. 'Maybe she'll be OK.'

'Yeah, but I won't be,' he replies. 'I'm supposed to keep her safe. It's my *job*.'

I sigh. How is it that the one thing that feels right in my life is the one thing that is wrong in my dad's?

Gillian

Gillian Cummings Can't believe it's almost year 12 retreat time. Time is flying! #hooray

A loud knock on my bedroom door wakes me up. Dad calls out my name. I glance at my phone. It's 6.54 a.m., which means that whatever he wants to talk about must be important. I throw on a cotton dress over my singlet and pyjama shorts and hope he doesn't want to schedule an emergency photo shoot. Right now, we're about a month shy of the election and at least once a week his campaign staff hijack our kitchen and living room to discuss stats, promo opportunities, and, occasionally, ways to jeopardise the opposition. It's enough to turn a person off voting — not that I am even eighteen yet. But, I remind myself, it's good blog material.

'Hurry up, Gillian,' Dad's voice booms in between the knocks.

'I'm coming, Dad, just one second.'

I open the door, and find my father brandishing the day's paper centimetres from my face.

'What is the meaning of this?' he asks.

I peer at the headline. 'Well, I suppose it's a good idea,' I say sleepily. 'If everyone else has to commute to work, I suppose people on the dole should too. After all, "nothing in life should be free if you're able".'

He glares at me. That was a slogan from his early career that he now cringes over.

'Not that,' he says sternly. 'Underneath it.'

'"MP's daughter in nude photo scandal",' I read out loud. 'Yeah, and what's that got to do with —' My eyes widen and I snatch the paper out of his hands, looking at it more closely.

MP'S DAUGHTER IN NUDE PHOTO SCANDAL

Sydney MP Peter Cummings will have something else riding against him in the coming election, with reports that his blogger-daughter Gillian has been posting scantily clad photos of herself to friends on social media. The two images, posted anonymously to Sydney Confidential via a USB stick, show the seventeen-year-old in states of undress, doing what appear to be menial tasks around what is assumed to be her bedroom. The teenager, who attends the prestigious Holy Family High School in Sydney's Inner West, launched her blog, *Diary of a Pollie's Kid*, earlier this year and has quickly earned a respectable following. But despite her legions of followers, she has recently been subjected to a barrage of cruel taunts and comments that urge the teenager to 'go die', or realise she's as 'repugnant as a diseased elephant', prompting newer calls from anti-bullying groups for greater monitoring of hateful comments on social media. The two images bear the markings of a screenshot, suggesting they were sent or obtained via social networking site Facebook. This latest drama is yet another drawback for the teenage girl, who was snapped late last year vandalising a Croydon street with friends as part of her school's muck-up tradition, and for her father, who is battling strong odds as he contests his seat and runs for the premiership in the upcoming election. Only time will tell if his party's slogan 'family comes first' will play out in his office's dealings of the situation at such a critical time.

I bury my head in my hands for a moment. When I look up, Dad is walking off.

'Well, are you coming?' he asks, turning around at the top of the stairs. 'I'm sure you know we have a lot to deal with.'

He makes a coffee in silence and paces the kitchen until Sammy's school bus arrives. He takes Sammy out to the minivan, while I wait in the kitchen, dreading what's to come. A few seconds later, two familiar members of his staff walk into the house. Janine is tapping on a tablet and James is talking into a phone headset, but they both still motion for me to make them each a coffee.

Moments later, the gadgets are put aside and the four of us are sitting at the dining-room table, newspapers sprawled before us.

'So I've been on the phone with 7.30 already,' Janine says. 'They're very interested in running a story on what's happened. This could be a great opportunity for us to paint the picture that we want — and if they pay, we could then donate the money from the interview to help some sort of teenage crisis centre or bullying refuge in the area, and have the local press there.'

Dad nods curtly.

'Meanwhile, both Facebook and Instagram are yet to bow down to the pressure to remove the comments from her profile,' James says.

'Um, why not?' I ask. 'That stuff is nasty.'

'Sweetie, we have to think logistically in terms of your father's career,' Janine says, smiling insincerely at me. 'You're so lucky to have a father who's supported your quest for fame, but look at where it's landed him. So why don't you leave it to professionals like us to rework the situation into a win?'

'Huh?' I ask. 'You mean manipulate it?'

'Ah, we prefer to talk in more positive terms,' James says.

'Dad, this is ridiculous,' I say, pleading with him. 'I'm your daughter. Do you want me constantly seeing comments telling me to neck myself? I've done nothing to incite that rage, I don't understand where all this came from.'

Janine snorts.

My father and I both look at her.

'Um, Peter, we need to make sure we paint the right picture,' she says, ignoring me. 'Just an innocent, hard-working girl who is trying to make something of herself as a writer, who's been taken advantage of.'

James nods enthusiastically. 'The fact that she's trying to make her own way instead of relying on you has a lot of appeal,' he says. 'Sends out all the right messages.'

'OK, fine,' I say. 'I just want to know how the hell they got "scantily clad images" of me. I don't have a boyfriend, and Mum can't wait to get me into Weight Watchers — who would I send pictures to and why would I even bother?'

'You don't use Snapchat?' James asks.

Dad looks confused.

'It's a messaging app for photos,' I explain to Dad before turning to James. 'And yes, I use it, but, again, I have never sent dirty pictures to anyone.'

'Do you take your computer to school?' he asks.

'Sometimes. Why?'

'Does it have a webcam? Have you ever left the computer unattended? Say, when you asked a teacher a question, or photocopied something, or went to the bathroom?'

'Uh, yeah ...' I respond slowly, not sure where this is going.

James and Janine exchange looks, while my father and I look on, more puzzled than ever.

'There's a chance your computer could have been hacked by someone at your school.'

'I don't understand,' my father says, looking at them. 'Are you telling me that someone from Gillian's school could have hacked into her computer in as short a time as it would take her to go to the bathroom, and then waited till she was at home and getting undressed to film her?'

'That's right,' the man says.

'This is a joke,' my father says, standing up and smoothing his tie. 'People can't go around filming girls in the privacy of their own home! Think of the child protection concerns!'

He turns to face the buffet and I watch him tap his fingers on his lips — a gesture he does when he's deep in thought.

'James,' he says, turning back around, 'call the office. Have Mark draft up a bill that would enable the government to punish hackers who do this. Get Roslyn to do a search of anti-bullying groups or support groups for victims of sexual crimes so we have some people to liaise with should we make a donation — so we'll need 7.30 to pay upfront. Janine, you call 7.30 and agree to the interview — we'll do it, but only after the election, so that if I lose we'll be able to lay some blame on my daughter's situation. Then call a press conference for 3 p.m. so that I may make a statement.'

'Yes, sir,' they chorus, jotting down notes.

'My wife's up in bed,' he says, looking at the phone. 'She was in a great deal of shock when saw the paper. She'll need a massage or something, so have Roslyn arrange one at The Darling Spa. Then have her meet me for lunch at 1 p.m. at the office, so we can debrief her too, and see what she can be of help with.'

They nod and make their way outside, again affixed to phones and tablets.

'Gill,' he says, turning to me, 'you'll need to go to school. I'll contact your principal from the office this morning. She has to put a stop to this ridiculous behaviour. And I don't want you using that computer again — I'll send someone to buy you the best model out there and we'll have the IT guy do some checks on our internet security. And for heaven's sake, don't do anything stupid. If I had known that your blogging career was going to cause this many problems, I would have put a cork in it — the internet is worse than politics.'

'But, Dad, what about the photos? Can't we sue? I don't want them online. They're humiliating.'

'Look at me, Gill,' he says. 'Does it look like I have time to speak to a lawyer? I'm too busy trying to salvage my career so you can continue to live in this grand house, go to a fancy school and have a future.'

I nod, watching as he slips on a blazer and inspects himself in the hall mirror.

'As soon as we have applied some pressure to the situation and stifled the bleeding, we'll work on the photos. Who knows, they might even be good for your "career".'

He walks out the front door and leaves me standing in the hallway, feeling dirty and ashamed, even though I have done nothing wrong. I look at the big clock in the living room. In forty-five minutes, my father was able to mobilise a team and decide on a media strategy for dealing with a crisis, yet he could make no attempt whatsoever to give me the emotional comfort I so desperately craved.

And so I went to school feeling rejected and unloved, physically feeling as though the hole in my heart was getting bigger, no longer pumping blood to that part of my body that gave me the will to live.

RYAN

Ryan Fleming Hamlet, you are killing my life. #HSCEnglish

'Mr Fleming, may I please see you before you leave?' Mr West says as the bell rings.

I walk up to him, my bag on my shoulder.

'Ryan, I couldn't help but notice you didn't hand in your final English assessment yesterday.'

'No, sir, I left it at home.'

'That's unlike you,' he says, picking up the eraser and wiping down the whiteboard. 'Not only is your HSC grade riding on this assessment, but also your chances of winning the St Jerome Medal. Charlie Scanlon is hot on your tail.'

'I know, sir,' I say. 'But she has plans, and, without soccer, I have nothing. That medal — well, the scholarship — it no longer makes a difference.'

He sighs and puts down the eraser. 'You shouldn't fail your assignments to make some sort of statement.'

'But, sir, I'm seventeen,' I reply bluntly. 'I'm genetically programmed to want to make statements.'

He raises his eyebrows, and in the gesture I can see his ambivalence. He's not going to bother to lecture me, because whatever fire moved him to take this job has since been put out by hundreds of other thick, know-it-all teenagers before me, and he just doesn't care any more.

'I want it on my desk tomorrow,' he says finally. 'And I'll make you a deal — I need an additional senior representative at the Speak Now public-speaking contest on Friday morning. I have three year 11s and two year 12s, including Miss Scanlon. If you'll be the third, I won't penalise you.'

'Yes, sir,' I say.

I think about his words as I walk through the halls. All the teachers seem to be gunning for me to win that scholarship, and I have no idea why. They obviously think some healthy competition would do me good, and from the outside Charlie is the ultimate competition for me: fierce, spirited, confident. But they can't see what's beneath the surface. She isn't just my opposition any more — she's also a part of me, occupying a part of my heart that I didn't know was there.

Is this what love feels like? I think. Standing in the open space of the quad, I can't help but feel as though I have been backed into a corner.

———

The opposition and I wind up sitting next to each other on the bus on the way to the Speak Now session on Friday morning. Across the aisle, we both watch one of the year 11 students frantically making notes.

'What do you think she's doing?' I ask Charlie.

She shrugs. 'Beats me. I mean, how can she be preparing? We don't even know what the topics are yet.'

'Maybe she's psychic,' I suggest.

'I wonder if she can foresee the punishment I'm going to dish out to Lauren Pappas,' she says, looking out the window. 'Because I can't seem to decide on one.'

'Oh, you're going to fight fire with fire, are you?' I ask her sarcastically. 'That's smart.'

She rolls her eyes. Things have been awkward ever since I kissed her, but they're worse than ever now thanks to the whole Gillian's-hacked-webcam thing; it's like we're back to where we started.

'Don't talk to me about being smart,' she says after a moment. 'Not only do you hang out with terrible people like her and David, who, by the way, is an absolute dick for the way he treated Tammi at the party — yes, Gill told me what happened — but you also let them treat you like crap too.'

'Wow,' I say, raising my eyebrows. 'You're even more opinionated than usual today.'

'Stop living in denial, Ryan. You hang out with bullies and you're so blind to them bullying other people because they have so easily bullied you.'

'What are you talking about?' I say, incredulous. '*You* seem to bully me more than anyone I know. I'm actually scared of coming to school because I never know what cannon you're going to fire at me on any given day.'

'I can't offer you advice about how to deal with bullies if you don't ask for it.'

'That's funny, because you offer me all sorts of other advice that I've never asked for.'

She gestures to my leg, and I redden.

'That scar is nothing compared to what's going on in your head,' she tells me seriously.

I sigh. 'I might regret asking this, but what do you mean?'

'The scar will fade with time,' she says. 'But if you don't start getting your dream back, then eventually it's going to be too late. Meanwhile the guy who took your dream away because of his stupid idea to ride a four-wheeler over a sand dune is now pursuing it, and you're just sitting on the sidelines watching it all unfold.'

'How do you know how it happened?' I ask her. 'I mean, I have a vague idea — something about girls and how much they gossip — but that's a bit sexist isn't it?'

'Please. It's all everyone could talk about when I first got here,' she says. 'Ryan Fleming: school captain, soccer star, gorgeous, smart, nice. Why did he have to get on that bike and ruin our prospects of winning the Sydney Schools Soccer Tournament or whatever the hell it's called? Never mind whatever personal prospects he had ruined.'

'Not pros*pects*,' I say, turning away. 'Pros*pect*. Just one.'

'The biggest one, though, right?'

I just nod. There isn't anything to say.

'Who says it's ruined?'

I look at her like she's the dumbest person I've ever met, instead of the smartest. 'Um, the doctor who spent four hours in surgery trying to fix my knee. The physiotherapist. The coach.'

'And did you get a second opinion? A second physio? Did you ever go into the backyard and actually try to kick a ball around?'

'What would be the point?' I ask her.

'To go beyond the limitations other people have set for you,' she says. 'Don't take your injury at face value. Give yourself a chance, and if it really doesn't work, then at least you know for certain that you did everything you could.'

'I'd never play the same,' I mumble, looking at my feet.

'No, probably not,' she agrees. 'But the way people spoke about you made you sound like a god on the field, so you'd probably still play better than a hell of a lot of people out there.'

I'm quiet for the rest of the bus ride, mulling over her words. She might be the exact type of person whose face I would love to smash in if she were a guy, and yet she's teaching me more than I ever thought possible.

Inside the hall, surrounded by words and arguments and speeches, I'm thinking about my own inner debate. For and against. To play or not to play. To dream or not to dream.

We get let out for a half-hour break. Mr West asks me if I know what I'm going to talk about. And even though I planned to speak about the environment, I tell him I'm going to be talking about my generation's potential to do more than download TV shows, to pursue things more important than Instagram followers and to dream about things bigger than fame.

He smiles, and puts a hand on my shoulder. 'Good to see some of that old spark back,' he says.

I find Charlie outside on her iPad, looking frustrated.

'Look at this!' she says, showing me a photo of Gillian with a crude drawing of a penis next to her smiling face.

'That's disgusting,' I say.

She looks at me tersely, then turns away.

'What, you think my friends did that?' I ask her.

'I don't know,' she said. 'But they definitely made it OK for others to get in on it. It's so infuriating.'

'What do you have against them?' I ask her.

'Nothing except the fact that they are just so insensitive to the people I care about.'

'So you care about me, do you?' I ask, smirking.

Her eyes are like slits as she gives me a death-stare. 'Ryan, get over yourself,' she says slowly. 'I care about Gillian. How can they be so mean?'

'It's like a witch hunt! You have no proof my friends did the webcam thing.'

'It's not just Gillian — every single person they've put down to make themselves feel better are victims. You and Tammi included. You think I don't see how Lauren talks to Tammi? Maybe if Lauren stopped and thought about who Tammi is, she might learn a lot from her — like how to not do stuff just because it's trendy or because some guy is pressuring you to.'

'You know about that?' I ask. 'Jeez, nothing is private any more.'

'Playground gossip, Ryan. Wake up! Why do you blind yourself to what's happening around you?' she asks. 'Why can't you accept that our generation is not shiny or beautiful or smart, but completely insensitive and stupid and self-centred?'

'Well, actually, my talk is —'

'I just can't get over it,' she says, shaking her head. 'No matter which way I look at it, Lauren's aspirations for fame are in no way jeopardised by what Gill is doing, so why is she treating her that way? It's crazy. And by your silence you're just letting them get away with it.'

I don't say anything.

'I'm going to go,' she says, standing up. 'Think I need a little bit of space.'

Her phone beeps as she starts walking off. She stops in her tracks to read the message, and by the almost imperceptible slump of the shoulders I know it's from Pete.

'I'm not the only one who's blind, you know,' I call out. 'If you opened your eyes, maybe you'd see that he doesn't really care about you.'

She turns to face me, her eyes narrowed. 'Oh yeah?' she says. 'How do you know?'

'How many times has he ignored your messages?' I yell, walking up to her. 'How many times has he come to visit you? How many times has he shared links he thinks you'd like on your Facebook wall? All the stuff that you do for him.'

She bites her lip.

Shut up, I tell myself. *You can see you're hurting her, so shut up.* But I can't.

'I mean, it's so obvious that you're the one putting in the effort,' I finish.

'Don't you dare talk to me about effort and what's obvious,' she says.

'Save it, Charlie,' I say. We're standing so close our noses are almost touching. 'This is the only time that you are wrong and I am right.'

She blinks. I can't tell if she's trying to restrain her tears or her anger; I'm too mesmerised by her smell, the colour of her eyes, that little freckle on her right cheek, to care.

'I'm never wrong,' she says defiantly, and I can't help but admire her for that. She's more of a champion than half the guys on the soccer team.

'You're the one who's always going on about women's worth,' I tell her. 'Why are you chasing someone who doesn't know yours?'

'Because he's the closest thing to a man I've found in a teenage guy,' she tells me, vindictive and venomous.

And I know then that I don't have a chance in hell with her.

THE YEARBOOK COMMITTEE
Minutes for September Meeting

Recorded by: Gillian Cummings
Meeting Chair: Ryan Fleming
In attendance: Everyone

The Playlist: N/A
The Snacks: Burgers, fries and milkshakes.

Agenda:

* Location Change: We met outside the library as per usual,
  and spent about eight minutes trying to decide between
  a public library or Charlie's house, which I guess Ryan
  felt awkward about. Then Ryan found out it was Matty's
  eighteenth birthday, and we all got really excited (well,
  mostly excited — Charlie and I also felt a bit crap because
  we had no idea, but Matty said it was OK as he never
  actually told us when it was). So we all caught the train to
  town and went to Burger Project, where the burgers are
  amazing and the milkshakes taste like heaven. We sang
  'Happy Birthday' out loud when Matty came out of the
  bathroom — he walked past our table like he didn't know

us and went to sit by himself until Charlie made him come back. We then decided that our subsequent meetings should be in the public library, because we're going to be spending a lot of time there studying anyway.

* Progress Update: Matty reckons we're about 79% there. He calculated this by checking the number of completed pages in the entire template/document.

* Camp Coverage: All completed, thanks to a lot of teamwork (and, Matty says, Red Bull being on special at Coles).

* Deadlines: Charlie said that Ryan is doing a bad job of tracking our tasks so she is taking over. Ryan did not argue. The rest of us pretended not to notice that the two of them had hardly been speaking at all.

* HSC Wish Dish: I had an idea that we put all five of our names into a dish, then each draw a name, and write that person a 'good luck for the HSC' note. Charlie gave me a death stare (I hope for my sake she doesn't get Ryan) and Matty asked 'Why can't we just tell the person?' and I giggled and said that he never talks as it is, but he didn't respond. Which means he is definitely mad (and not as understanding and mellow as I previously thought he was). Ryan said it was a

good idea. So we did it, and we decided that we're only allowed to open the notes in the privacy of our own home on the morning of the HSC — and no one else is allowed to know what the note says.

Questions for Mrs H:
* Can we at least use a classroom if we can't use the library?

Action points for next meeting:
* Meet the deadlines that Charlie gives you! We're on the home stretch, people!
* Study for the HSC next month.

Charlie

Charlie Scanlon feels like she's journeyed to the ends of the earth.

Katy Coolidge-Brown Nope, just Sydney.
#comehomecharlie

I didn't think I could hate this school any more, but then I found out about the year 12 retreat: a three-day weekend in the mountains that's supposed to be 'spiritually and mentally nourishing', in preparation for the barrage of exams we're about to take. And much as I hoped it would be cancelled, the day finally came for us to board the buses and set off.

We've now been here for three hours. Meditation sessions aside, it's clear this is going to be three days of personal hell. Here I am spending every waking moment — well, every moment really — with people I wish lived on another planet because I sincerely believe they don't belong on Earth.

And as usual, I seem to be the only one feeling miserable. Everyone else seems so happy.

'I can't believe there are only a few weeks left of school!' Sally Parsons screeches next to me, using her oar the wrong way even after I've explained how to do it twice.

'Can you please concentrate, Sally?' I ask her. 'You're not paddling how I told you to.'

'Oh, please,' she says. 'As if we're going to beat them anyway.'

'Not with that attitude we won't,' I mumble.

Sally Parsons — a girl who has come to camp with long acrylic nails, false eyelashes and a curling tong for her blonde hair extensions — is probably one of the last people in the world I would want to be alone on a raft with. And yet here we are.

We've just made the raft out of barrels, and are now racing the boys around the lake in it. None of the girls actually wanted to get on said raft, so Sally unfortunately drew the short straw. And now she is driving me insane.

'They're really good, aren't they?' she says. Ryan and David are already at the halfway point; we've moved about three metres.

'Because they're focusing.'

'God, how hot are Ryan's arms,' she says, staring. 'Even maimed, he's still amazing.'

'He's not maimed, Sally,' I say. 'He hurt his knee, but surgery fixed it. He's fine.'

'Is it true you guys hooked up?' she asks in a hushed tone, even though there's no one around to hear us.

'No,' I say, bluntly.

'Are you going to?' she asks. 'Lauren will be so jealous.'

'I won't have a chance to hook up with *anyone* if I have to remain on this raft for the rest of my life because you won't paddle,' I tell her. 'And I have other concerns in my life beyond Lauren Pappas, or any other girl for that matter.'

'I'm sorry,' she says, sticking her oar in the water again. We move another metre, but I think it's the water that's moving us.

'Are my undies poking out of my pants?' she asks, looking behind her.

'Sally, seriously, does it matter out in the middle of a lake?'

She shrugs.

Another two metres. We're now about a quarter of the way. The boys have reached the bank and are dismantling their raft.

'Are you sure my undies aren't —'

But she can't finish her sentence because my hand has just taken on a life of its own and pushed her into the water.

'Charlie, I am going to kill you!' she says, spitting water. 'There are eels in here — and my hair is ruined!'

'Oops,' I say, biting my lip and ignoring her scrambles to get back onto the raft.

The whistle blows from the bank. Ms Richards looks so stern I'm actually afraid for my life. One of the camp activity organisers comes out in a canoe to tow us back to shore.

'Charlie Scanlon, I am really getting fed up with you,' Ms Richards says, as I put my shoes on. 'What a ridiculous stunt.'

I try to ignore Sally, as she squeezes water out of her hair, and her friends, as they surround her in solidarity. I am literally being communally death-stared.

'It was just a little water,' I mumble.

I would bet that payback is just around the corner.

Lesson #1 in life: Always trust your instincts. Especially when the next day's activity involves a waterfall jump and people who want revenge on you. We're in the middle of listening to the instructions from the guide, when I notice one of Sally's best friends hovering nearby.

Slowly, she comes up behind me. Then she whispers an 'oops' into my ear, and pushes me with all her might into the freezing water metres below. As I'm falling, my foot clips a large rock, but before I can cry out from the pain, the force and iciness of the water knock the breath out of me.

Seconds later, the guide that dived in after me (in an entrance a lot classier than my own) carries me out of the water.

'She's hurt her foot,' he calls out, as a crowd gathers around us.

'Eww, her foot's all swollen,' one person says.

'Maybe it's sprained or something?' another says.

'Should we take her to the hospital?'

'Perhaps,' the guide says, looking at Ms Richards who has just come over.

'Well, the nearest hospital is over an hour away,' she says. 'She just slipped — I'm sure she'll be fine. We can ask Mrs Hendershott's opinion when she arrives tomorrow.'

'Are you sure?' the guide asks, looking concerned. 'We could drive her …'

'She'll be fine,' Ms Richards says again. 'It was just a little water.'

———

It's the early hours of the morning and I'm fast asleep, having taken three Panadols before bed, when a knock at the cabin door wakes me with a jolt.

I ignore it and try to go back to sleep, but there's another knock. I sigh, limp out of bed and open the door to find Ryan Fleming hovering tentatively in the hallway, as if he can't decide whether to come in or not.

'Ssssshhhhh,' he whispers, holding his hands up in front of him, as if to placate me.

I look out in the hallway to make sure the coast is clear, then motion for him to come inside. He's fully dressed, but only in shorts and a t-shirt, even though it's pretty cold outside.

'What are you doing here? Are you crazy?' I ask, not entirely sure which question I'd like answered first. I glance over to Gillian who is sound asleep, her light snores muffled by the pillow that she has her head buried in.

'Batshit crazy, I'm thinking,' Ryan replies, 'But it's too late for me to stop now.'

'Stop what?' I ask.

'I'll tell you when we're no longer in earshot, OK?' he says. 'You're going to need to change your … err, outfit.'

I peer down and realise I'm in my nightie, and redden. Ryan has the decency to pretend he wasn't looking at my boobs. I motion for him to turn around, throw my denim cut-offs on underneath my nightie, and slide on a tank top and a jumper.

'Well?' I ask.

He nods and motions for me to follow him, and, against my better judgement, I do.

Out in the corridor, my limping is not helping with the creaky floorboards. He turns around and gives me a death-stare, and I shrug. As if I can help it! He rolls his eyes, then puts his hands out in a permission-seeking gesture. I nod, and he lifts me up effortlessly into his arms. I swallow. That scent from his jacket — from that night out in Melbourne — is even stronger on his skin, and it's making me nervous.

He carries me down the corridor and outside into the clearing. Instead of stopping to explain, he continues towards the car park.

'Ryan Fleming, if you're thinking you can take advantage of me while I'm in this sorry state, you have another thing coming,' I hiss.

He keeps walking.

'I mean it, what are you doing?' I ask, peering up at him.

'I'm trying to keep quiet, but as usual you're insisting on making things difficult.'

He reaches a black hatchback, sets me down and fumbles in his pocket. He pulls out a set of keys, then opens the passenger door.

'I suppose I better explain before I expect you to voluntarily get in my car with me at 3 a.m.'

My face says it all.

'I didn't like the way Ms Richards fobbed you off today when you complained about your foot hurting,' he says, looking down at the floor.

'She didn't fob me off,' I say. 'She didn't look my foot properly to see how bad it actually was.'

'Well, if it's as bad as you say it is, we should get it looked at.'

'Looked at by koalas and wombats?' I ask, puzzled. 'Or are you going to go all new age on me and ask the forces of nature to heal me underneath a black sky and crescent moon?'

'I'm taking you to the hospital, you idiot,' he said. 'I had to wait until everyone was asleep ... and for my phone to charge.'

I give him a quizzical look.

He exhales loudly, opening the door. 'I need the GPS,' he admits. 'Now will you get in the car?'

I let him help me into the car and he turns on the engine — but he only switches on the headlights when we're a safe distance away from the cabins.

'I can't believe I'm running away from camp,' I groan, burying my head in my hands.

'Relax,' he says. 'We might be back before anyone realises.'

'Seriously, we should go back now before we get caught.'

The dark road is suddenly illuminated by blue and red flashing lights. Ryan looks in the rear-view mirror and swears under his breath. 'What could be worse than cops?' he asks.

He pulls over and rolls down his window just as a young cop approaches us.

'Evening, guys,' he says politely. 'Licence please.'

'Evening, officer,' we reply in unison. Ryan hands over his licence and looks over at me with a half-smile as the officer returns to his car.

'If I make it out of this alive, Fleming, remind me to never go along with any of your plans again, OK?' I tell him.

'Fine by me,' he says, shrugging. 'I'm not the one in need of medical care.'

I turn and look out my window.

The officer returns and shines his torch over the back and front of the car.

'So what are two teenagers like yourselves doing out at this time of night?' he asks.

'My cousin and I are camping with some family friends while our parents do a tour of the Barossa Valley,' Ryan says, motioning to me. 'We told her that the stone fence on the property wasn't solid, but she just had to see for herself, and, well, she fell off. At first we thought it was fine, but *apparently* it's giving her a little grief — you know what women are like — so I'm taking her to emergency.'

'Uh-huh,' he says, shining his torch over my foot, which is purple and swollen.

'See?' I say, wincing.

'Please, officer,' Ryan says. 'It is an emergency, after all. I have no offences to my name. I'm even the school captain.'

'Also,' I butt in, 'it's a free country, and we've broken no laws.'

Ryan turns and grits his teeth at me.

The policeman shrugs. 'Fair enough, kid,' he says finally, slipping his torch back onto his belt. 'You two drive safe. Hope your foot heals just fine.'

'Thank you,' I say, flashing my biggest smile.

Ryan doesn't wait for the policeman to get back in the car before he's back on the road again, ignoring my laughs at his 'I'm the school captain' line.

How can such a nerd be the most popular guy in this school?

I awake in Ryan's arms to the noise of the hospital emergency department, and realise I must have dozed off in the car.

'You can put me down now,' I tell him as we approach the reception desk.

'It'll look more … urgent this way.'

He explains what happened to the nurse, and she tells us to sit down after taking our details. We sprawl over the chairs, trying to remain awake.

I realise I'm wearing his jacket — he must have put it on me in the car — and hand it back to him.

'You had goosebumps on your arms,' he says. 'I figured you were cold.'

'Thanks,' I say.

Time goes by slowly.

'Has it only been forty-seven minutes?' Ryan says, struggling to keep his eyes open. 'Feels like hours.'

'Welcome to the emergency department,' I say.

'I really thought we would back before anyone knew,' he admits, making an apologetic face.

'Well, you're an idiot,' I say.

Finally I'm taken into a room, where a nurse comes in to wheel me over to X-ray. I leave Ryan in the room, pacing. When I come back, he's curled up in an armchair, staring at his phone. He steps out when a doctor comes to tell me I have a sprained ankle, which he will return to bandage shortly.

'What's the go?' Ryan asks, yawning as he walks back into the room.

'A sprain,' I say. 'He's going to bandage it.'

'Ouch,' he says, scowling. 'Well, since we've been here a little longer than expected, I should make a phone call. There's no reception in here.'

I watch him leave as a young nurse comes in with some juice and toast.

'Is he your boy?' she asks.

'No, just a … good friend,' I tell her.

'He's certainly very cute,' she says. 'Wish my man would look at me the way he looks at you.'

I'm silent, unsure of what to say. When I don't engage her in further conversation about 'my boy', she shrugs one shoulder and walks out the door.

Ryan returns, his feet dragging along the floor.

'You should get some more sleep,' I tell him. 'You look totally exhausted.'

He shrugs. 'I'll be OK,' he says, settling in the armchair.

'You can't drive back if you haven't slept,' I point out.

'Yeah, but I can't sleep in a chair,' he says. 'I just can't.'

I look at him for a moment then bite my lip nervously. 'We could share the bed?'

He laughs quietly, the tips of his ears turning pink. 'Yeah, great idea,' he says. 'I'd just make the mangled foot worse.'

I turn away to face the window, not wanting to admit I'm disappointed. But minutes later, he shuffles in next to me.

'I got cold,' he whispers. I lean against him and he inhales, but he doesn't say anything.

I sleep like a baby.

I wake up feeling drowsy and confused. It's 11 a.m. and Ryan is nowhere in sight. I don't have time to ponder his whereabouts because then Mrs H walks in, coffee in hand, a half-smile on her face.

'And would you look at who we have here,' she says.

'It's not Ryan's fault, Mrs H,' I say quickly. 'If I didn't whinge so much about my foot, he wouldn't have felt compelled to do it. You know how he is, he's so damn helpful. I'm not even that nice to him, if you ask me, but it's just —'

'Spare me the rant, Charlie,' she says.

'We're really sorry,' I say, hanging my head. 'Well, I am.'

She waves her hand at me. 'You should be sorry for sneaking out, yes. But you shouldn't be sorry for tending to injuries that should have been attended to by the staff. I know they thought it was safer to wait for me to arrive, but your foot's obviously in pretty bad condition.'

I shrug.

'Well, they're not doctors ...' I say, my voice trailing off uncertainly.

She smiles, then takes a sip of her coffee. 'It's certainly the most exciting start to a camp I've had as a principal,' she says. 'So does it hurt?'

I shake my head. 'Not as much as high school.'

She chuckles. 'Holy Family's not so bad,' she says. 'I think you'll slowly figure that out.'

I swallow and look down at my lap.

She hesitates, and then says, 'Some boys aren't worth getting into trouble for, Charlie. And some girls — when you're a student like Ryan — aren't worth getting into trouble for either.'

I look at her quizzically. 'I don't know what you're getting at, Mrs H.'

'Then you're not as clever as I thought you were.'

Matty

Matty Fullerton So maybe, just maybe, photography is up there with music.

Gillian Cummings So maybe the yearbook is bringing some good to your life ;)

The first thing I notice when the bus drops me off in front of the apartment block is the open window. The curtain is fluttering in and out, as if celebrating its freedom after months trapped inside.

I scowl, confused. And when I let myself in the front door, the box of Lite n' Easy ready meals sitting on the coffee table doesn't lessen my confusion at all.

I look around. The air seems fresher, clearer, and I realise the back door is also open.

'Mum?' I call out. 'Are you OK?'

She calls out from the bedroom where I head to find her sitting on her bed, staring outside her window. There's a half-finished cup of tea and the core of an apple on her bedside table.

'Your principal is here,' she says, holding her knees to her chest. 'She brought the food that's on the table. She wants to speak to you.'

'What?' I ask, my face reddening.

'She's on the balcony,' she says, cocking her head towards it. 'She's calling a doctor. One who does house calls.'

My eyes widen. Nothing is making sense.

I start for the door, but the sound of Mum's cracking voice stops me.

'Why would you tell her?' she asks me. 'Couldn't you let me work it out?'

'You haven't done anything in eight months. As if you were going to work it out.'

'It's better than being ambushed and humiliated,' she says, still looking out the window. She sighs and closes her eyes. 'Why would you tell her? Answer me.'

'I never told her anything,' I say, taken aback. 'Even when I got questioned about parent–teacher night, I kept my mouth shut.'

'Well, she's here now, so go out and fix it.'

I roll my eyes and walk out of the room, muttering, 'Just like I fix everything else.'

Mrs H is standing on the tiny balcony. She hangs up the phone when she sees me.

'You should have told me, Matthew,' she says.

I shrug. 'I'm already the scholarship kid in a fancy school,' I reply. 'How much charity am I supposed to take?'

'As much as we can give,' she says simply. 'And student welfare is not charity.'

I sigh. 'She says you've called a doctor?'

'Yes, she's on her way,' she says, sounding exasperated. 'Frankly it's about time. This should never have got this far.'

'I can't do everything,' I mumble.

There's a loud knock at the door and we look at each other.

'That'll be Dr Talbot,' she says. 'I'll send her in to your mother.'

Mrs H sits in the kitchen with me while I unpack the Lite n' Easy meals and divide them between the fridge and freezer. I suddenly realise I could eat the entire box in one go — it's been that long since I've had a proper meal.

'How long has it been like this?' she asks as I put the lid back on the box.

'A while,' I answer vaguely.

She raises an eyebrow.

'It's felt like ages,' I admit. 'But what was I supposed to do? I owe some loyalty to the person that she was.'

'You're a wonderful boy, Matthew,' she says. 'I really wish I had known.'

'Do you want a tea or something?' I ask, desperate to change the subject.

She nods, and I rifle through the cupboards for some biscuits. I don't have any, so I put a lolly on the saucer, then feel like an idiot and toss the lolly bag back in the pantry.

'I called your boss at the juice bar,' she says. 'He told me you've been working a lot. And that you do some sort of catalogue route as well. Am I right in assuming your mother has not been working and you've been paying the bills?'

I feel like the teabag inside the cracked china mug in my hands — trapped in hot water. I nod.

'How are you managing?' she asks. 'They're not well-paying jobs.'

'Mum has some savings put aside for when I go to uni,' I explain.

'Oh, Matthew, you shouldn't be using your university money.'

'Well … I doubt I'll go to uni,' I say honestly, as if that makes it OK. 'I'm thinking of becoming a photographer or a band manager actually.'

It's quiet for a moment and I realise I'm breathing a lot faster than usual. She puts her tea cup down and looks at me earnestly.

'Mrs H, is this intervention legal?' I ask.

She doesn't answer the question. She just talks to me about welfare and adulthood and my future and all these other concepts that at the moment seem entirely foreign to me.

'It's not so bad,' I say at the end of it all. She knows that I'm lying. And she knows that I know that she knows.

I feel embarrassed. I look at the floor, my shoes, the paint chip on the cupboard — anywhere but at her.

'Mrs H, how did you find out?' I ask.

'It doesn't matter,' she says after a moment. 'There's no one else, is there? No family?'

'Um, not really. No dad, no grandparents. It's just me and Mum. Always has been.'

She sighs. 'That doesn't make it easier.'

I say nothing.

She takes her cup to the sink, pausing to look out the window. 'It means so much to her that you go to Holy Family. You did it for her; now she needs to get better for you.'

I swallow. 'It's not that easy,' I tell her. 'She doesn't listen, doesn't talk. There's a wall there.'

'Matthew, this troubles me so much,' she says. 'You should *not* have been dealing with this on your own. You should have come to me sooner.'

'I've had a lot on my plate,' I say. 'Talking wasn't the priority.'

'Yes, but your wellbeing is paramount,' she says. 'As a child, you should always be the priority.'

I'm silent, chastened. Chastened enough for myself and for my mum.

Mrs H pauses for a moment then continues. 'Matthew, these are the seeds of your future that you are planting today,' she explains. 'If there's anything that I can help with, then I would like to try. At least until your exams are over. This is your time now — yours and yours alone.'

I nod.

The doctor taps lightly at the doorway and motions for me to come into the living room. I look to Mrs H and she follows, standing in the doorway while I sit down on the couch.

Dr Talbot talks about school and how a home environment needs to be stable for a child, but all I can hear is static.

Then she tells me she has booked my mother in for a psychological assessment next week.

'She might try to get out of it,' she says, 'so I guess it's on you to make sure she attends.'

'He's had enough "on him",' Mrs H snaps.

Dr Talbot looks from her to me. 'I'm just pointing out the facts,' she says, handing me a card. 'Call if you need anything.'

She closes the door behind her.

Mrs H rolls her eyes. 'Good Lord, if that's what professional help is like nowadays we're in trouble. She was no help at all.'

I move to stand up, but she gestures to me to stay seated. 'I'm going to have a private word with your mother.'

She walks down the hallway. I wait until she's out of sight, then tiptoe after her until I'm within earshot.

'Mrs Fullerton, you have to understand the gravity of what Matthew is going through,' I hear her saying. 'I don't care what that doctor says, asking him to attend a doctor's appointment with you on the first day of his HSC exams is not on.'

'It's OK, Mrs H —' I say, walking in.

'Matthew, that is enough,' she says, glaring at me. 'You've yet to graduate so you're still one of my pupils, and I demand that you pay your future the attention it deserves. Even if you intend to stay at home caring for your mother for the next few months or years of your life, eventually you will want to move on, and having your Higher School Certificate behind you makes it that much easier to move to something that is both practical and beneficial.'

'OK, but —'

'And I will be asking the supervising staff to make sure you are at each exam.'

'OK,' I mumble, defeated.

'Will you need anything else from me, Matty?' Mrs H asks.

I shake my head.

'Ring the school if you need anything,' she says. 'My extension is on the fridge, I don't know if you noticed it.'

'I wasn't paying attention,' I say.

'Don't be afraid to reach out to your friends either,' she tells me. 'You might have got used to being leant on, but I know you can count on them. I'm sure of it.' She turns to my mother. 'Ms Fullerton,' she says, looking at her the way she looks at a student, 'I hope you follow through with Dr Talbot. I care about my pupils as though they were my own children. Had I any idea what Matthew was dealing with earlier, I would have been able to offer more support.'

My mother doesn't say anything.

'Please do not be ashamed by the taboo surrounding mental illness,' Mrs H says finally. 'It is nothing to be ashamed about.'

'You've made your point,' my mother mutters.

Mrs H nods a quick goodbye to the both of us and lets herself out the door — my very own Mary Poppins giving me a spoonful of sugar when I needed it the most.

I'M PANICKING.

A text from Gillian wakes me up on Monday morning and I realise it's here. Everything that I have been told my future hinges on. I pray to a God I'm not sure I believe in for my classmates, for Mo's sister, for every student who — unlike myself — actually cares.

But still, I have studied. I've revised, done practice exams and written silly little rhymes to remember words and terms, because maybe on some level, I too believe that it might change my life. And now here it is. The first exam.

I reply with a blunt *You'll be fine* and leave it at that. I'm ninety-nine per cent sure it was her that couldn't keep her mouth shut about my mum, but I'm not ready to confront her just yet.

I quickly run over my study notes, put on my school uniform, then rush out into the kitchen for a speedy breakfast. I'm about to leave the apartment when I notice Mum's keys on the entrance table. Like I need the added drama of a missed appointment today.

'Wasn't your appointment at 8.30 a.m.?' I ask, walking in to her bedroom without knocking.

She rolls over and looks at me, her eyes still groggy.

'I postponed it,' she says. 'She gave me an afternoon slot.'

I realise I don't have time to waste following up the story. I need to believe her.

'Well, make sure you go,' I tell her. 'You're still good-looking, you know. There's no need to stay inside the house forever.'

But she doesn't laugh. She just stares out the window.

'Ok, well, wish me luck then,' I say, pausing at her bedroom door.

'Matty,' she says slowly. 'Don't go. Stay, and come with me.'

'I have to go,' I tell her tersely. 'Because I don't want to look at myself the way I'm looking at you. With disappointment.'

I storm out the door and head off to the bus stop, panicked that after my efforts and resolve, I'll be late. But I'm not, and I feel a rare sense of affinity when I arrive at the school hall and see that everyone is as tense as I am.

I turn off my mobile phone and head into the hall, hoping that the future will hold more for me than my past. But sitting at that desk doesn't do me much good. I stare at the questions before me, thinking that they might as well be in another language. Suddenly my future is obscure — something I can't envision, a language I can't speak, a prospect I can never touch.

The questions might as well be about my mother's illness — something that I will probably never understand. Like I didn't have enough mysteries in my life to contend with.

This year, I had tried to forge friendships with people across the great divide. But someone I trusted has ratted me out, and now I just want to retreat back into the shell where I really feel like I belong. On my own — because I am the only one I can count on.

Tammi

Tammi Kap Me at my desk today: Can't study any more / it's almost over / checks snapchats on phone / studies for 2 minutes / WTF does this mean / chocolate cravings / let me look at formal dresses / focus Tammi / yuck, pimple / back to studying / my head hurts.

I'm sitting in the gazebo in the park, studying for my Business Studies exam, when someone sits down next to me.

'You make me feel like Indiana Jones searching for lost treasure,' Mike says, smiling.

'Yep,' I say sarcastically. 'I'm a regular diamond in a hay stack.'

'What's this?' he asks, gesturing at my papers.

'Study notes,' I say. 'My HSC has just started.'

He pretends to pull out a notebook and tick something in it. 'Year 12,' he says slowly. 'So you're seventeen, eighteen?'

'Eighteen,' I say, smiling. 'I repeated kindy.'

He laughs and I give him a funny look.

'So even though I'm nineteen and not a student, I've been doing a bit of study of my own,' he says seriously.

'OK — and?'

'I've been carrying out some extensive research on whether or not you're a figment of my imagination — because I never got a call and it's been ages since I last saw you.'

'Yeah, I lost your number, sorry,' I say, making a regretful face.

'You should be sorry,' he points out. 'Do you know how many weird looks you get when you walk around a park asking people if they've seen a beautiful clown?'

I crack up laughing.

'OK, I didn't *really* do that, because it's not like I could even explain the whole clown thing,' he says.

'It doesn't matter now,' I tell him. 'That part of my life is over.'

'You don't sound happy about that, ironically.'

I shrug.

'Year 12 passes, you know,' he tells me. 'And all the drama that comes with it goes with it too.'

'It's not just year 12 I'm worried about,' I tell him, looking out at the park.

'I can't help you if you won't give me anything to work with,' he says pointedly. 'All I know is that you're in year 12 and working as a clown to save up and study off-campus. I don't know where, I don't know when, I don't know why.'

'Well —'

'Oh, don't ruin the mystery,' he warns, smiling.

Two police officers pass by in front of us. One of them must recognise me as Dad's daughter, because she smiles at me.

'Pigs,' he says, shaking his head. 'Can't stand the effing police.'

'Wow,' I tell him. 'That's some attitude. Common, but probably misinformed.'

'Trust me, I'm well-enough informed.'

I roll my eyes, thinking this might be a conversation for another time. Or never again, depending.

'Do you ever feel like your life is mapped out before it's even really begun?' he asks me, pulling out two phones.

'Please, you're talking to a girl.' I counter. 'We have all the same stuff to contend with as boys, but we also have to deal with lesser pay *just because*, or male colleagues thinking we can't do the same job as them in the same way. We're still fighting stereotypes.'

'Everyone is fighting stereotypes and judgement in one way or another,' he says. 'You just have to find a way to deal, a way to unwind, and a way to keep going.'

'Sounds like a well thought-out plan,' I tell him. 'So what's your strategy? And do the two phones work into it?'

'Ha! One's for business, the other's for pleasure. As for the strategy– that's a foolproof method that will probably make me a millionaire one day, so consider yourself lucky that I'm about to share it with you for free.'

'OK,' I say, intrigued.

'I deal by having a good support system around me,' he says. 'That's essential. I'm in the family business — whether I like it or not. I've learnt to milk it for all it's worth, and then I use that money to help me relax and unwind a little. And I keep going because I know that I have to. We all have to earn our keep some way; we can't all be heirs to racing fortunes or children of political dynasties.'

I shrug. 'I bet they have their own problems too,' I point out, thinking of Gillian.

'Yeah, but there's still a class division in society,' he tells me. 'It's not like in Downton Abbey or whatever the hell it's called, but it's there. So deal, unwind, keep going … and repeat.'

I sigh. 'You know, I'll probably have to hunt you down and kill you if I remember that instead of this stuff,' I tell him, pointing to my notes.

'Trust me, my stuff is worth remembering.'

'Yes, well, so are my Business notes, because I need them to pass my HSC and figure out something to do with my life.'

'Because clowning around doesn't pay enough?'

'Not quite,' I say.

One of his phone beeps and he looks down at it.

'Duty calls,' he tells me. 'Do you remember the mantra?'

'"Deal, unwind, keep going … and repeat,"' I tell him proudly.

'See?' he exclaims. 'An excellent student. I bet you'll ace all of your exams.'

I laugh.

He starts to walk away, then turns around. 'Are you planning on celebrating once the HSC is over?'

'Yeah I guess so,' I tell him. 'Doesn't everyone?'

'Well, if you really want to celebrate, these will help.'

He thrusts a small ziplock bag with two green pills in it into my hands.

'Oh, I don't think these —'

'Relax,' he says. 'They're not illegal, they're not detectable, and you're not going to get in trouble for them. They're made from these cultural herbs or some shit, and they're amazing. Just don't take them both at once if you're worried.'

He waves goodbye and heads off. I stare at the packet in my hands. Against my better judgement, I slip it into my pocket.

I'll probably throw them out anyway.

THE YEARBOOK COMMITTEE
Minutes for October Meeting

Recorded by: Gillian Cummings
Meeting Chair: Ryan Fleming
In attendance: Everyone

The Playlist: Matty chose 'Bad Blood' by Taylor Swift.
Tammi had a confused look on her face, so he tried to
pass it off as a subliminal message for Ryan and Charlie,
but I knew the real reason — he knew that I was the one
who did it.

The Snacks: Vitamin water and Gatorade (Tammi's
Mum); wheat crackers, cheddar cheese, and ham (Ryan's
grandma); and tuna and cracker lunch kits (Charlie's mum).
It was obvious that the families were getting into HSC-
nurture mode. Except mine, because she is always 'busy',
and Matty's, for obvious reasons. I did chop up some carrot,
celery and cucumber sticks, though. (Charlie said they were
called crudites, but I had never heard of that word so I will
stick to calling them sticks ... lol).

Agenda:

* Graduation Day Material: It was decided that we would ask Mrs H if we can hire a cheap photographer (a sibling of a student maybe?) to take photos of the ceremony. We are all responsible for sending one or two things to Charlie so she can write some text about the day — funnies, anecdotes, reflections etc.

* Final Tasks: It was decided that Tammi will get the staff photo for this year, and Ryan will collect the funniest teacher comebacks to student remarks. They will work on the staff pages together. Matty's job is to take the file to the printers after he and Charlie do the final check. And my job is to call the printers and make sure the requested extension is not going to cost extra to have our books ready in time.

* Formal: It was decided that we will stick to our plan to hand the book out at formal. We will leave two blank pages at the back with the heading 'Formal Memories' for people to write and stick photos in.

Questions for Mrs H:

* Token gift or small payment in school budget to allocate to photographer mentioned above?

* Can we get an extension of just ten days? If we have until mid-November, we will still have time to pick up the yearbooks in time for our formal on December 5th.

Action points for next meeting:
* Meet up for a champagne brunch at Charlie's house in lieu of next meeting, where we will toast our success, and see the book before it is distributed that night.
* Give ourselves a pat on the back when we do!

Gillian

Gillian Cummings FINALLY. #graduating

Lauren Pappas We'll be rid of you forever!

David DeLooka LOL Pappas, you crack me up.

I ring the doorbell one more time and hear a thud and a torrent of swear words before Matty finally opens it.

'How long were you going to ignore me for?' I ask.

He rubs his knee furiously, then scowls at me. 'Dunno,' he says, shrugging. 'How did you find my house?'

'I followed you home after the Maths exam,' I explain. 'Well, I followed your bus in my car.'

'Remember all those times we sat together at lunch and you would go on and on about how you needed a life?' he asks. 'Today I agree with you.'

'I drove you here once, remember?' I say. 'So I didn't think it was a big deal. I just forgot which building it was. They all look the same.'

He rolls his eyes. 'Poor people's houses often do,' he mutters.

I give him a gentle shove.

He closes the door behind him. 'Talk?' he asks.

We sit down on the stairs.

'I knew you would tell her,' he says, shaking his head. 'But I thought you would pick a better time.'

'I'm sorry,' I say, 'I really am. But I kept quiet hoping that you would come to your senses and then the HSC was, like, there, and I panicked. Mrs H needed to know. I hoped you'd get disadvantage points.'

'I don't need you to take care of me,' he says sternly.

'Someone has to,' I exclaim. 'You haven't been able to catch a break this year.'

He picks at his shoe, staring out at the road. 'And you know what? I'm fine with that — it's character-building.'

I roll my eyes. 'You think you're so hard, don't you?'

'I've been relying on myself since I was a kid,' he explains. 'You might not get it, but this is who I am. I don't share, I don't open up, I don't want anyone caught up in my jam. As my friend you should have respected that.'

'I know that … sort of,' I say. 'But I still wish you would have let me apologise.'

'Gill, a "sorry, not sorry" is not my thing, and that's the kind of apology I would have got from you,' he points out.

'You know me too well,' I mutter. 'Forgive me?'

'Always,' he says.

I scoff. 'That would have been good to know three weeks ago,' I say. 'You know how hard it was going through exams without being able to talk to you? I was dying.'

'What, couldn't you draw some hope from your wish-dish note or whatever?'

'Don't mock the wish dish,' I say, looking at him. 'I got a really sweet note from Tammi.'

'Yeah, because you deserve one,' he responds. 'And she needs better friends ... Well, at least you seem fine. According to the internet anyway. Guess your dad's PR team are pretty effective.'

I shrug. 'It's all for show,' I tell him.

'Don't I know it,' he says. 'I've decided to delete my Facebook.'

My eyes widen. 'Delete, like, full-on get rid of it? Not just deactivate it so you can study?'

He laughs at my reaction.

'Wow,' I say. 'That's awesome.'

'Yeah,' he says. 'Time for a fresh start, post high school. Tomorrow it all ends.'

'You *are* coming to graduation though, right?' I ask. 'And David's party?'

'Dude, I don't even know why you're going to David's party,' he says. 'That guy is a see-you-next —'

'Don't say it,' I say, slapping my hand over his mouth. He laughs again, and I rest my head on his shoulder. It's quiet for a moment; we're both watching the sky turn a pretty swirl of pink and orange.

'Come on,' I say, finally. 'You have to come. It's our last high-school party!'

'I was never one of you guys,' he says, smiling. 'Not really anyway.'

'What, and you think I am?' I ask. 'Lauren put water on my chair in the exam room yesterday. I sat in there for two hours with a wet bum and I'm still going.'

'I don't get it,' he says, shaking his head.

'Neither do I … She must be really obsessed with me,' I say, striking an exaggerated pose like I'm more fabulous than the simple girl that I really am.

He looks at me, narrowing his eyes as if he's trying to understand something difficult.

'No … I don't get why you just keep … going,' he says.

'I won't let her bully me out of my high-school memories,' I say defiantly. 'I'm just as entitled to them as she is.'

He smiles at me approvingly.

'Sammy is so lucky to have you,' he says after a minute. 'I bet you teach him so much.'

I stand up to leave and give him a quick hug before making my way down the stairs.

'Hey, who'd you get?' I ask from the bottom.

He leans over the railing and smirks at me. 'I thought the wish dish was a secret,' he says, winking.

I make a face at him and he puts his hands up.

'They're your rules,' he says, laughing.

―――――

My parents don't make my graduation ceremony. There's a press opportunity at the opening of some fancy new wing at a private hospital. My mum thinks getting the hairdresser to blowdry our hair together at home counts as suitable mother–daughter bonding time before the ceremony.

'We'll get the video,' she says, as she grabs her designer bag and rushes out the door. I just give her a half-arsed smile in response to her half-arsed parenting.

I look over my school uniform one more time and make sure I look perfect, then kiss Sammy goodbye and leave for school.

At least I know that he and Elliott will be there, cheering me on.

Outside the school hall, I am surrounded by people brandishing cameras and mirrors, posing with their families and adjusting themselves for the final walk under the school hall's sandstone arch before they are officially free.

I take a quick Snapchat video, blowing a kiss to the camera, and post it to my followers. Then, as I'm slipping the phone back into my blazer, I feel a pair of hands close over my eyes. I whip around and find Charlie standing there, arms folded in her signature pose.

'OMG, you look good,' I screech. 'You're wearing make-up.'

'Yeah, photos and all that,' she says, smiling mischievously. 'I do have to act like a girly girl sometimes, you know.'

She looks around. 'Did you see Lauren Pappas? She's wearing these gigantic heels — I hope she stacks it.' We burst out laughing.

'You don't mean that,' I say, nudging her.

'Of course I do!' she exclaims, grabbing my hand. 'Come and see how huge my mum is now.'

'It's so lovely to see you, Gill!' Charlie's mum exclaims when we find her. She starts fixing my cap and adjusting the cape on top of my uniform. 'I bet you're glad all those exams are over?'

I nod, smiling, trying not to look at her boobs, which are huge.

'You'll have to come visit after baby is born,' she continues. 'When Charlie moves back to Melbourne, I'll be all alone.'

My eyes flick to Charlie, who bites her lip and looks away.

'Of course another girlfriend is abandoning me,' I say to Charlie later, as we're about to make our entrance. Teachers are walking up and down the line, thrusting lit personalised candles in our hands.

'I'm not abandoning you,' she hisses. 'What a complete waste of money,' she says, scowling at her candle. She blows it out.

'Whatever,' I say. 'Are you nervous? I am.'

She scoffs. 'What for?'

'I dunno. But I'm so glad they decided to do this after the HSC. Most other schools do it when the students finish in term three, but what's there to celebrate when you're still turning up for exams and stuff?'

A cameraman appears in front of me.

'Gillian, how does it feel to be graduating?' a reporter next to him asks.

I give her a confused look. 'Um, who are you?'

'We're from the Channel Nine News. We're doing a segment on your dad and how he must really be "all for the people" if it means missing your graduation.'

I shake my head, caught completely off-guard.

'Do you mind?' Charlie steps in. 'This is a private moment.'

'How about just a sound bite?' she says.

'A what?' I ask, flustered.

'God, do they want to film you doing a poo as well?' someone behind me asks, snorting and laughing with their friends.

I redden, but shake my head. 'Please leave,' I whisper to the reporter and cameraman.

Inside, our hour-length ceremony is one of speeches (boring), award presentations (predictable — the same people come first every year) and lessons on the real world (looong). And then — the awarding of the St Jerome Medal — which is pretty much the high-school equivalent of winning the lottery.

It goes to Charlie! I literally whoop with joy, rising up out of my seat as she goes up to accept it.

She smiles and gives the shortest award speech I've ever heard in the six years I've been at this school. It's just a thank you to the teachers, thanks to her mum and stepdad and a thanks to the women who inspired her to make something of herself.

'I hope every girl graduating today doesn't let society diminish her inner spark,' she says, finishing with the peace sign and a quip of 'Girl power!'

A few people in my grade exchange looks. I love that she's never at a loss when it comes to making a statement.

We walk out of the school hall for the last time, to the applause of all the younger students, and out into the sunshine where we throw our hats in the air, hug one another and take photos with our family and friends. I pose with Sammy and Elliott, and Sammy says he was so happy to come see me become 'a growed-up'. After a few snaps, Elliott tells me it's time for him to take Sammy home. I give Sammy a big kiss and thank him for coming to watch me. He wipes his face where I kissed him, and then gives me a super huge hug goodbye.

A second later, the reporter and the cameraman are back.

'Gillian, how do you feel about your parents not being here?' she asks, as he shoves the camera in my face.

'Oh my God, you're all over her like a wet suit,' Charlie says, coming over before I can respond. 'She's totally fine; stop ruining her graduation.'

The man gives her a dirty look and she sticks her tongue out at him. I look on with amusement. Then the reporter and cameraman walk away, muttering to each other.

I turn back to Charlie. 'So I don't actually think I *am* fine with the fact that my parents aren't here,' I tell her. 'It kind of sucks. I mean, what was the point of them even having kids if they're not going to invest time and effort into raising them?'

'Gill, don't let it ruin your day,' Charlie says, rubbing my back. 'It's not worth it.'

I look at her sadly.

'Cheer up,' she says. 'You're not the only one. Here comes Matty. He's probably been waiting around the gates, hoping that his mother would turn up.'

'*It is finished*,' he says, smiling at us. 'Even I don't have a song for this feeling.'

We hug him excitedly and ask where he was earlier.

'I came late,' he whispers. 'I slept in. I thought, *Screw it, what does it matter now? I need the rest.*'

'Can't argue with that,' Charlie says. 'So, Gill tells me you're not going to that party either?'

'Either?' I exclaim. 'Wait — what? You're not coming?'

She looks at me as though I'm stupid. 'As if I would.'

'Puh-*lease*,' I beg. 'I really wanna go!'

'God knows what for,' Matty says.

'I'll see,' Charlie says, relenting. 'But you should come over before the party. Help me pack my mum's hospital bag. She still hasn't done it and her due date is in two weeks.'

The crowd starts to dwindle and I realise I haven't snapped a photo with my friends yet.

'Selfie time!' I squeal, gathering them close. Matty shakes his head and tries to escape, but Charlie grabs him.

'If I'm doing it, so are you,' she growls.

I take a few photos, Charlie and Matty grimacing in all of them.

'Any more pictures or can I go now?' he asks.

'Yeah, let's get one with Lauren Pappas so that when I'm so happy and successful in the future I can look at it and remember to come back down to earth.'

'Ahem,' Tammi says, coming up behind me. I crack a smile and bite my lip.

'Relax,' she says. 'I was just hoping I could get a picture with you guys.'

Her mum takes one of us and I ask Tammi where her dad is. 'Working,' she says. 'Don't worry, you're not the only one.'

I give her arm an affectionate squeeze and gesture to Matty and Charlie. 'These two aren't coming tonight.'

'Wait — what?'

Both of them wave their hands in front of their faces, going into all sorts of excuses.

'Well, you should both come,' she says. 'You can hang with me.'

I give a snort of laughter and realise she looks offended. 'Sorry,' I say, clearing my throat. 'But what about Lauren?'

'She'll be fine,' she says. 'She'll probably be pashing everyone in celebration.'

Ryan comes up to us, beaming.

'Charlie, congrats on the medal,' Ryan says. 'You deserve it.'

'Yes!' Tammi echoes. 'You should be so proud of yourself. You came into the school out of nowhere and blew us all away.'

'I'm good at that,' Charlie says, winking. Ryan looks at her admiringly and I wish the look was enough to melt her ice-queen heart.

'Do you mind if you take a photo of the yearbook team, Nan?' Ryan asks his grandmother.

We smile enthusiastically — even Charlie — then take another one making silly faces.

'David's parents are away this weekend and he has the house to himself,' Ryan says to us. 'So he's having a party. We're raising money for Movember so there's going to be a cover charge and it's BYO booze, if you want to come.'

We all look at him with amusement.

'You're so delayed, bro,' Matty says, tapping his chest and walking away.

———

I go home and change out of my school uniform before heading over to Charlie's. She's in the shower when I arrive, so I sit with her mum in the kitchen as she fusses about getting drinks while filling me in on the weekend away she and Stan are taking to Berry.

'We leave tomorrow morning,' she says excitedly. 'It's my first road-trip from Sydney.'

I smile at her politely. 'Um, aren't you worried about …?'

She points to her belly. 'About this? God, no … Charlie was ten days overdue. I still have two weeks.'

Fair enough, I think.

Suddenly I notice an odd expression come over her face. 'What?' I ask.

'Sorry,' she says. 'I'm just curious as to how you're going after … everything that's happened.'

'Great,' I say, shrugging.

She looks at me with a combination of professional experience and parental concern.

'I can't afford you, Mrs Reynolds,' I say.

She smiles. 'Don't be silly,' she says, putting a plate of biscuits on the bench before me. 'It's totally normal for you to be feeling a little down. Big changes in your life, a busy family, and the whole media and blogging business — it's gotta be tough. You're just a kid; you deserve a chance to act like one.'

I don't say anything.

'Ohh, this baby is sitting on my bladder so comfortably it must think it's a chair,' she says, tapping her belly. 'Baby Buttercup … Mummy's bladder is not a seat. Excuse me while I go to the bathroom, love.'

She waddles away and I smile to myself, wondering how the hell Charlie could still be desperate to move to Melbourne given that she's going to have a baby brother or sister around. I grab a biscuit off the plate then turn around and glance at the house.

A picture on the wall catches my eye. It's a wedding photo — Charlie's mum in a super-tight ivory dress that hugs her boobs (her pregnancy attire is not any more subdued), a bunch of red roses in hand, smoothing Charlie's hair, presumably right before she walks in front of her mother-bride down the aisle. I knew Charlie was in a bad mood on the wedding day, having just found out about the plans to move to Sydney, but I had no idea how much. It's usually the bridesmaid comforting the bride. I laugh to myself and think that perhaps Charlie will be fine making that move back to Melbourne when the baby is born after all.

Nearby, there's a picture of her mum and stepdad — Charlie's mum is smiling happily, and he's affectionately kissing her belly. Even though I can only see his profile, he looks so familiar to me. Or maybe it's just because Justin Timberlake posed the same way with his wife's belly. Who knows.

I grab another biscuit, wander over to the bay window and peer outside. The sprawling yard, filled with gorgeous garden roses, is beautiful. There's even an ivy-decorated iron gazebo with several peacock chairs arranged in it.

Charlie's right, I think. *She really doesn't belong here. Not just in this house, but in this whole show-offy city.*

Mrs Reynolds returns and joins me at the window.

'I'd love to say it's all me, but Stan hired a decorator,' she says.

'I'm trying to find Charlie in it,' I say, looking around the house. 'But it's hard.'

'She's in the nooks and crannies,' she replies, looking around. 'And in here,' she says quite quickly afterwards, putting her hand to her heart.

'I don't think I'm very much represented in my parents' décor either,' I admit. 'Not that my dad cares about that, but Mum does. Our fridge is bare — no school awards or childhood photos. She does have pictures on the walls, but most of them are those stiff, posed kind of photos.'

She peers at me closely and I feel myself redden slightly. She seems to notice, and lightens the mood again.

'Ah, everyone's different,' she says cheerily. 'I'm sure your mother wants to keep the memories of your childhood all to herself instead of sharing them with the world.'

'Yeah, maybe,' I say, shrugging.

'I'm going to go check on her royal highness,' she tells me, looking at her watch. 'She has short hair — I have no idea why she needs to spend so long in the shower.'

'I don't want you to trouble yourself going up the stairs,' I say.

'Because I look like I couldn't make it up there without breaking a step?' she asks knowingly. 'I'll be fine. Plus we pay for the water and, more importantly, she has company she needs to visit with.'

I give an embarrassed half-smile and mumble a thanks as I watch her take each step carefully and slowly.

I head back to the window, but this time notice the little corner alcove that must be Charlie's mum's study. Peeking inside, I recall Charlie telling me her mum was doing a PhD on teens or something, something I had totally forgotten. I find myself staring at her bookshelves, gliding my hands over books with titles like *What's Happening to our Girls?* and *Living Dolls: The Return of Sexism.*

I'm curious about her work. I wonder if she interviews people with a recorder, like a journalist would do. I wonder what she does with their information — is it anonymous? Does she have to get some sort of clearance to use teenagers' information? I know my dad was once in charge of a big 'working with children' project, making sure that people who work with kids were properly accredited, but when I thought of those people, I always thought of teachers and camp volunteers and religious bodies who run youth-group nights — researchers never crossed my mind. I guess his work was more far-reaching than I could have imagined and for a moment I'm sad that we don't have the sort of relationship where we could talk about it.

I finger the piles of paper on her desk and think about how far Charlie's mum has come. Eighteen years ago, when she was unwed, pregnant and alone, she might have felt lost and terrified; now she was married to a loving, wealthy guy, practising as a psych, doing a doctorate, and about to have her second child. At that moment, Charlie's mum's life gives me a little hope for my own, and I like that I can look forward to something bigger, brighter and better.

Then my eyes fall onto the words 'blogging' and 'social media' and I'm suddenly more than curious. I scan the page and realise that Charlie has recounted — with extremely vivid detail — almost every problem I have had this year to her mum. My rocky relationship with my mother, my best friend who moved away to become something, the bad reputation at school thanks to bullies and the idiots who believe them, the constant trolling on public forums, even my concerns about my body image are there, spelt out as if I had no right to privacy. *Gosh,* I think, *is this for her PhD? Are people going to read this? Will they know it's me?*

'It's not what you think,' I hear Charlie say as I spin around, anger and betrayal burning my cheeks.

'Really? It seems pretty obvious what it is.' I hold up the paper. 'Or maybe you're going to try to convince me otherwise because of the way that I let people walk over me because I — here, let me read it out — have an "overwhelming desire to be liked"?'

She takes a deep breath and rubs at her temples.

'Look, let's just talk about it,' she says. 'I'm sure once you hear —'

'Don't give me that crap,' I reply. 'You've been in my ear this whole year telling me I shouldn't let people bully me, starting with my mother and Pappas and people on the internet. But you've been telling me what to do and when to do it, which is almost as bad. I thought you were just being my friend, but it turns out I'm being used as a case study!'

'Gill —'

'You think you're so immune from teenage bullshit,' I tell her. 'But you just proved to me that you're the same as the rest of us. I can't believe this whole time you had an agenda. *I hate agendas!*

Couldn't you just have asked me if I wanted to be interviewed? So I could at least have had a say in what is said about me in this thesis?'

She shakes her head but I stare her down, eyes narrowed.

'It wasn't about you,' she starts to say, but I don't buy it. Not after what I've seen and read. 'It was me, she does this with all her pa—'

'It's so obviously about me,' I tell her, my voice cracking. 'Do you know how hard it's been seeing myself reflected in the eyes of so many different people, and all those reflections being negative? My parents, those stupid PR people that work for my dad, *our class*? I thought that I was at least safe with you. I thought you were my friend, but you've turned me into a case study. In your mother's thesis. Without me knowing.'

The more I say, the less I want to believe that, after everything I've been through this year, I also have to contend with this.

'No, it's not what you think,' she pleads. 'It was mostly for me, to —'

'I just don't know how to deal with this,' I interrupt, my voice heavy. 'I am panicky and hurt and I don't even feel like I can breathe properly any more.'

'Please, Gillian, you have to hear me out,' she says. 'You're only getting half —'

'Oh, there's more, is there? Great, even better.'

'No, that's not what I'm saying.'

'I don't want you coming with me tonight,' I say bitterly. 'You don't even wanna go, so don't come. You broke Ryan's heart, then mine — why don't you go after Matty and Tammi next?'

I watch her recoil in horror.

'You think you're fixing things, but you just made it all worse,' I say, scowling. And when she takes a step towards me, I realise I can't take it any more.

'I have to get out of here,' I whisper. I don't even give her a chance to respond. I just charge past her and out the front door.

Outside, I break into a run, breathing loudly and heavily as tears stream down my face. With each foot that pounds the pavement, I find my desire to escape it all growing; I wouldn't be surprised if I suddenly had the power to never stop running.

But every runner stops when they reach their destination, and mine wasn't just far away. In that moment I realise that I will never reach my destination because I simply have nowhere to go, and no one who cares enough to come find me anyway.

I am all alone.

RYAN

Ryan Fleming No one wants to be the Fun Police.

David DeLooka Lol Bro, I told you!

I relive the moment over and over again.

She won it. I worked for it for years and she breezed in out of nowhere and won it. It was the only thing I had left after soccer and now it was gone, and I had nothing.

Except her ... and she was going too.

A knock at my door shakes me into reality.

'Are you still upset about the medal?' Nanna asks, coming into my room.

I shrug. 'Honestly? I don't know,' I admit. 'I'd be more upset if I knew what I wanted to do.'

'Does Charlie know what she's going to do?' she asks.

'Yeah, of course — she's always so sure about everything,' I say. 'She's planning on doing Law at Monash, where she'll probably boss everyone around, make the lecturer change the course and come top of every class.'

Nanna smiles at me knowingly. 'It sounds like you like this girl,' she says.

I sit up. 'Yeah,' I admit. 'But the thing is, she's so complicated, and I have enough complications.'

'But maybe it's like maths, dear — two negatives in your life might make a positive.'

I smile. I decide to chase the positive.

———

I head to David's afterwards and find a bunch of the soccer guys there, slicing lemons and limes, moving furniture and stacking drinks in tubs of ice.

'I can't believe she trusts you with this house — and her stuff,' I say, looking around. 'Does your mum know many people are coming tonight?'

He sneers. 'Yeah, as if I told her I invited my whole Facebook friend list.'

I do a double-take. 'What?!' I ask. 'What do you mean you invited everyone on your Facebook list?'

'Pfft,' he replies. He cocks his head at me and calls out to the rest of the boys, 'When do you think Fleming got so sissy?'

'Round about the same time he let a girl beat him for the St Jerome Medal,' someone answers.

'She deserved it,' I call back. I'd been saying it endlessly — now I just needed to believe it. 'Seriously, Davo,' I try again, 'you said the other day that you were only having people from school and some friends from your soccer club. What happened?'

He shrugs. 'I thought I'd make it a little more exciting.'

'But what if hundreds of people show up?' I ask.

'You really need some booze in you, pronto,' he says.

I roll my eyes. 'I'm just trying to look out for you, man.'

'Don't,' he tells me bluntly. 'I'm sick of you babying me.'

'Ouch,' someone says behind him.

I shake my head. 'Maybe I just won't come tonight,' I say, walking away.

'That's not what I'm saying, Flemo. I want you to come — just as the guy you used to be, and not the fun-police guy that you've turned into,' he says. 'I want this party to be off the chain and memorable. Lots of music, dancing, laughs … the whole package.'

'Suit yourself,' I tell him, knowing that I'll inevitably be the one to help him clean up the mess afterwards.

———

It's only 9 p.m., and already the mess looks like it's going to need special tactics to clean. Maybe magic even.

People are milling about, inside and outside, and I swear I don't even recognise half of them.

'What do you think makes them act like that?' I ask Charlie, who has appeared next to me to give a searing look to a bunch of girls dirty dancing with each other, while some guys look on enthusiastically.

'Do you really want me to get into that now?' she asks. 'Besides, don't pretend you don't love it.'

I make an exasperated face. She just gives me her annoying smirk and asks me if I've seen Gillian.

'I assumed you guys would be coming together,' I reply.

'That doesn't answer my question,' she says, irritated.

'Sorry,' I tell her, rolling my eyes. 'I haven't seen her. Try outside.'

I wander over to the kitchen and find Lauren, David and Amanda mixing something in that high-powered, do-it-all blender that David's mum spent a grand on.

'What if it tastes so bad that no one can even drink it?' I hear Amanda ask. 'It'll ruin everything.'

'Let's hope it still gives us something worth filming,' Lauren replies, as David pulls off the lid and inspects the orange contents. 'Ryan!' she exclaims. 'I've been looking for you all night! Wanna dance? For old times' sake?'

'Sure,' I say, as she grabs my hand.

We head to the living room where the DJ is, and I ask her if I even want to know what the hell they were making.

'Think of it as a festive cocktail,' she says, smiling. 'A little something to make the night more exciting.'

'More exciting than this?' I ask, looking around.

'Sometimes I wonder what happened to that guy I had the hots for,' she says, shaking her head. 'Relax, will you? It's our last party before formal!'

She grinds up against me and I realise that I really must have changed. Once upon a time, I had the hots for her as well. Popular guy, popular girl — we were such a cliché. Everything she did and said was a tease, a turn-on. But after the accident, well, everything changed. And all of a sudden, I could see her for what she was: a shallow, selfish bully. Just like my best mate.

Charlie was right. Charlie. The girl who came out of nowhere and suddenly occupied my every thought. Even tonight, when I was supposed to be celebrating the end of my schooling life at a party I had excitedly planned with David for years.

A year ago, Charlie would have been the most annoying person I had ever come across. A self-righteous know-it-all who was the voice of reason for a generation that wanted everything but reason. A generation who took risks, rebelled, revelled, rioted and ran rampant. In real life and on the net.

But now, for me, the fog of high school was starting to clear. And Charlie was the reason; she was the reality I craved after living in a bubble for so long. With or without the soccer career, she was the mirror I needed to look into every single day of my future, to remind me to *be more*.

Which is why, when Lauren comes up close to me and plants a kiss on my lips, everything stands still. And despite the crowd swarming around me, I only see one face in the mess of tangled, sweaty, dancing bodies.

Charlie's. Betrayed, bruised, a little broken. In that instant, I was just another let-down in her age bracket, in this school, in the small circle that was her Sydney life.

Charlie

I hear the screen door bang shut again a few seconds after I'd slammed it myself, and I know he's coming after me.

I quicken my pace, heading further out into David's backyard, away from the party, away from everyone, especially Ryan.

'Charlie, wait up!' he yells. 'That wasn't what it looks like.'

'It doesn't matter what it looks like,' I yell back, not bothering to turn around. 'Because I don't care.'

'Well I do,' he says, catching up with me and grabbing me by the hand.

'Don't touch me,' I say, firmly. He lets go and I miss his hand instantly. But I can't put my heart on the line. Not again. 'Fool me once, shame on you. Fool me twice, then shame on me.'

'Just let me explain.'

'I'm sick of explanations!' I shout, blowing my fringe out of my face. 'She's always there — I don't want to be in the way.'

He looks at me like I am stupid. 'You're not in the way,' he says.

'That's funny,' I scoff. 'I always seem to be.'

He grabs my hand again. 'Well, you're not. Trust me.' .

He starts to say more, but I interrupt him.

'Do you know what it's like?' I ask. 'I don't always want to be judgemental. I don't want to be mature all the time. Sometimes I want to laugh and live and be just like everyone else my age. OK, so I don't want to take stupid selfies and, yes, I know about the political situation in the Middle East and the economic crisis in the EU and I can't stand Kim Kardashian, but I'm still a teenage girl, which sucks because everyone prefers Lauren Pappas over there and the smart girls like me have to wait until their thirties to rock.'

'I think you rock now,' he says quietly.

'Cut the crap, Ryan,' I tell him. 'You also think your stupid friends in there rock.'

'It's hard, OK?' he says. 'Some of my best memories ever involved those guys. I don't see you bugging Tammi about why she still hangs out with Lauren even though she's suddenly chummy with Gillian too. I don't have to question my loyalties for you.'

'Well, don't,' I say. 'And for your information, I have tried to speak to Tammi. Although I think, with her, even though she sees what they're doing, she's just too scared to do anything about it. But she'll come around.'

'But you won't be here to see it,' he says quietly. 'Because we're all a massive let-down in your life and the quicker you move, the quicker everything will get better. How can it not occur to you that you might have problems in Melbourne too? Maybe it's not the city you're in ... maybe it's just a part of getting older.'

'Why are you so hung up on me going back?' I ask, irritated.

'Because I like you,' he says, putting his arms out. 'I want you to see all the reasons why you should stay. A new baby, your new friends ...'

'What friends, Ryan?' I ask. 'Gill isn't even talking to me. The only reason why I came to this party was to make sure she was OK. But I must be the only person in this entire city with a decent bullshit detector, because while I was trying to talk to her, Lauren comes up and spins some stupid line about having a drink together to "patch things up", and Gill goes ahead and buys it.'

'Well, if you're so worried just go inside and talk to her…'

'I just told you she isn't talking to me!' I exclaim. 'You know my mum's a psych, right? Well, just like Gillian likes to record everything about our meetings, my mum likes to treat our serious D and Ms like one of her sessions, so she can see how much progress I make as we work through an issue.'

'Like one of her patients?' he asks, confused.

'Exactly,' I say, sitting down on the grass. 'Well, as you can imagine, I've had a lot to talk about this year, including everything Gillian was going through … and then Gillian comes over and snoops around Mum's desk and thinks the notes are going into Mum's thesis.'

'Ahh, shit,' he says.

'So you can imagine why I'm over it,' I say, picking at the grass. 'Just go inside, leave me alone — don't waste your time on me.'

'Everything else is a waste of time,' he says. He sits next to me. 'But not you. You make time stand still and life make sense.'

I open my eyes and roll onto my stomach, then turn to face him. He lies beside me. Our eyes meet, noses touch, lips come together.

'Seriously,' he whispers. 'Give me a chance.'

I pull away, but he's looking into my eyes so intently I feel a little scared.

'I've given you plenty of chances,' I say honestly.

'I'll probably need plenty more,' he replies. 'But I'll try. I'll stuff up and fix it and try again.'

I turn away. I can hear him sigh and I love the fact that I've flustered him, because I hate the way he flusters me.

'What's the point?' I ask. 'Seriously, what's the point?'

'This,' he says, turning my face to his and kissing me. It's different to the time at the dance-a-thon. More urgent, more serious — like there's more thought and feeling behind it. Ryan presses himself down against me. My hands reach out to the warmth under his shirt, and I wonder if he's going to pull them away.

He doesn't. He just continues kissing me, his lips never leaving mine. I realise I haven't paused to take a breath; it's like I need those lips more than I need air. And then one of his hands slides up the outside of my thigh, and I pull back.

'I don't want to lose my virginity on the floor of someone's backyard,' I tell him honestly.

'Who said anything about losing your virginity?' he says, smiling at me. 'You chicks are always jumping to conclusions.'

I give him a dirty look then smile, because I can't help it.

We sit and hold hands and just look up at the stars.

'I'll be good for you, you know,' he says. 'You're always so tense; I can balance you out.'

I shake my head, smirking. 'It's not my fault the world needs some hard truths.'

'It's not your job to save it,' he tells me. 'You'll kill yourself in the process.'

I give him a serious look. 'My mum's always saying the same thing,' I say finally. 'She kept telling me it was going to kill me, worrying about Gillian.'

'She's right, though; you came here looking for Gillian, and she's fine,' he tells me. 'She's here, having a good time. Maybe it was you just obsessing; you always want to correct things you have no control over. Idiots … and girls who want to dance in rap videos.'

I smile.

'I like your status updates,' he says, nudging me. 'But if you move to Melbourne, they won't be enough.'

'Are you asking me to stay?' I ask.

But he's stopped paying attention. He furrows his brow. 'The music's gone off …' he says, standing up.

We hear a shriek from inside the party and look back at the house.

'That's weird,' he says. 'Everyone's just hovering at the back door.'

He looks at me apologetically. 'Sorry, I better see if there's anything wrong. David's probably passed out somewhere now.'

'It's OK,' I say. 'I'll come with you.'

He leads me inside, where I can immediately tell the atmosphere of the party has changed.

We walk into the living room together, where we can only just make out a girl with long hair convulsing on the floor, completely encircled by people.

Shit! Ryan and I push through the crowd together, and it feels like time is standing still.

'Get away from her!' I scream to some dickhead from year 11, who is filming her on his iPhone. He starts to say something back, but Ryan grabs him by the shirt and shoves him at the wall, and then everyone is quiet. No one dares to say anything or move.

'Oh my God, it's Tam,' Ryan says, the shock draining his face of colour as we kneel beside her. 'Do you know first aid?'

I breathe heavily. Why did I have to be such a know-it-all? I can't run now. I look at Ryan, silently pleading with him to help me in any way he knows how.

'Open the windows!' I call out to no one in particular. 'Hurry!'

'She's not moving as much any more,' Ryan says, looking at me. 'Does that mean she's coming down?'

'Coming down or calming down?' I ask.

'I don't know, whatever,' he says. 'It's not like I know what's wrong with her.'

'Maybe it's just dehydration?' I say. 'Was anyone with her? Lauren? Anyone?'

'I dunno,' one girl says. 'She kind of staggered in here; she kept saying something about being ill upstairs.'

'Trust Tammi,' Ryan says. 'She's such a policeman's daughter that even if she was collapsing she would still want to clean up after herself.'

'Her dad's a cop?' I ask. 'God, this just keeps getting worse.'

Ryan and I both look at each other helplessly. The party, swarming with people only minutes before, has suddenly dwindled in number.

'We need to call an ambulance,' I say to Ryan after a moment. 'It doesn't look good.'

Lauren appears out of nowhere, and crouches down next to Tammi, her face ashen.

'Oh my God!' she exclaims. 'I was outside having a smoke. What happened to her?'

'We dunno,' Ryan says. 'Charlie says we need to call the ambos.'

'You can't!' she cries, looking at me. 'Her parents will kill her!'

'Really, Lauren?' I ask. 'How are they going to kill her if she's dead, because that's what we seem to be dealing with right now.'

I pull Tammi's hair from her face and start wiping away her sweat with my shirt, feeling my face reddening with the pressure of the situation.

A girl in the crowd asks if she should look up what to do on her phone, but someone tells her that we don't even know what's wrong with her. *Or we won't admit it*, I think.

'Ryan, call triple zero right now,' I tell him again. 'I know you guys might get in trouble, but she's in danger.'

But Ryan doesn't hear me. He's in some sort of daze, staring at an orange splodge on Tammi's shirt.

'Ryan,' I shout, just as my phone beeps. A text from Stan.

Mum's in labour. She reckons it's going to be a quick one, just like yours. Catch a cab to Royal Prince Alfred, she wants you there more than she wants me.

'Fuck,' I say out loud. Talk about the worst timing ever. 'Someone call the ambulance!'

But no one moves. They just stand around like statues. I pull out my phone and dial triple zero, stuttering as I talk to the operator.

'Oh, the address?' I ask, panicking. I spot Lauren in the small crowd and shove the phone at her. 'Here, you tell her the address, or find David.'

She doesn't argue and gives out the details of David's address.

When she hangs up, Ryan is looking at her sternly, hands at his temples.

'Lauren,' I hear him ask as the sound of sirens gets louder. 'That cocktail that you were making: what exactly did you put in it?'

Matty

Matty, it's Ryan. Tammi's sick at the RPA. Have you seen Gillian? I can't find her anywhere. Call me.

I stare at my phone for what seems like ages, then the reality of what it says hits me and I start to panic. I wrestle my way through the crowd and storm outside.

'Leaving already, Matty?' the bouncer asks. 'That's unlike you. Didn't like this band's sound?'

'No, they were great,' I say, flustered. 'There's just an emergency with some friends. I, ahh … need to make a call.'

I dial Ryan's number and he picks up straight away.

'Thank God,' he says. 'Do you know where she is? Apparently she was at the party too, she was with Tammi for most of the night, and now Tammi's in an ambulance on the way to RPA and I don't know what's going on.'

'She isn't with me,' I say quickly. 'I'm at a gig. Last I heard she was heading there with Charlie.'

'No,' he informs me, 'they had a fight. And Charlie left after the ambos came. She texted me saying her mum's in labour and she had to go be with her.'

'I'm sure everything's OK,' I tell him. 'It has to be, right?'

'I don't know any more, Matty,' he says. 'I wish I did.'

'Did you actually see Gillian tonight?'

'No,' he admits, and I can hear the strain in his voice.

'OK, let's not freak out,' I tell him. 'Maybe she left early. Did you check everywhere?'

'Yeah, I think so,' he says, puffing. 'I just tried the yard again.'

'OK, while you keep looking, tell me what happened with Tammi. How did you find her?'

'I was outside, and I heard a scream,' he explains. 'So I went in, and she was just lying there, surrounded. Maybe she had too much to drink? I dunno … She'd been drinking some of Lauren's "special cocktail" — but there was nothing bizarre in Tammi's drink, Lauren said she made enough for a few people who all drank it. And then Tammi came into the room, said something about being ill upstairs, and just collapsed.'

'So did you check upstairs?'

He goes quiet for a moment. 'Oh my God. She wasn't saying she'd been *ill* upstairs,' he says, dread in his voice. 'She was saying *Gill's* upstairs.'

And then my battery goes flat.

I don't know how it happens, but the bouncer puts me in a cab, gives the cabbie a fifty-dollar note, and the next thing I know I'm storming through the emergency ward of RPA. I don't even know if Gillian's there, so when I smash against the reception desk and say her name, I'm hoping I've just blown out the situation in my mind; that Gillian just got bored and left the party early.

But the receptionist nods and my worst fears are confirmed. She has just been admitted.

I ask the receptionist if I can see her.

'Are you immediate family?' she asks.

'No,' I say. 'But I'm the one who cares the most.'

She gives me a sympathetic smile. 'Sorry, immediate family only.'

'I just need to know she's OK,' I beg.

'I'm sorry, sweetie,' she says. 'Like I said, immediate family only.'

But her parents don't care, I think.

'And Tammi Kapsalis?' I ask, feeling weird about using her full name. 'Tamara, sorry.'

'Yes, she arrived a while ago. She's with the doctors. I can't tell you any more.'

I sigh, defeated, then walk over and take a seat.

'You shouldn't stay here,' she calls out to me. 'It's 1 a.m.'

'Trust me, I'm all she has,' I tell her.

She shrugs and gets on with her job. A few minutes later, she comes up to me with a Post-it.

'Put your name and number here,' she says. 'Home and mobile. I'll do what I can.'

'If it's all the same,' I say, 'I'm just gonna stay here. My mobile's dead anyway.'

She smiles politely and walks away, and I slump back into my chair.

Poor Gillian. We all thought it couldn't get any worse after the webcam hacking; God knows what has happened to her now. And Tammi! How did she get involved? I grab my phone to text Ryan, to ask more questions — and then I curse myself for using it to record snippets of the band showcase at the bar.

I start feeling claustrophobic, so I head outside for some fresh air. But I can't escape the feeling of the world closing in. I sit next to a man on a bench, and try to slow my breathing, but I can't. It just gets more rapid.

'You OK, kid?' the man asks, with the faint trace of a foreign accent. 'You're breathing like my wife during one of her contractions.'

I shake my head, my eyes welling up with tears. 'Something's happened to two of my really good friends,' I tell him. 'And they won't tell me anything because I'm not family.'

He nods sympathetically and a jolt goes through my body when his eyes lock on mine. For a second I feel like I've seen him before, in a distant dream. But it's probably just my shock talking.

'Sometimes it's better,' he says. 'Not seeing them. My wife convinced me she doesn't want me there at the birth. Too much happening, you know?'

I nod, but my friend's not giving birth. She's … something else.

A policeman appears before me. 'Are you Matthew Fullerton?'

I nod quietly.

'I'm Tamara Kapsalis' father, Nick,' he says, extending a hand. 'Were you at this party my daughter was at?'

'No, sir,' I tell him.

'So you don't know what she's had to eat or drink tonight?'

'No, sir,' I say again.

He sighs. 'Has anyone in your grade ever sold or taken synthetic substances?'

'As in party pills?' I ask.

He nods.

'Not that I know of,' I say honestly. 'But I was never part of Tammi's crowd.'

He grunts. 'She's having her stomach pumped,' he says. 'You kids have so much at your disposal, but you're not very bright. What about the other girl. The politician's daughter?'

'She's my best friend,' I say in a hushed tone.

'That's why you're here?' he asks.

'She means a lot to me,' I say. 'They both do.'

'It could be a while,' he says. 'I'll ring someone to come get you. You shouldn't be here alone.'

I watch him walk away, then bury my head in my hands.

The stranger hasn't moved, and I find his presence oddly comforting.

A phone beeps. His, not mine.

'A girl,' he says, leaping up. 'I have a daughter!'

'Congratulations,' I say, giving him a half-smile through my sadness.

He shakes his head, smiling. 'Life is a wonderful thing,' he says.

A few minutes later, Charlie leaps outside and into his arms. She doesn't notice me.

'A girl!' she says, excitedly, embracing him. 'She says she can't pick a name.'

'Shall I go up?' he asks earnestly.

'Sorry, Stan, she wants to get cleaned up first.'

'Of course,' he says, deflated.

I stand up and she finally sees me.

'Oh my God, Matty!' she exclaims. 'Ryan's not replying. Is this where they brought Tammi?'

'Yes, but we don't know anything yet,' I tell her. 'About her or Gillian.'

'Gillian?' she asks, confused. 'What are you talking about? Gillian was fine.'

We look at other, bewildered, as if we're communicating in two different languages.

'She was upstairs, I think she might have been unconscious …' I say.

'Unconscious?' she whispers, stunned. 'For how long?'

'I don't know,' I tell her. 'Ryan said he found her, like, forty minutes ago.'

She gasps. 'She must've been out for ages then …'

'You two know each other?' the man asks. We both nod through our shock.

'I'm sorry, Chi,' he says. 'I guess that means they were your friends too. I'll be right back. I'm just going to ring your aunty.'

We both watch him walk off.

'Charlie,' I say after a moment, 'I thought you guys were going to the party together?'

She bites her lip. 'We had a fight,' she says, sighing. 'Gill thought I was giving my mum info about her for Mum's thesis. But I've been talking to Mum about *everything*, just as a way to deal with it. I need help too, you know.'

'Because you've been really hung up on the trolling and everything — trust me, I know,' I say.

'Exactly,' she says, her eyes watering. 'But Gillian just stormed out of my house. So I followed her … and she wouldn't talk to me. She wanted to have a drink with Lauren instead.'

I swallow hard, trying to keep my emotions down.

'Let's talk about something else,' she says. 'It could be all fine, right?'

I nod, unconvinced, but I feel like I owe it to her. I feel like I've ruined a happy moment by being here.

'So … is that Stan?' I ask. 'He has an accent.'

'He was a Polish exchange student at our school once,' she says. 'Isn't that cute? His real name is Stanislav Rezynoliki, but he changed it to Reynolds because no one could spell "Rezynoliki". He went to Sydney Uni too, which is why he's bugging me to go there.'

A sudden shiver comes over my body and she notices it.

'He went to our school?' I ask.

'Yeah, why? Why are you acting weird?'

I realise I'm breathing extremely fast again.

'Matty, you're scaring me. Sit down,' she says, dragging me to the bench. I sit down and put my head between my knees. 'What's wrong?'

'I just have this weird feeling,' I tell her.

'Should I go get a doctor?' she asks.

I shake my head and look up, noticing a figure coming towards me. As she comes into full view, she looks tired, worn, more aged than ever, but so beautiful at the same time.

'Mum!' I say, embracing her. 'What are *you* doing here? Are you OK?'

'The cops said you needed me,' she says, sadly. 'I figured it's about time I stopped failing you. Are your friends OK?'

I start to reply, but a stunned look comes over her face as her eyes are trained on something behind me. I follow her line of vision to Stan.

And then my mother falls to the floor.

She comes to on a chair outside one of the wards.

'You fainted again,' I tell her, grabbing her hand. 'Here, have some water.'

She doesn't look at me.

'This Stan guy,' I say. 'Did you run into him at the supermarket?'

'Matthew, don't,' she says. 'I'm tired.'

'So am I, Mum,' I exclaim. 'I'm sick of being in the dark. I deserve to know.'

'And so do I,' Stan says, emerging from around the corner.

'What were you doing, hiding there?' she asks him.

I stand to attention — confused, scared, uncertain. He looks at me for a moment, then at her.

'I had to see for certain if it was you,' he says quietly. 'You're still so beautiful, it's like you haven't changed.'

She grunts.

'But obviously you're still good at keeping your cards close to your chest.'

Her face reddens, and her eyes fill with tears. I drop her hand and wipe my own on my pants. I'm so sweaty, and my heart is beating loudly in my chest.

'We used to be married,' Mum says, turning to me.

'And pregnant,' Stan adds.

'Jellybean,' I say, filling in the puzzle.

Stan raises his eyebrows. 'He knows?'

'No,' I correct him. 'I've been snooping.'

'So where's Jellybean now?' I ask.

'We killed him,' he whispers.

'Stan, don't start that again,' she says. 'Please.'

'Start what, Anna? It devastated you, but you went through with it anyway. You couldn't care for a baby with Down's syndrome. Or you could, but you just let the doctors bully you into believing you couldn't.'

I look at her, shrinking down into her seat.

'I didn't know it would hurt so much,' she says.

'You forget how well I knew you,' he says, as he reaches for her hand. She looks at him sadly. 'How much I fought to be with you. Despite our differences. We could have done it.'

'Well, why didn't we?' she asks.

'Because you said it was your body, your choice ... whatever the line was,' he points out. 'I had to respect you.'

'But you couldn't respect her enough to stay?' I say, finding my voice. For her, for me, for Jellybean.

'He stayed, he stayed,' she says, giving him a half-smile. 'For ages. And for months I would wait, see if I was given another chance. I bought ovulation kits and made him shelve his business plans — I was desperate to fall pregnant again.'

'And then one day I told you I couldn't take it any more,' he admits, swallowing. 'And I left.'

'I found out three weeks after you walked out,' she says sorrowfully.

'And you didn't think I deserved to know?' he asks, hotly.

'You were so adamant,' she says defensively. 'You were convinced we had done something so bad that it would never happen for us again. And you never called me.'

'You could have told my lawyer!'

'I was done!' she says. 'Just like you said you were. I left you free to concentrate on your business, build another life. You had already sacrificed so much for me.'

'I was so happy fifteen minutes ago,' he says, looking at her. 'I thought I had left you in the past. But now you're back, wrecking my present.'

He shakes his head and starts to walk away.

'Wait,' I say. 'What about me?'

He stops for a moment and looks at me sadly. 'Your mother made a decision for her family,' he says, cocking his head towards her. 'And I have another family now. One that wants me around.'

He disappears as quickly as he came into my life, and I shrink to the floor, gasping for air, alone again.

Tammi

Tammi Kap is sorry.

The smell hits me first and I know I'm in a hospital before I even open my eyes. When I do, my fear is realised: Dad is with me, sitting in a chair on the other side of the room.

'Thank God,' he says, exhaling. 'Your mum and I have been worried sick.'

'So how much trouble am I in?' I ask.

'Do you really want to know?' he replies, standing up.

'Well, if I'm going to be stuck here for a while yet, I might as well have something to mull over,' I say bitterly.

'Hey,' my father roars, coming over to me, 'don't you dare take that tone with me. I'm not the one who put you here. What were you thinking, Tamara? Honestly, what went through your head?'

'Let's say, hypothetically, you really wanted to know what "went through my head",' I say. 'I promise you that you wouldn't be able to handle it.'

For a moment, he's silent. Then he says, 'Do you know what it's like for me? I go out and police the meanest, grittiest people and parts of this city, yet I have no control over my daughter. Do you know how humiliating that is? Do you know what it was like, telling people at the station my daughter had to have her stomach pumped because she was taking drugs at a party? I had to be the father that I have felt sorry for countless times over the years; the father who discovers their kid has done some stupid thing and not come out of it the same. Or not come out of it at all.'

'Look at me, Daddy — I'm still the same,' I say.

He walks across to the door. 'Not to me you're not,' he says, before leaving.

I must doze off because when I open my eyes again, he's back where he was. In the chair near my bed. My protector. Guardian of my life. I don't know if I should love or hate him for it. I'll probably never know.

'I'm sorry, Dad,' I say quietly. 'Really. I know I stuffed up.'

'I know teenagers, Tammi. I know they want to experiment. I know you're a good kid, but you made a foolish choice. A choice that could have cost you your life.'

'I know, but I thought I was being careful,' I point out.

'Careful how?' he asks.

'I took a tiny bit of the pill. A really small dose. I didn't drink, and I stayed with friends.'

He scoffs. 'Tammi, when you say you stayed with "friends", who exactly are you referring to? Half of the party were off their faces when the cops arrived.'

'Cops? At David's house?'

'How do you think you got here, Tamara?' he asks, bitterly. 'Cops and paramedics. Thank God.'

'Come on, Dad,' I beg. 'You were young once. Plus it's not like I took anything illegal.'

'Tammi, you took a synthetic drug!' he exclaims. 'They're sometimes worse than the ecstasies and the heroins and the meths. They haven't been around long enough for us to know their dangers.'

Woah. 'I had no idea,' I say. 'I was told they were herbal.'

He sits on the edge of the bed and holds my hand. 'Did you give them to your friend?' he asks.

'Yeah, why?' I ask.

'She hasn't woken up yet,' he says. 'And she might not.'

'We had the same amount,' I say, my voice hoarse. 'So how come I'm awake and she's not?'

'I'm not sure,' he says, getting up. 'Other people might take the same thing and be OK. Doesn't make it worth the risk.'

I go quiet and bite my lip.

'That orange drink your friend Lauren made you? Gillian's was spiked,' he explains, pacing my bedside. 'I only know because Lauren told me. Apparently it was supposed to be part of some joke. They wanted to film her doing something stupid and play the video at the formal. I don't get your generation, in all honesty.'

'We're not all the way you think we are,' I whisper.

He shrugs and leaves the room.

When he returns, it takes a lot of effort for me to try to sit up.

'Any news?' I ask.

'The doctors say it was the combination of alcohol, that drug you gave her and whatever they used to spike that drink that caused her vitals to shut down. I'm sorry, honey, but she didn't make it.'

I start to cry silent tears that turn into sobs, and then howls. Howls that I'm sure they can hear in the next ward. I cry for what seems like ages — until the sun fades into blackness, until my father leaves. For hours and hours, I cry for her lost youth, and for my own, which took hers away, until I have no tears left to weep.

———

The next day, I'm allowed to go home. There are flowers all over the house. I cut every single flower off its stem one by one and burn them in the backyard. Mum doesn't say anything when she comes home and sees my destructive art.

Two days later, Ryan, Charlie and Matty come to visit.

I cry as soon as they walk into my room. Every single one of them looks haggard, gaunt.

'I'm sorry,' I whisper.

'Hey, it's not your fault,' Matty says, while Charlie sits next to me and rubs my arm.

'I gave her the pill,' I tell them. 'It *is* my fault.'

'No, because if she just had the pill she might have recovered, like you did,' Ryan says. 'You didn't know about the prank.'

'And, what, now her trolls get away with it?' Matty asks.

We all go quiet.

'Do you think they will even learn?' Charlie says bitterly.

Ryan doesn't say anything, and neither do I. I can't defend them any more.

'It could've been any of us,' Matty says, sullen. 'How many of us really think about what we're doing when we're trying to play a joke or prove a point?'

'I bet they don't think that way,' Charlie says. 'They'll still refuse to see it. Their part in all of this.'

'I don't know,' Ryan says, shrugging. 'I can't speak for David, but Lauren — well, let's just say she's learnt her lesson.'

Charlie rolls her eyes. 'Too little, too late, don't you think?' she says bitterly.

They look at each other for a moment and she shakes her head, then looks away. He has the pained expression of a person that can never do anything right.

'Come on, guys,' Matty says quietly, his deep voice cutting through the tension. 'Gillian wouldn't want this. Any of it.'

I nod and look down at my lap. 'She cared about this yearbook so much. She'd want us to stay friends.'

'And she'd want us to be there for Sammy,' Matty adds. 'Can't we focus on that?'

'Poor Sammy,' Charlie says, rubbing her temples. 'Alone in that house with those parents. I was so focused on hating Lauren that I forgot about him. How's he doing?'

'Better than his parents, I think,' Matty says. 'Neither of them are handling it well, Gillian's mum especially. She kind of looks like shit.'

'Shame it took all of this for everyone to wake up,' Charlie says. 'What a fucked up world we live in.'

Everyone goes quiet, and I realise that their efforts to make me feel better have been for nothing.

Tears well up in my eyes again. 'Distract me,' I say, my voice cracking. 'Please. Tell me something else.'

'Well, Charlie's my sister,' Matty says quietly.

'Huh?' I ask, my head shooting up.

'Turns out Charlie's stepdad, Stan, is my dad,' he says. 'He and my mum were married once. She fell pregnant, but they found out at twenty weeks that the baby had Down's syndrome, so she had the baby aborted. And then she couldn't fall pregnant for ages, so he left. By the time he was out of her life, a pregnancy test came back positive, and that was me. He never found out.'

'Wow,' I tell him. 'Is this why she's been a little down?'

'Well, she actually saw him a year ago or so. He was shopping with Charlie's mum, and she panicked. And apparently I made the situation worse by introducing her to Sammy at work that day.'

'But why would the abortion thing come up seventeen years later?' Ryan asks.

'Some women feel immediate relief, others make peace with it really quickly, and then there are some whose grief hits years, even decades later,' Charlie says. 'I think seeing Stan and Sammy after so many years in the one day was just the equivalent of a bomb going off in her system.'

'That's scary,' Ryan says. 'You never know what someone is hiding.'

We go silent.

A while later, Ryan and Charlie leave. Matty stays behind.

'Are they a couple now?' I ask, gesturing to the door after they've walked out. Matty shrugs, but a hint of a smile appears on his face.

'Well, they're not *not* a couple, if you know what I mean,' he says. 'They go everywhere together, she bosses him around, and he looks like he's won the lottery when she does, even though they pretend to fight about it.'

'So not everything has changed.'

Matty chuckles and moves from the chair to the edge of the bed. 'I think they're afraid to come out and admit they're together; Charlie isn't even sure whether she's moving yet …'

He trails off. It's quiet for a moment, and I can tell he has something on his mind. Thankfully, I don't have to pry.

'Was Gillian happy?' he asks. 'Before it all …'

I swallow, then nod. 'She was mad at Charlie,' I say. 'But when she got to the party she just wanted to forget about it and enjoy herself. We were hanging out together; she was having a good time. She believed Lauren was really trying to patch things up. She was … optimistic.'

'And you really didn't know the drink was spiked?' he asks. 'Sorry — I'm just trying to make sense of it all.'

'No, Matty,' I say quietly. 'I promise I didn't. But I had the pills. I thought they were herbal.'

'She didn't have to take it, though,' he whispers. 'Please don't blame yourself.'

He looks at his watch and tells me he has to go. Despite their shaky meeting, Stan has agreed to let him meet his new half-sister today.

'I'm happy for you,' I say when he tells me.

'Happy,' he says, biting his lip. 'I think that's a foreign concept to us now.'

I watch him leave, then curl up into a ball and wipe a tear away.

Hours later, I'm thinking about Ryan's words. *You never know what someone is hiding*, he'd said. And suddenly I'm not just upset, but enraged.

Everything about Mike makes sense: the enigmatic personality, hatred of the police, the two phones.

I hop out of bed and slip on my shoes, determined to have it out with him. After all, I know where to find him — every drug runner has a zone or a 'hood'. Isn't that why he was always hanging around at the park?

I'm halfway down the hall when I realise I have nothing to fight with.

Dad once said to me: 'Arm yourself with evidence, smarts and strategy to get the outcome that you want.' But right now, I have none of these things. And taking down one runner isn't going to get me the outcome that I want. If I want to make a real difference — to prevent another episode like the one I have survived, and which many others have not — I have to play the big game.

I'd watched every *CSI*, every true-crime and forensics show I could get my hands on. But I was no longer content to be on the outside looking in. I was no longer content with being called too frail or feminine. But most of all, I was no longer content to be fighting my true calling.

I was going to change my university preferences, and enrol in a Bachelor of Policing.

Gillian's story had reached its horribly sad conclusion, but maybe I could someday rewrite someone else's.

RYAN

Ryan Fleming Lost.

No one answers their phone any more, I think, hanging up. Everyone's probably still in shock, reliving that night. So I send out a group text message:

I think we need to add some sort of postscript/note to the end of the yearbook. If you want to help me write it, come to mine at 6 p.m.

No one replies.

———

At about 7 p.m., when I've convinced myself I'll be writing it alone, they turn up. One by one, like ghosts from a life I lived long ago, they wander through my house to the back veranda, where I now spend my days sitting and staring out into a sky that was once filled with more promise than pain.

We write without laughing, or joking, or fighting. We just spill it all out. And then Matty saves it to a USB stick that he tucks into his pocket, and reminds us that the yearbook goes to the printer tomorrow.

Ryan

We exhale — a big, collective sigh of struggle and sorrow.

One week later, I get an email telling me that the yearbooks will be delivered to our formal venue that afternoon, the day before the big night. I take the car to greet it, like it's a long-lost friend I'm desperate to see. And when I open the first box, pick up a book and flip through it, everything just comes flooding back: forty weeks of teenage angst, thirteen missed soccer games, eleven assignments, seven stressful HSC exams, three late-round university applications and no St Jerome Medal.

Oh, and one epic task that cemented a now-unbreakable bond between five strangers who became four friends and a memory.

The yearbook committee had started out as a random bunch of people who walked the same halls, sat the same exams, shared the ordinary school experiences that became extraordinary as we learnt to look beyond one another's façade, Facebook profile picture, group of friends. Who knew that after all those meetings, the five of us would not only accomplish what we set out to do, but become better people just by knowing and learning from each other?

Charlie: the feisty snob with a big heart, who taught us all not to accept the limitations placed upon our lives.

Tammi: the girl who started out as a victim, but who eventually taught us to follow your gut and not let anyone else get in the way of what you want.

Matty: the guy who single-handedly kept his mum afloat, and defied all the negative stereotypes about our generation, and never said a word about it.

And Gillian: the girl who had so little love and still gave better than she got.

I've been in a lot of teams in my lifetime: scout teams, soccer teams, debating teams, track teams. But this team is the one that has found a permanent place in my heart. If I ever forget how to be a good guy and how to treat my fellow man, then I know that their experiences will remind me.

As we evolve from children to adults, our outlooks change. Goal posts shift, strategies are altered, and the game gets a lot more demanding than we ever imagined it could be. And life suddenly becomes as unpredictable as a sand dune — one wrong choice and everything falls apart, drags you under.

Mrs H once said that we should leave the world better than when we entered it. At the time, I didn't understand what she meant. But this year, in Studies of Religion, I learnt about the apostle Paul, who once wrote that we could have great knowledge and a faith that could move mountains, but if we didn't have love, then we were nothing. And if we speak without love, then what we say is just noise. Sure, his exact words were 'booming gongs and clanging cymbals', but it's all noise, white noise.

St Paul could probably say a lot about noise. And faith that could move mountains. In fact, he was so dedicated to his Jewish faith that he made a mission of stoning Christians, until God Himself asked him what the go was with all the persecution, and he stopped letting the noise in his head affect the love in his heart.

That's the thing about choices. They're an act of knowledge, of faith, of love. It's how we make them that sets us apart, because every single day, worlds are colliding, and our choices shape so much more than just our own story. And if we want to change this world for the better, then we must be the best possible version of ourselves, because who we are in each moment is our gift to the universe. This is what the present is: when the sum of one person's past meets a world's collective future.

I've spent so much of my high-school life listening to noise. And maybe there'll more of it in my future. But, like St Paul, I've had a little change of heart. He owed his to the voice of God, but I owe mine to the yearbook committee. And I'm so thankful.

Notes from the Wish Dish

Hey Tammi,

I thought you were a massive doormat when I met you. I hate girls who are like that because, to me, they have not made anything of the rights they have been granted by women who protested and burnt bras and fought for us. You always seemed so afraid to me. Afraid of David, afraid of Lauren, afraid of disappointing everyone. Like you didn't see the bigger picture. But over the last few months, I really got to see that you are not a doormat. You were just different to me. It must have been hard realising that the guy you liked for ages wasn't the person that you thought, and I bet it takes real character to still accept a person who has a lot of flaws. The thing about me is that I always go in guns blazing. I fight first, talk later. But you let people get things off their chest, be themselves and you still do your own thing on the downlow. You are the embodiment of that saying 'live and let live'. I think that is a great quality to have, and I think the way that you give everyone the benefit of the doubt —

and the calm way you approach everything — will make you an awesome police officer. Good luck in the HSC.

Charlie

PS Just quietly, I think in a few years' time you will look back and be glad you were the one to break it off with a guy who goes by DeLooka instead of DeLuca on the net. Trust me.

———

Charlie,

I didn't have friends when I started here two years ago. My friends were rhythms and beats and melodies. But even though I was sort of alone, I was still happy. Then when I started year 12, cracks started appearing. And suddenly the music wasn't enough to keep me going.

And then this chick from Melbourne with an attitude and another chick who I thought was just a prissy pollie's kid show up and start asking favours of me, and changed everything. These two girls were like salt and pepper — so different, but they each had so much flavour. You were feisty and in control and Gillian was happy-go-lucky (or whatever the expression is). You two have balanced everything out for me, and I finally feel like I have some support, even though I have no solid answers about anything. I am so thankful to you both for holding me up. Life just tastes so much better with you guys around.

Keep rocking,

Matty

PS: Damn, I was supposed to wish you good luck in the HSC as well. But I don't think you need it. The HSC should be afraid of you killing it. I know you will.

PPS: Please stay here. I know I'm not the only guy who thinks you should ;)

————

Gillian,

Here's a good-luck note for your HSC! I have been following your blog and I am amazed at how much it has grown. It's like, WOW, you took something so basic that we all use (the internet) and basically started a business on it. You will make a great business woman one day.

Also, while I am writing this, I want to say I'm sorry about everything. I know we stuffed up. We were trying to be your friends when Sylvana moved away, but then Lauren got so upset about that night, and when she gets an idea in her head …

You know what? I shouldn't blame everything on her. I have a role to play in this as well. But I am trying. I have never been brave. It's funny, because I really want to be a police officer. But I was never brave enough to stand up to Lauren, or David, or my dad. And it's strange because these are the people I love more than anything — and I should be able to be honest with them. Maybe that's why I can be such a moll to complete strangers, or people who are not close to me, like you.

Anyway, I can't stop thinking about that night at the party. You were the first person in my life to tell me that I should be loved unconditionally, and you made me realise that every person who meant something to me had conditions for how I should be. I was just living up to someone else's ideals.

But that's not me any more; I am going to be different. I will still love those people, but I won't let them walk over me. Thank you for teaching me more than any textbook ever could. David will probably have a massive party when the HSC is over (he has been talking about it for ages *rolls eyes*). You should definitely come with Matty and Charlie, and this time I will be proud to call you guys friends.

From Tammi

To Matty,

It feels weird writing a note to a guy. Especially if you've hardly ever spoken to him. But I thought this was a cool idea and I am kind of surprised at how the whole yearbook thing turned out, so I don't really mind doing it. I guess I just wanted to say I'm sorry I never really got to know you over the last two years. As the school captain I should have made you feel more welcome, done more beyond the school tour I gave you on your first day, the one that Mrs H made me do. I guess I always thought you were a bit of a loner. You hung out by yourself all the time, with your headphones on, and when the teachers didn't notice you had that black hoodie on top of your blazer, which made me (and a lot of other people) think you were strange. Weren't you ever hot in there?

But now I see you were just ... above it all. And, dude, I really like that about you. I like that you do your own thing, and don't care what anyone thinks. You just seem to see beyond everything ... and stay away from drama. And the photos you've been taking for the yearbook have been pretty cool too.

Anyway, I know you don't want to go to uni, but I really want to wish you the best for the HSC. The last year has taught me that our biggest dreams need back-up plans, so study hard, in case the music thing doesn't pan out. But I bet it will, because I have never met anyone more hard-working. I bet you will go on to manage some global superstars. If you ever meet Taylor Swift, can you call me? It would be good to see her legs in real life.

From Ryan

Dear Ryan,

I know it probably didn't feel like it this year, but I think you did good. Sure, the soccer thing is still uncertain at the moment, but I hope you learnt something about yourself this year. And I hope it is the same thing that I learnt about you. You see, so many people in the grade thought you got school captain because you were popular and smart and good at sports, and we didn't think you deserved it. You just stayed in your bubble with your (now ex-) girlfriend and your crew. You hardly spoke to any of us.

But over the last year, I was really impressed with you and the way you handled your friends. I know you can't change people, but I could see that you were trying to help them to see the light. Good on you for trying, but people grow up in their own time.

Anyway, I just wanted to tell you that I think you are an amazing leader. If you think back to our first meetings, you had a bunch of people who either hated each other's guts or had never even spoken to each other, that you had to nudge into doing tasks they didn't want to do. And yet you never let any of us get out of the work, and we ended up making a pretty good yearbook, one that I am super proud of. I can't wait to see it in print. What I am trying to say is that you are a good leader. One who really gets in the thick of it. I honestly admire that about you, and I can see why Coach still wanted you to go to soccer games and stuff. You have that quality that makes people listen, learn and want to do better. Just because you can't kick goals, doesn't mean you won't motivate people to kick theirs. I bet that will be just as rewarding, and I wish you all the best for the HSC, and for your future.

From Gillian ☺

PS Sorry I wrote a lot. All that blogging practice!

Acknowledgements

I'm so blessed to be able to do what I love and call it work, but I am even more blessed because of the stellar support system that has made this book a reality.

Thank you —

Selwa Anthony and Drew Keys, for the encouragement and guidance.

My team at HarperCollins Australia: Chren Byng, my wonderfully creative and clever publisher; the beautiful Cristina Cappelluto; and my patient and adept editor Rachel Dennis who wrangled the book into its current state. Thanks also to Bianca Fazzalaro, Amanda Diaz, Tim Miller, Gemma Fahy, Libby Volke and Graeme Jones. A special note for Jacqui Barton, for her ongoing efforts at taking my books into high schools, and to Stephanie Spartels for her gorgeous work on both the outside and inside of the book. I still adore the orange cover.

Melina Marchetta, for being an inspiration, and for offering her time, energy and feedback at every corner.

My biggest champions: my parents, siblings and extended Lebanese family. And to those that encouraged me across continents, cities and social networks, in particular Ahmed Mahmoud, Rachel Hills, Tammi Ireland, Fiona MacDonald, Scarlett Harris, Gabby Tozer, Nathan Azzi, Danielle Binks and Tara Eglington.

My sisters: Marie-Claire for being my right hand in everything I do, and Josephine for being an anti-ageing cream for my brain. Josie, I really appreciate how much time you invested in helping me to fine-tune this story.

Special mention to my mother-in-law, Glenda Anderssen, for her help with my baby at many a turn; and to my father-in-law, David Christie, and his partner, Christine Downing, for reading everything I write with great (and much appreciated) enthusiasm. And to Sarah Tarca from Girlfriend magazine for her constant support in all my writing endeavours.

To the surprise cheerleaders of the #loveozya community: school teachers, writers' festivals, media outlets, book stores, book bloggers and social media fans who have supported my author adventure so far. Thanks for all the love.

Finally, to my great loves Jam and Crumpet. James and Alissar, you bring so much love, joy and anxiety to my life, and are the sweetest blessings. I hope I make you proud.

About the author

Sarah Ayoub is a freelance journalist based in Sydney, Australia. Her work has appeared in various print and online publications, including *Marie-Claire, Madison, Cosmopolitan, House & Garden, Sunday Style, The Guardian, Cleo, Shop Til You Drop, Frankie, Yen, Girlfriend* and more. She has taught Journalism at the University of Notre Dame and spoken at numerous industry events with the Emerging Writers' Festival, NSW Writers' Centre, the Walkley Foundation, Vibewire and more.

She is the author of *Hate Is Such a Strong Word* and regularly runs writing workshops at Sydney high schools.

To find out more about Sarah, follow her on:

Facebook: www.facebook.com/bysarahayoub
Twitter, Instagram and Snapchat: @bysarahayoub

HATE IS SUCH A STRONG WORD

'Finally a book that
tackles the big issues –
and the ones all girls
face (frizzy hair, formal
dates, and what to do
about *that* boy).'
**Sarah Tarca,
Editor of *Girlfriend***

SARAH AYOUB

Seventeen-year-old Sophie hates Monday mornings, socks worn with sandals, and having to strategise like she's a battle sergeant every time she asks her parents if she can go out. But she especially hates being stereotyped because she's Lebanese.

When New Guy, Shehadie Goldsmith, is alienated at her Lebanese school because his dad's Australian, she hates the way it makes her feel.

Like she's just as prejudiced as everyone else.

Like she could make a difference if she stopped pretending she's invisible.

Like the attraction between them might be too strong to fight …

But hate is such a strong word … Can Sophie find the strength to speak out — even if it means going against everything she's been brought up to believe?

A brilliant debut novel about identity, love, culture and finding your place.

Turn the page for a short extract from
Hate Is Such a Strong Word …

HATE IS SUCH A STRONG WORD

I take my phone out onto the veranda, where I can watch the sun set over Bankstown, the area I've lived in since I was born. Although it's still daylight, boys are setting off illegal fireworks despite their mothers' fearful warnings. Older girls are heading out to parties, all dressed up, while their fathers lament their daughters' short childhoods and even shorter skirts. And I lament the fact that I won't be attending the globe's biggest party tonight – even in the limited way I've come to expect as a social nobody.

I can't decide which is worse: being sick of always missing out, or constantly having to explain why I'm missing out, which, trust me, is just as humiliating.

I call my best friend, Dora Maloor, to deliver the verdict.

'Nawwwww,' she wails. 'Why does he always limit your socialising to people who share your DNA?'

'I dunno,' I mumble, trying to keep myself from crying. I'm ashamed to admit that I care so much, even to her. 'Have fun on my behalf.'

'I'm sick of having fun on your behalf, Skaz,' she says. 'You've got an unhealthy attitude for a seventeen-year-old. You need to build up the courage to express yourself. It's the only way you're going to have the fulfilling life experience you subconsciously desire.'

I roll my eyes. 'What new-age hoo-ha have you been reading? That doesn't even make any sense.'

'Well, neither does a seventeen-year-old who can't stand up to her father.'

'Seriously, what am I supposed to do?'

'Um, stand up for your right to enjoy your youth,' she says, stating the obvious. 'His Stone Age 1950s Lebanese village rules have got to go. What's the reason this time? He's usually okay with you coming over.'

'One of their friends is holding a dinner at his restaurant tonight. Mum doesn't really want to go, but she is, so I have to babysit.'

'A dinner beats the little backyard soirée that my brother and sister are throwing. Although at least at my house there'll be hot boys to perve at, even if my brother's friends smile patronisingly at me.'

'At least someone's smiling at you,' I point out.

We chat for a bit longer, then I hang up and lie sprawled on the veranda floor, resisting the urge to strangle myself with the cord of my pink mobile extension handset, something Mum bought me after seeing a daytime TV segment on the effects of mobile phone radiation on the brain.

I know no one will hassle me out here, but I also find it ironic that my safe haven represents everything that bothers me. Hiding on the veranda allows me to see the outside world, but there's no way I can touch it. It just stretches out before me, while the ties of my upbringing keep my feet firmly rooted in my father's house.

I turn to look through the glass sliding doors at what's holding me back. Mum is eyeing herself in her bedroom mirror as she applies a particularly unflattering shade of red lipstick. I hear her complaining about her wrinkles, and how a new year is only going to age her. Dad is watching the LBC news direct from Lebanon, totally unaware that Mum's ramblings are his cue to say something loving or supportive.

She focuses her attention on me instead, muttering something to herself before yelling, 'Sophie, stop wiping the floor with your clothes and come here and help me.'

I scramble inside.

'God give me patience,' she wails in Arabic, raising both hands in the air. 'God give me patience to endure the torment of watching my practically adult daughter lying on the floor and catching dust that I'll have to handwash out of her clothes.'

'Mum, your floor's cleaner than the plates of most restaurants because of your incessant need to clean it!'

She gives me a look and I decide to drop the attitude. I don't want her giving me a job to do when I just want to whinge. I stand there for what seems like ages while she fiddles with her hair, her shirt, her jewellery.

'Sophie, do I look fat?' she asks eventually.

I wince, hoping she doesn't see. 'No, Mama. You look lovely.'

My white lie doesn't convince her. She looks in the mirror, eyeing the body her children have given her.

A career woman might pass my mum in the street, see her wide hips, lined face and tired movements, and pity her because of the choices she's clearly made in life – to live for others. But Mum doesn't see it that way.

'A housewife is a career woman, Sophie,' she often tells me. 'She work every day, but she doesn't make money, she makes people. She turns a lazy man into a hard-working husband, and together they grow smart, strong babies like you. Well, until the baby is seventeen and tells me she's not hungry and won't eat the *shish barak* I make for her.'

I used to love my mother's *shish barak*. The little dumplings of mincemeat smothered in warm yoghurt sauce were just the cure after a tough day in primary school when I'd worn the wrong uniform and she'd have to come and save me from detention. Nowadays, she knows I won't let her save me. Hell, I don't even tell her what's wrong any more.

But where do I start with what's wrong? Not going anywhere on New Year's is the tip of the iceberg. I feel like I don't have a say in my own life. It's as though I'm invisible, defined only in the relative: dependable daughter, sister, student and friend. Is it so wrong that I want a little more?